CAST OF CHARAC

C000076698

Abercrombie "Filthy" Lewker. The noted mountaineer, and amateur detective.

Georgina "Georgie" Lewker. His lovely, loving and long-suffering wife, a former actress, who knows how to keep her husband in check.

Vera Crump. A self-confident but abrasive young schoolmistress.

Ted Somerset. A level-headed but somewhat spineless young man, whom Lewker trusts sufficiently to appoint as his Watson.

Gay Johnson. An adventurous young rock climber given to solo climbing.

Leonard Bligh. Gay's boyfriend, with whom she had quarreled.

Hamish Macrae. Gay's former fiancé.

Janet Macrae. Hamish's sister, an agreeable and lively young woman.

Paul Meirion. The temporary Warden of the Cauldmoor Youth Hostel and a self-styled student of the dark arts.

Bodfan Jones. A cherbubic little Welshman in his middle years.

George Roughten. The jovial landlord at the Herdwick Arms.

Ben Truby. A gloomy old shepherd who is a firm believer in the Old Ones.

Sir Walter Haythornthwaite. The Deputy Chief Constable, an expert on watercolors, a gentleman farmer, and an hospitable host.

Mr. and Mrs. Crake. Owner of the farmhouse where the Lewkers were to be staying on their holiday.

Detective-Inspector Grimmett. An old friend and ally of Lewker's.

Sergeant Daniel Miles. Mrs. Crake's cousin and Grimmett's assistant.

The Abercrombie Lewker novels

The Detective Novels

Death on Milestone Buttress (1951)
Reprinted by The Rue Morgue Press (2000)
Murder on the Matterhorn (1951)
The Youth Hostel Murders (1952)
Reprinted by The Rue Morgue Press (2006)
The Corpse in the Crevasse (1952)
Death Under Snowdon (1952)
A Corpse at Camp Two (1954)
Murder of an Owl (1956)
The Ice Axe Murders (1958)
Swing Away, Climber (1959)
Holiday with Murder (1960)
Death Finds a Foothold (1961)
Lewker in Norway (1963)
Death of a Weirdy (1965)
Lewker in Tirol (1967)
Fat Man's Agony (1969)

The Spy Novels

Traitor's Mountain (1945)
Kidnap Castle (1947)
Hammer Island (1947)

The Youth Hostel Murders

by Glyn Carr

Introduction by Tom & Enid Schantz

The Rue Morgue Press
Lyons / Boulder

The Youth Hostel Murders
© 1952, 1953 by The Estate of Glyn Carr
New material
© 2006 by The Rue Morgue Press
87 Lone Tree Lane
Lyons CO 80540

ISBN: 0-915230-98-4

Printed by
Johnson Printing

PRINTED IN THE UNITED STATES OF AMERICA

About Glyn Carr

If you look upon a mountain climb as taking place in a large, open-air locked room, then Showell Styles was right to choose Glyn Carr as his pseudonym for fifteen detective novels featuring Abercrombie Lewker, all of which concern murders committed among the crags and slopes of peaks scattered around the world. There's no doubt that John Dickson Carr, the king of the locked room mystery, would have agreed that Styles managed to find a way to lock the door of a room that had no walls and only the sky for a ceiling. In fact, it was while Styles was climbing a pitch on the classic Milestone Buttress on Tryfan in Wales that it struck him "how easy it would be to arrange an undetectable murder in that place, and by way of experiment I worked out the system and wove a thinnish plot around it."

That book was, of course, *Death on Milestone Buttress*, which first appeared in 1951 and was published for the first time in the United States by the Rue Morgue Press in 2000. Upon its publication Styles' English publisher, Geoffrey Bles, immediately asked for more climbing mysteries. Over the next eighteen years, Styles produced another fourteen Lewker books (fifteen, counting one last, currently lost manuscript) before he halted the series, having run out "of ways of slaughtering people on steep rock-faces." But before Lewker put away his ice axe and ropes for good, Styles managed to send him to Switzerland (*Murder on the Matterhorn*), the Himalayas (*A Corpse at Camp Two*), Austria (*The Corpse in the Crevasse* and *Lewker in the Tirol*), Scandinavia (*Lewker in Norway*) and Majorca (*Holiday with Murder*). The present volume, *The Youth Hostel Murders*, was set in Cumbria, the northernmost part of England. Many of his books were set in the place Styles no doubt loved the best, Wales, where, in 2005, he died at the age of 97 after a long, rich life.

The foreign locales included some of the places Styles had himself visited, first during the period he refers to as his "tramp" days from 1934 to 1937, and later as the leader of a Himalayan climb in 1954. Somehow he never managed to find a way to send Lewker to the Arctic, where he led expeditions in 1952 and 1953.

While Lewker professes to be new to detective work in *Death on Milestone Buttress,* he certainly was no stranger to danger and adventure, having served in Department Seven of the Special Commando Branch of British Intelligence during World War II. In fact, when Styles was searching for a character to solve murders among his beloved mountain peaks, he needed look no further than to three of his thrillers, published a few years earlier under his Styles byline. Abercrombie Lewker debuted in *Traitor's Mountain* (1947) when he revealed himself, in the guise of a tramp, to another British agent: "He was immensely broad, in general shape resembling a pocket-flask, and his rusty elongated bowler crowned a rather pouchy countenance fringed with a bush of black whisker. His expression was the expression of a dictator travelling incognito. His stained and bulging raincoat was buttoned to the neck with six buttons."

Although the events in that novel were based on Styles' own experiences in the Royal Navy during the war, the author and his fictional creation bore little physical resemblance to one other. Styles' jacket photos from the period show a lean, very fit-looking man, obviously capable of taking on the most arduous of climbs. Lewker, on the other hand, is described as short, bald and fat, and people are always amazed to learn of his climbing feats. Yet, size notwithstanding, Lewker is an imposing figure, perhaps the finest Shakespearean actor of his day, with a booming voice and an often irritating predilection for quoting the Bard at the drop of a hat or a corpse. His wife Georgina is obviously deeply in love with him—and he with her—but she knows that one of her primary roles is to keep his pomposity from running away with itself and getting him into trouble. Ego aside, "Filthy," as his friends punningly call him, is generous to a fault and always willing to lend a hand to friend and stranger alike, as is evident in *The Youth Hostel Murders.*

Filthy is also a man of old-fashioned (or perhaps time-honored) values, and chivalry is one he holds most dear, which explains, in part, why he turns detective to solve a young woman's moral dilemma in *Death on Milestone Buttress.* Other aspects of this first novel (and subsequent ones) may puzzle or amuse modern readers grown used to the casual sex that permeates today's books and movies, not to mention television programs. In 1951, it was still possible for a proper girl to be ruined—or at least think of herself as being ruined—by having sex outside of marriage.

But the real fun of the Lewker books lies in their depiction of life in mountainous regions of the world and in the love Lewker and his fellow climbers share for their chosen sport. Filthy is reluctant to embrace the kind of extreme technical climbing that was an outgrowth of Hitler's desire to see Germans demonstrate Aryan supremacy by climbing many of Europe's impossible North Faces. Nor is he willing to use words like "hiking," preferring to call such treks walks or tramps. If Shakespeare didn't use the word, why should he?

In addition to being an accomplished climber himself, Styles has written scores of books on the subject, ranging from guides to climbs in Wales to a full-fledged standard history of the sport, *On the Top of the World* (1967). Styles' love for the mountains and climbing comes through so strongly that it is almost impossible to resist the urge to put down one of his climbing mysteries and head for the nearest mountain trail, though those of us who live in places like Colorado can't help but be amused when Lewker appreciatively sniffs the clean mountain air at a thousand—or even three thousand—feet above sea level.

But even the most sedentary readers can enjoy these stories. Those who prefer to do their mountaineering from the comfort of an armchair need not worry about being unfamiliar with the terminology or techniques of the sport. Styles is first and foremost a storyteller, having written many books for children as well as historical novels, and he never forgets that the first role of the professional writer is to entertain.

Tom & Enid Schantz
April 2000
Revised in 2006
in the Colorado mountains

The Youth Hostel
Murders

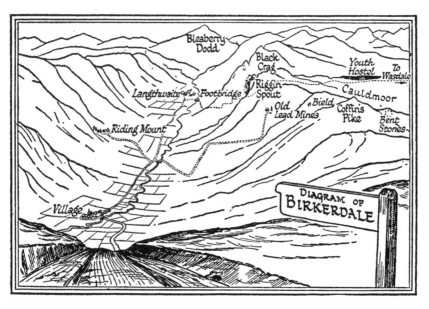

Sketch of murder locale done by Abercrombie Lewker

CHAPTER I
BUT WHO COMES HERE?

"THE TOMATO SANDWICHES ARE RATHER SQUASHY," remarked Georgina Lewker, frowning at the limp specimen she held between her fingers.

She was sitting on the running board of her husband's vast and venerable Wolseley, which stood axle deep in the roadside grasses. The mellow sunshine of the late August afternoon glinted on her neatly braided hair, mercilessly showing up the gray strands among the pale gold, and accentuated with its relief of light and shade the comfortable rotundity of her figure in its tweed suit. Georgie, had she realized this, would not have cared. She had the priceless gift—perhaps it was a legacy from the days when she had been Georgie May, the darling of Variety—of appearing at home in any setting. The yellowing hazels that bordered the lane, the blue Cumberland fells that peered distantly over them, had no quarrel with her golden-brown dumpiness.

Receiving no answer to her comment, she repeated it in a louder tone. A curious hump or mound, half-hidden in the grasses, stirred slightly and a voice like the Great Bell of Kiev replied.

" 'Why, thus it is, when men are ruled by women,' " it boomed.

"Filthy, you promised!" said Georgie severely. "No quotations—and that was *Richard the Third*, too!"

"My dear," intoned the voice reasonably, "you cannot expect that I, after playing Richard of Gloucester for eleven weeks in the greatest production of Dick Three ever staged, should be able—nay, or willing—to bar forever from these lips the noble lines which—"

"Rubbish! You just drag them in whenever you think they fit the case.

Do try and snap out of the actor-manager and remember you're on holiday, there's a dear. I'm sorry the tomato sandwiches are squashy, though."

"Granted, granted—so am I," agreed the voice. "That is to say, not squashy but sorry. Tomato sandwiches are always squashy. Hence my apt comment in the words of the Bard. You may remember that ere we started on this journey I respectfully tendered my opinion—based on years of picnicking—that tomatoes, if they are to be picnicked upon, should be carried whole in some suitable receptacle. That opinion was rejected."

"So it was," admitted his wife. "Well, let's say you were right for once, shall we? I gather you don't want a squashy sandwich?"

The oracle did not deign to reply. Georgie ate the sandwich herself, gazing contentedly at the lifting horizon of mountains, blue-shadowed now under the westering sun.

"You know," she announced, "I'm going to like this part of Cumberland."

"Wait till you see Birkerdale," rumbled the voice sleepily.

"I am waiting," protested Georgie, "though I can't think why. You can't talk about men being ruled by women now. Who insisted on stopping here to have tea, although we're only seven miles from the farm where we're going to stay? You did—and I didn't even question it. And now you aren't having any tea, and I'm dying for a wash in hot water."

"I want you to see Birkerdale at its best," said the voice, gathering sonority as it proceeded. "I want you to see the long shadows of the fells stretching across the narrow fields, the whitewashed village, the tiny church with its twisted yews. I want you to see the bowl of the valley's end filled with purple dusk, and the great heads of the mountains tipped with sunset gold. It is worth loitering a little while here that you may come into such a place at close of day."

Georgie was touched. "Of course, darling. It's nice of you to plan it for me." She took a Thermos from the case beside her and unscrewed the top. "Do have a cup of tea. I made it just your strength."

"No, thank you, my dear."

"But you must be thirsty."

"I am indeed thirsty," admitted the voice, "but tea is not the desideratum. The time is not yet. In Birkerdale village—"

"Abercrombie Lewker!" Georgie sat up very straight and her voice was accusing. "I *know* why we had to stop here. All that talk about letting me see Birkerdale at evening was just phooey—you don't want to get in before the village pub opens!"

The curious mound among the grasses heaved, and Mr. Lewker sat up. To anyone who had not seen the famous actor-manager on the stage, it would have seemed odd that a voice so magnificently deep and expressive should proceed from a short, very broad, undeniably stout gentleman with a pouchy countenance like that of a rather dissipated Buddha. He wore on his head a handkerchief knotted at the corners, which he snatched off as he got to his feet, revealing a large bald head decorated with untidy tufts of black hair above each ear. The lane, the hazel clumps, and the distant mountains seemed to shrink and form themselves into a stage setting as soon as he began to speak.

"Is it to be thus traduced," he boomed dramatically, "that I have worked for another's pleasure? Am I to receive no credit for having arranged for you to stay at the only mountain farm in England whose nearest neighbor is a celebrity who once asked you to call on him? Can the imputation of selfishness—"

"Don't be ridiculous, darling. Sir Walter invited us both—and anyway, he's Deputy Chief Constable as well as an expert on watercolors, so he's probably heard of how you sometimes play at detectives."

"Play at—" The phrase appeared to stick in Mr. Lewker's throat. He brushed the accumulated pollen from his coat sleeves, conveying outraged dignity by the gesture. "Sir Walter Haythornthwaite," he said in measured tones, "is doubtless as well-informed in the constabular capacity as he is in the Aristarchian."

Georgie rose and began to stow sandwiches and Thermos in her case.

"Long words butter no parsnips with me," she said with decision. "Opening time or no opening time, I want to finish the journey and get the dust off my skin. *En voiture*, darling!"

The actor-manager heaved a windy sigh and glanced at his watch.

"Half an hour to go," he observed. "Now sits Expectation in the air. Prudence demands a speed of fourteen miles an hour along this lane, which, by a happy coincidence, will bring us to the village at the very moment when the Herdwick Arms opens its hospitable doors. I believe they keep a very passable bottled grapefruit juice."

"We'll stop, then—but for five minutes only," conceded his wife, getting into the big tourer. "Come along."

Mr. Lewker climbed into the driving seat and started the engine. The ancient car lurched with dignity off the grass verge and rolled away down the lane towards the mountains.

The road to Birkerdale, which leaves the coast road some miles short of Gosforth, climbs a little over a shoulder of hill to avoid the marshy lower reaches of the River Birker where that adventurous stream becomes at last sedate before winding with increasing muddiness to the sea. Thus the newcomer to the dale—there are not many such, for it is far from being a guidebook beauty-spot—approaches it from above, by a road that has at times seemed to lose itself in boggy moorland; and the effect of discovery is all the more striking for that fact. Mr. Lewker, who had visited Birkerdale in his energetic youth, and Georgie, who was seeing it for the first time, were equally charmed with the prospect that opened below them as the aged Wolseley rocked slowly over the hill-brow.

The whole length and breadth of Birkerdale (it is no more than three miles long by half a mile wide) lay before them, its flat patchwork of fields smiling in the level sunshine beneath the circling sweep of enclosing mountains. The village, set almost exactly in the center of the valley, looked like a child's toy village with its few whitewashed houses and tiny church, and the humpbacked bridge over the Birker. They could see the white road winding on up the dale, never far from the silver river, until it turned half left and appeared to end at a large gray stone house set in a kind of alcove of the hills on the northwestern side of the valley.

"Riding Mount," said Mr. Lewker, in reply to his wife's question. "That is where your celebrated acquaintance Haythornthwaite lives, the world forgetting, but not by the world forgot. That white house, in the trees at the very head of the valley, is Langthwaite."

"The road stops at Riding Mount," remarked Georgie. "Don't say we have to walk the last mile!"

Lewker negotiated a steep turn on the zigzag that was bringing them down into the valley bottom before replying.

"The old road continues by the stream as far as Langthwaite," he said. "It runs between stone walls, which is why you cannot see it. Incidentally, they seem to have made a new road up to the old lead mines. I wonder if there's been a revival of industry in Birkerdale since I was here in '37."

"Oh, surely not—the place looks as if it had been asleep since the Spanish Armada. There's not a building in sight except the village and Riding Mount and our farm. And—look!" she added suddenly. "Isn't that a waterfall, high up on the right?"

The descending road had brought them to a point from which they could look up at the mountainsides on the southeast side of Birkerdale. These were steeper and more craggy than those on the Riding Mount side, and from a dip in their sun-gilded rank a glittering streak of falling water sprang, to lose itself in the ravines and boulders of the lower slopes.

"That is Riggin Spout." Mr. Lewker, having safely brought the old car down to the level road of the Birkerdale strath, sat back in the driving seat and gazed round him with satisfaction. "Comely," he pronounced. "That is the word for this. 'How comely it is, and how reviving,' as Milton exclaims."

Georgie turned to stare at him.

"If it makes you quote anyone but Shakespeare, darling," she said, "it must be positively intoxicating."

"Let us say 'rejuvenating,' my dear. Nothing has changed in Birkerdale since I was a lad on my first walking tour."

His wife smiled at him affectionately. "For your sake, old boy," she returned, "I hope that's true of the beer."

The car lolloped over the switchback bridge that crosses the shining Birker and they were in Birkerdale village. The seven or eight solid old houses of whitewashed stone which constituted the village were already in the spreading shadow of the mountains, and the rank of twisted yew trees that stood in front of the venerable little church looked black and somehow sinister, Georgie thought suddenly, against the sunlit meadows beyond. The Herdwick Arms, moreover, had not the comfortable welcoming air of the old inns she knew in the south country; the only indication of its inn-ship was the almost illegible lettering on the lintel of its door which stated that Geo. Roughten was licensed to sell Ales, Wines & Porter. The door was open, however, and Mr. Lewker, having parked the Wolseley beside a worn mounting block, lost no time in hustling his wife inside.

The place was bare, with typical north-country contempt for appearances. But the flagged floor, the scrubbed benches and table, the little bar, and the landlord himself, were all exceedingly clean. Geo. Roughten had the look of having just undergone a cold shower and brisk toweling. His round red face, with short gray sidewhiskers, shone so cheerfully upon the somewhat gloomy room that it had almost the effect of firelight. He wore a gray pullover over a collarless shirt, but the shirt was spotless and the cuffs starched.

"A grand evenin', sir and madam," he beamed, as they came in. "Rain's to come, though."

"Oh, I hope not!" said Georgie, seating herself at one end of the long table and pulling off the yellow kerchief she had worn in the car. "We're only just starting our holiday."

The landlord's sharp gray eyes twinkled at her.

"Ay—you'll be the London lady and gentleman stayin' oop at Langthwaite," he nodded. "Well, Mrs. Crake'll look after you. What's it to be, sir?" he added quickly to Mr. Lewker, who was growing impatient.

"Beer, one pint, and let it be in a tankard," boomed the actor-manager. "And for you, my dear?"

"I think I'd like to try some porter," said Georgie. "I see Mr. Roughten's licensed to sell it, and I've often wondered what it's like."

She flashed a smile at Mr. Roughten, who nodded gravely at her as he operated the beer-pump.

"Porter, madam," he replied, with an accent curiously refined for a Cumberland innkeeper, "was a dark beer specially brewed to the taste of the London city porters in the eighteenth century. There was a 'stout' porter—stout being the same as strong, d'ye see—and stout's the only kind o' porter we can sell you today."

He set a foaming tankard in front of Mr. Lewker with a flourish.

"I will not have you guzzling bottled stout, Georgina," said her husband firmly. "One grapefruit, Mr. Roughten, if you please."

" 'Tesn't a lady's drink, stout," approved the landlord, hastening to obey. "Grapefruit, now, that's full o' vitamins." He transferred the contents of a small bottle into a glass and placed it before Georgie. "I know that's good because I've seen where it came from—Gan Shemuel. That's a Jewish village in Palestine. I was there in the War. Miles o' grapefruit trees."

"You were in the Army?" queried Mr. Lewker, setting down his half-emptied tankard.

"R.A.S.C.—driver. Finished up a sergeant." The landlord leaned folded arms on the bar and settled himself for a chat. "Funny thing, that. I got invalided home, d'ye see, and then posted to a depot near Liverpool. First job I got after VJ Day was running a transport operation—where? Why, up this very dale!"

"Where you had not been for many years."

The landlord darted a shrewd glance at Mr. Lewker.

"Ay. You're quick, sir. 'Tes my manner o' talk, I don't doubt, as told you that. Left here to go to London when I was a mere lad—'twas Sir Walter helped me to get a job there, spite o' my old dad's grumbling. A fine gentleman is Sir Walter Haythornthwaite, sir. We think a lot of him in Birkerdale."

There was enthusiasm in his tone. Georgie, who had been favorably impressed by Sir Walter, was pleased.

"Don't you find it very quiet here after London?" she asked.

"Ay, nice an' quiet, madam. The old Dad, he died four year ago an' left me the pub. I'm well enough off here with Sir Walter as my landlord. There's not much happens in Birkerdale, it's true."

" 'Cept sudden death."

The voice that interjected this remark was like the croak of a raven. It came from the farthest and gloomiest corner of the room by the fireplace, and though Mr. Lewker and Georgie both turned to see who had spoken, they could make out only a shapeless figure huddled in a corner.

" 'Tes old Ben Truby, th' shepherd," explained Mr. Roughten in a hurried whisper. "He means the young chap as were found dead in Riggin Spout at Whitsun. Been climbin' alone on Black Crag an' fell into th' beck an' over th' fall. Death by misadventure, coroner said. But I reckon 'tes dommed foolishness—beggin' your pardon, madam—the way these rock climbers go on. Stayin' at th' new Youth Hostel, he was."

"Ah, yes." Mr. Lewker drained his pewter and felt benevolent enough to encourage the garrulous landlord. "It is on Cauldmoor, I am told. Was that new road up by the lead mines made for the Youth Hostelers?"

"No, sir. 'Tes the old road, but Government mended it when the Jerry bombers began. They stored art treasures in the lead mines, you see. That was the transport job I mentioned a while back—cartin' the stuff back to the Reynolds Galleries in Liverpool, where it came from."

"An' sudden death near cotched ye at it, George Roughten," croaked the voice from the shadows.

"Now, Ben," remonstrated the landlord uncomfortably.

"Mortality doth flavor his speech," observed Mr. Lewker. "Another excellent pint, if you please."

"But what does he mean, Mr. Roughten?" inquired Georgie.

Mr. Roughten was drawing ale, and concentrating upon the operation.

" 'Twas nothin', madam," he said. "Only when I was drivin' a load down from th' mines my steerin' went wrong. It's steep, that hill. I jumped clear just as she went over. She crashed down two hundred feet an' bust into flames. All the stuff—art treasures, like as I said—was burnt. Lucky it was insured. An' lucky the chap as came with me from the Galleries, art expert chap, had decided to walk down 'stead o' ridin'. Winter o' 1945, that was."

"So things do happen in Birkerdale sometimes," Georgie remarked.

"Ay." The landlord, leaning across the bar with a cautious eye on the shadows by the fireplace, spoke in a confidential whisper. "There's some folk hereabouts says 'twas witchcraft as sent my truck off that road. Coffin's Pike's an evil place, they say—'twas why the lead mines failed. I'm not one to believe in such things, but it's got about as witchcraft made that young fellow fall to his death, too. Old Ben says—"

"Me 'twas as found t' boady," said the sepulchral voice from the shadows.

"Now we're for it," muttered Mr. Roughten. "Now, Ben," he went on more loudly, " 'twas three young hikers goin' up to th' Hostel as found him, as you very well know."

As he spoke a picturesque figure came shambling out from the shadows by the fireplace, like a troll emerging from a cave. He was a tall old man with scanty gray locks and very long and muscular arms. His gaunt body, bent like a question mark but still suggestive of great strength, was clad in an old velveteen coat with tails, much patched tweed knee breeches, and huge nailed boots. His face was weather-browned and bony, and the inordinate length of his bristly jaw gave him a horse-faced appearance which instantly reminded Georgie of Wordsworth. The mild, rather watery eyes might have been a poet's, too, had it not been for a shifting, glinting light which flickered in them as Ben Truby turned them upon the visitors. It hardly needed Mr. Roughten's significant dumb show behind the shepherd's back to tell them that here was a mind a little out of gear.

"It mubbe three childer see'd it fust," the shepherd conceded grudgingly, "but 'twas me they came runnin' to, up in my la'l bield yarnder. Me 'twas 'at went nippity to pull it out, an' me 'twas 'at got t' laads an' a stratcher to bring it down."

"Ben's got a kind of stone cottage up on Cauldmoor," explained the landlord with a touch of apology in his tone. "Sir Walter grazes a few sheep, and Ben's shepherd to Sir Walter, d'ye see."

"A few sheep!" repeated the old man contemptuously. He had a habit of twitching his bushy eyebrows up and down rapidly when he was annoyed which was oddly frightening. "Eighty head he've got, an' ye can carl eighty head a flock, George Roughten!" He turned to the two southerners again, his pale eyes rolling from one to the other. "But 'tes about t' boady Ah'm tellin'. A young chap 'twas, like as George Roughten tells ye, not above twenty year of age Ah racken, wi' black hair an' dressed up in t' duds like as these climbin' folk wears. Ye wudna think he was dead, not excep' ye saw t' girt hole in t' back of his head where t' rocks had brokken him in when he fell."

"You see, sir and madam," put in the landlord, looking like a somewhat anxious cherub endeavoring to play the role of Chorus to a goblin, "these rock climbers, of late years they've made what they calls rowts—that's to say, ways of climbin' up—on Black Crag, an' Black Crag—as you'll know, sir, havin' been in these parts before—it stands up beside the Riggin Beck, just where it takes a dive over into Birkerdale, bein' then called Riggin Spout. Any young rashpate fallin' off these rowts, d'ye see, would fall slap into the beck, with maybe a bounce or two on the way, an'—"

" 'Tes my story, George Roughten!" broke in the shepherd angrily. "You quiet down! I was a sergeant afore you, my laad," he added venomously and with apparent irrelevance, "aye—an' knew Sir Walter afore you, for all your talk. Served him man an' boy, I have, which is more'n you can say. So let me finish my crack!"

Mr. Roughten turned away, with a wink and a shrug for his customers; but his round face was a darker red. Ben Truby shook his ragged locks as a dog shakes himself after a skirmish and returned with gusto to his tale.

" 'Twas nigh dusk afore we got him down," he said impressively. "Me an' eight other laads, wi' a few from t' Youth Hostel to help. We tipped him off t' stratcher more'n once, for 'tis a dommed rough trod from Riggin Spout. Stiff he was, an' t' girt hole in his head—"

Mr. Lewker, with an eye on his wife's slightly frowning face, interrupted firmly.

"Very interesting, Mr. Truby," he boomed. "But, do you know, we are not really anxious to hear any more about the body. 'Why should calamity be full of words? Windy attorneys—' " He caught Georgie's reproving glance and cut the quotation short. "In brief, Mr. Truby, permit me to refill your glass."

The shepherd, after a momentary hesitation, decided to accept this bribe and shambled off into the corner to fetch his mug.

"Don't mind him, sir and madam," whispered Mr. Roughten hastily. " 'Tes a lonesome life, is Ben's, and this accident kind o' made a change for him."

Ben Truby came back with his empty pint mug and banged it on the counter in front of the landlord with a truculent air.

"See ye fills it proper, George Roughten," he croaked. And then, turning to face the others, "Ah'll give ye a friendly warnin', measter an' missus. George Roughten'll tell ye Ah'm turned foolish, but Ah'm a sight wiser'n him in some things. Don't go pokin' about oop Cauldmoor way. T' Old Ones don't like it."

The sunlight had gone from the dale, and the reflected light from the fields beyond the narrow windows no longer relieved the gloom of the barroom. The gaunt figure of the shepherd was singularly impressive as he bent forward with his pale eyes fixed on his listeners. Georgie shivered a little and then laughed.

"But how mysterious!" she said. "What are the Old Ones, Mr. Truby?"

"Fairies an' such," put in the landlord disdainfully.

" 'Tes more'n fairies, my laad!" said the old man steadily, without troubling to turn round. "If ye'd seen what Ah've seen, oop there on Coffin's Pike, by t' Bent Stones—"

But he was not allowed to finish. Hurrying footsteps sounded on the stones outside the inn door and a thin young man in shorts entered, followed closely by a plump red-haired girl. Both were very much out of breath. The young man, disregarding the other occupants of the room, went straight to the counter.

"Mr. Roughten?" he demanded.

"That's me, sir," returned the landlord, looking curiously at the other's anxious face. "What can I do for you?"

The plump girl, pushing in front of her companion, answered.

"You can help us," she said in a loud and overconfident voice. "We're from the Youth Hostel. We want some men for a search party. There's a girl been missing since yesterday morning."

CHAPTER II
POOR KEY-COLD FIGURE

MR. ABERCROMBIE LEWKER HAS BEEN HEARD TO COMPLAIN that the case he afterwards called the Youth Hostel Murders sneaked up on him as imperceptibly as 'th' inaudible and noiseless foot of Time.' His wife, on the other hand, maintains that from the moment she saw the twisted yews in Birkerdale churchyard she had a sense of something hidden, something black and secret lying beneath the smiling peace of the dale; and that Ben Truby's mysterious hints increased that sense to such a pitch that if the entrance of the two Youth Hostelers had heralded the revelation of a murder she would not have been surprised. This annoys Mr. Lewker, who, since his association with the British Secret Service during the War and his machinations in the affair of the death on Milestone Buttress, considers himself to possess something of a nose for crime. All his nose told him when Ted Somerset and Vera Crump burst into the Herdwick Arms, however, was that the red-haired girl used an expensive scent and used it far too freely.

There was a short silence in the barroom after the girl's announcement. Mr. Truby, his mug halfway to his lips, stared at the two with the disconcerting blankness of one whose mental processes are very slow; Mr. Roughten fingered his chin and looked puzzled.

"Well? Are you going to help us?" demanded the girl impatiently.

"Bit late for a search party, miss," said the landlord dubiously. " 'Twill be dark before you've started."

"Well, you see," began the young man in mild tones, "we thought at first—"

"Don't waste time explaining, Ted!" said the girl peremptorily. "You're always explaining. Are you going to help us, or aren't you?" she added fiercely to the landlord.

Mr. Lewker, whose finely accurate ear had placed her as a schoolmistress as soon as she spoke, found himself pitying the children who were subject to her rule. Mr. Roughten, at a loss for a reply to so brusque a demand, hesitated, and with a *'Hah!'* of disgust the girl swung round to face the other occupants of the room.

"What about you?" she snapped; and then, apparently perceiving that she was addressing two strangers of a superior class, became suddenly rather too refined. "I'm sure I beg your pardon. But we must get a search party organized tonight. Will you please help me to make these men see how urgent it is? Oh—I'm Vera Crump and this is Ted Somerset. We're from Birmingham."

The young man at her elbow smiled in an embarrassed fashion. He had a thin, pleasant face, but his features had that vaguely unfinished air which is not uncommon among those who go directly and prematurely from school to office. He began to say something, but was instantly cut short by Miss Crump.

"I'm sure I've seen you before," she said momentarily forgetting her refinement and fixing rather prominent blue eyes on Mr. Lewker.

Georgie, who was used to this sort of semi-recognition, did her stuff.

"I expect you've seen my husband on the stage, my dear," she smiled. "Abercrombie Lewker, you know."

"Of course!" Miss Crump was distinctly thrilled. *"King Lear"*—at Stratford last year. Fancy, Ted!"

The actor-manager, in face of their combined stares of wondering admiration, tried to look modestly deprecating and, as usual, failed completely.

"I say," said the young man diffidently, "I don't think we ought to bother Mr. Lewker—"

"I'm sure you won't mind," cut in Vera Crump, talking him down determinedly and addressing Mr. Lewker, "but it's really serious. Gay—that's the girl who's missing—has been out somewhere for a night and the best part of two days. She may be lying with a broken leg, or worse, out on the hills. We've just got to look for her."

"You've left it too late tonight, miss," the landlord put in from behind them. "You'll leave it till first light tomorrow, if you take my advice."

"Well, I'm not taking it," returned the girl positively, without looking round. "The others have already started from the Hostel to Coffin's Pike and the Wasdale side. There's only five of them, with the Warden, and we must have more people to help us search the Birkerdale side and up to Bleaberry Dodd."

"I'd notify th' police if I was you," said the landlord.

Ben Truby spoke up unexpectedly.

"Ye're a fule, George Roughten," he croaked contemptuously. "T' nearest po-lis is eight mile away at Egremont."

"There's a telephone box half a mile up road," protested the landlord.

"Tallyphone if ye want," said the shepherd with scorn. "They've still to come eight mile, ha'n't they? The young leddy's reet enough. 'Tis a clear night an' a braid moon when t' gloamin' comes. We'll tak a look for t' lass."

"Good," rapped Miss Crump. "You're the shepherd, aren't you? Just the man we want. Can you get any others?"

"Ay, ay. Young Forster an' Jemmy from two doors away, they'll come if Ah asks 'em. Rackon Ah'll bring t' stratcher."

"Stretcher?" repeated Ted Somerset, startled. "I say, you don't think—?"

Ben Truby regarded him askance, looking in the increasing darkness of the room more like a malicious goblin than ever.

"Ye can think naught till ye knaws, laad," he croaked, his watery eyes fixed on the other's anxious face with a kind of evil enjoyment. "T' lass has likely come to harm. 'Tes more than sartin. Aye—if she've been layin' out on t' fells all night, there's no knawin' but t' Old Ones have took her. Or mubbe"—his eyes widened dramatically—"mubbe she've fallen like t' other one, wi' a girt hole in her head—"

"Peace, peace, thou venerable bird of woe!" Mr. Lewker's measured tones were commanding. "The girl is probably safe." He addressed Somerset and Miss Crump.

"If we are to act, we should act at once. The light is failing. Will you permit me to suggest a plan?"

"Yes, of course," said the girl eagerly.

Ted Somerset nodded; his thin face looked relieved. Lewker heaved himself to his feet, and at once his figure, for all its squatness, seemed to dominate the room as it invariably dominated the stage.

"Mr. Truby," he boomed decisively, "collect your two friends as quickly as you can. I suggest that you go up the track to the lead mines, or near it. Spread out on the fellside, shout now and then, and listen carefully for a reply."

"Wull we tak' t' stratcher?" demanded the shepherd, twisting his long head on one side like an aged vulture.

"It might be as well. Make for the Youth Hostel. There we shall join you, and we can then move on northward towards Bleaberry Dodd." He turned to the two Youth Hostelers. "Did you come down by the Riggin Beck?"

"No," Vera said. "We went with the others over Coffin's Pike and then dropped straight down to Birkerdale."

"Very well. You and Mr. Somerset will come in my car as far as Langthwaite. We shall then go up by the Riggin Beck path, searching as we go, and meet Mr. Truby and his compeers at the Hostel."

"I'll come with you," Georgie interposed. "I can help."

Her husband shook his head. "You are our line of communication, my dear. You will stay at Langthwaite. If there is need, we shall send a runner down to the farm and you may have to drive to the nearest telephone."

"Sir Walter up at Riding Mount, he's on the telephone," said the land-lord, plainly impressed by this display of organization.

"Excellent. Meanwhile, Mr. Roughten, I suggest that you telephone the police and tell them what has happened. They will take what action they think fit. Langthwaite, remember, is the place to which information will be sent. Is that clear?"

"Yessir." The landlord's response was the reaction of the ex-soldier to the voice of authority.

Ben Truby, having retrieved a blackthorn stick from the corner where he had been sitting, had already shambled to the door. Mr. Lewker and his passengers, coming out into an evening surprisingly light after the gloom of the Herdwick Arms, found the old man standing in the lane and gazing into the air. A pair of crows were flapping slowly homeward above the twisted yews of the churchyard, cawing as they went. The shepherd raised a gaunt arm and pointed to them.

"They knaws," he croaked in tones not unlike those of the birds. "They knaws. Ah'll bring that stratcher, measter."

He shot a faintly derisive glance at the four and stumped off along the row of houses.

"What a perfectly dreadful old man!" said Georgie, climbing into the back seat as directed by her husband. "Of course the girl will turn up all right in the end."

Mr. Lewker, who had conceived a dislike for Vera Crump, succeeded in maneuvering Ted Somerset into the seat beside him.

"It is a fact," he boomed, as he let in his clutch, "that nine out of ten search parties prove to be false alarms. But that does not relieve us of our responsibility of searching."

The Wolseley left the few houses of Birkerdale behind and held on along a narrow but well-surfaced lane running almost straight towards the head of the valley. The sun had quite gone from the stonewalled fields and sweep-ing hillsides and lingered only on Bleaberry Dodd, the shapely fell that closed the end of the dale, making its pointed summit glow like a ruby above the dusk-purple slopes. Overhead the sky was a clear apple green, the sky of an autumn evening although August had still a week of life. On the felltops there would be light enough to walk by for an hour or two, until the moon—a few days short of full—came up. But the two-thousand-foot walls of the valley, closing in and steepening as they approached its inner recess, had brought night prematurely to the river meadows. A mile or more ahead a gleam of yellow lamplight, seen intermittently through clustering trees, showed where Langthwaite stood in the very jaws of the mountains, and when the car had made half a mile from the village the lights of a large house came into sight some distance away on the left of the lane. Georgie leaned over from the back seat, where she was making desultory conversa-tion with Vera.

"Oughtn't we to call at Riding Mount, Filthy, and tell Sir Walter what's happening?" she inquired.

"Hardly worth it, my dear," returned her husband. "Pray restrain your social impulses for the present."

"Ape!" retorted Georgie, subsiding.

Conscious of a certain surprised tension beside him, Mr. Lewker felt constrained to reassurance.

"Marital badinage, Mr. Somerset," he said solemnly. "Incidentally, certain irreverent persons who address me as 'Filthy' do so not in reference to my habits but out of a childish delight in an execrable pun upon my cognomen."

Ted Somerset laughed rather shyly.

"The First Epistle of Timothy III:3," he said unexpectedly.

Mr. Lewker was impressed. In his experience, nine educated people out of ten imagined the phrase "filthy lucre" to have originated in Shakespeare. He said so, and added to his companion's embarrassment.

"Oh, I read a bit, you know, sir," he said confusedly. "Left school when I was fifteen and—and I'm in a bank. Got to make up for it somehow."

The touch of defiance in his voice left the actor-manager somewhat at a loss for a reply. An inferiority complex of this not uncommon sort is not easy to deal with. He drove on for a few moments in silence.

An excellent wrought iron gateway on the left showed where the drive of Riding Mount left the lane to wind through pastures and parkland to the big house which stood a quarter of a mile away close under the dark hillside. The good road surface continued only a yard or two past this gateway and then was carried off to the right, passing over the river by an unrailed bridge of iron girders to climb the steep slopes towards the old lead mines. The road to Langthwaite became a very bumpy cart track between drystone walls so close together that the wings of the big tourer all but scraped them. A deep, throbbing note made itself heard above the purr of the engine; it came from high up the fellside on their right, where a streak of white water hung beneath towering crags.

"Riggin Spout," murmured Lewker, half to himself. "There is a pool up there where I used to bathe."

"You know these parts, sir?" Ted remarked hesitantly.

"Yes."

Lewker's reply was brief. No one had ever called him "sir" in the days when he had first trampled up this valley, rucksack on back, a boy discovering his heritage. It came to him with a wholly irrational shock that the organ note of the fall had sounded unceasing through all the years since his boyhood, would continue to sound long after he was dead. It was this changelessness of the hills, he meditated, that gave them their especial and rather nostalgic charm; in a changing world they alone were steadfast, immutable.

A bump that jarred the very bones of the old Wolseley shook him out of this momentary mood. He changed into bottom gear and the car jolted slowly along the last half-mile of the lane. The slower speed gave Mr. Lewker more scope for consideration of the problem of the missing girl. He found one thing odd and voiced his thought.

"Why was this search party delayed until now?"

Somerset hesitated a moment.

"The Warden," he began, checked himself and began again. "I'd better start from the beginning. There's a party of four of us at the Hostel—Vera, myself, Gay Johnson, and Leonard Bligh. Leonard's Gay's boyfriend. They had a quarrel of sorts yesterday, and Gay wouldn't come with us to Wasdale. The three of us walked over there yesterday. Gay stayed behind. Mr. Meirion—that's the Warden—says she put on her climbing things and left after we'd gone, about ten o'clock. She didn't say where she was going."

"She is a rock climber?" questioned Lewker.

"Yes, and pretty hot at it. The rest of us are just walkers. But she's often said it's a mug's game to climb alone."

Ted Somerset went on with his story. He told it concisely and well—possibly because Miss Crump, out of earshot in the back seat of the open car, was unable to exercise her tyranny of interruption. The three had returned from their tramp to Wasdale at dusk the previous night. Gay had not come back from her solitary ramble. They had not worried unduly; for one thing, the girl was high-tempered and might have gone to another hostel for the night to spite Leonard, and for another the Warden, to whom they would have turned for advice in such a case, was not to be found.

"Gay had left some of her things at the Hostel?" asked Lewker at this point.

"Yes—including her pajamas," Ted nodded.

In the morning they had conferred with the Warden, who had by this time reappeared, and it had been decided that Leonard Bligh should walk over to the nearest hostel to Cauldmoor, on the Black Sail pass, and find out whether Gay had spent the night there. Bligh had returned at teatime, very worried, with a negative report. It was then that the belated search party had been hastily organized.

"I see," said Mr. Lewker slowly.

It was a common enough happening, he knew, since the postwar years brought a vast increase of youthful adventurers into the hills: some thoughtless youngster plunging off on an adventure of his own without telling his companions, failing to return at the expected time, setting in motion the nagging fear that "something might have happened" and the inevitable search party, and finally turning up safe and sound and wondering what all the fuss was about. Privately, Lewker considered that the girl Gay had very probably got tired of her young man—or, not inconceivably, of Vera Crump—and had deserted her party for the rest of the holiday. Still, she had not gone to the nearest hostel. And there were the pajamas——

"Here we are," he announced suddenly.

The bumpy lane had brought them to a stone-paved yard flanked by dark barns on one side and by ancient overshadowing trees on the other. The lit window of the farmhouse shone fifty yards away beyond the barns. Mr. Lewker turned the car so that it faced the lane, and switched off the engine.

"I've put the tomato sandwiches in the small rucksack," Georgie said briskly. "You may need them. You'd better share them with Vera and Mr. Somerset."

"Oh, we've lots of food, thanks awfully," said Miss Crump, getting out and shouldering a neat sack. "I've got bandages and glucose tablets as well."

As she spoke the door of the farmhouse opened and a woman's figure appeared silhouetted against the lamplight.

"Here is Mrs. Crake," said Lewker, climbing hurriedly out of the car and pulling a pair of nailed boots from beneath the seat. "You shall explain to her, my dear. We cannot waste more time. Come along, you two."

He made for a gap in the wall beneath the trees, Somerset and Vera following.

"Good luck—and be careful!" Georgie cried after them.

The vociferous welcome of Mrs. Crake as the good lady approached the car became more audible behind them and then was drowned in the noise of the river as they came across a field to the footbridge which Mr. Lewker remembered of old. They crossed it and took the narrow path beyond, winding among the dark shapes of giant boulders. The light was still good enough to pick a way, and the track, climbing gently at first over rock-strewn slopes, was fairly wide. Vera Crump lost no time in shouldering alongside the actor-manager, leaving Ted to plod in the rear.

"I'm sure you'd like to have the facts about this business," she began in her masterful voice.

"Mr. Somerset gave me a very concise account in the car," said Mr. Lewker rather shortly. He disliked perfume, even Duval's *Nocturne*, when it was used as lavishly as Miss Crump used it. The lady was not to be snubbed, however.

"I dare say," she said, careless of the fact that the young man was barely two paces behind, "but Ted's got a woolly mind. It's not factual. And he's no good at psychology. Now Gay Johnson was what I call temperamental." She implied that the word was her own invention. "If things didn't go just right for her she played hell, if you'll pardon the expression. I'm sure you know the sort of thing I mean, being on the stage."

"The leading lady temperament," murmured Lewker, feeling that it was expected of him.

"I knew you'd understand. Well, if it wasn't for one thing I'd say Gay had just gone off for a day or two in a fit of temperament."

"Her pajamas, perhaps?"

Miss Crump laughed shortly. "Oh, no. I'm sure Gay wouldn't stop to think about pajamas if she felt like rushing off somewhere to spite us. It was something else, something she said. Leonard Bligh, who is Gay's boy-friend—"

"Does that mean they were engaged?" queried Mr. Lewker. He was pleased to find that he could easily talk her down when he wanted to interrupt.

"You're rather old-fashioned, aren't you?" she said with kindly tolerance. "No, it doesn't. In my opinion, though, Gay was as deeply in love with Leonard as a girl of her temperament could be. Well, she and Leonard had a fearful quarrel, in front of myself and Ted—Gay liked to exhibit her emotions—and at the end of it Gay shouted at him 'You can sign off, Orpheus! This is where Eurydice does her stuff!' Then she dashed off and we didn't see her again. We call Leonard Orpheus by way of a rather silly joke," she added. "He carries a recorder round with him."

"I see. And what did you infer from Miss Johnson's classical ejaculation?"

"Well, Eurydice died and Orpheus tried to fetch her back from the kingdom of Pluto," Miss Crump explained kindly.

"You think Miss Johnson might have had the idea of suicide in her mind?" Lewker said, a little startled.

"I say, you know, Vera"—Ted Somerset spoke up from the rear—"Gay wasn't the sort of girl—"

"You know nothing about Gay," Miss Crump told him, without turning round. "I thought nothing about it at the time," she went on to Lewker, "but when she didn't turn up it occurred to me she might have intended us to think something like that—or intended Leonard to think it. Leonard's an impressionable type."

"But you do not think she meant it?"

Miss Crump considered, with the air of an authority on human mentalities.

"Not at the time," she pronounced. "But it's just possible she might have let her emotions affect her to that extent. Temperamental people do quite often."

"I would advise you to put the idea out of your head, Miss Crump," boomed Mr. Lewker firmly. "People who behave as you have described Miss Johnson as behaving are normally the last people to take their own lives. How old was this girl?"

"Twenty-two, but mentally about fifteen," replied Vera, completely undisturbed by his reproof.

"Hum. Well, I propose to halt here and put my boots on."

He sat down on a flat boulder and began to remove his shoes. The path had brought them round a low ridge descending from the tall mountain on their left, and was beginning to climb more steeply up a broken glacis of rocks and turf. The rumble of the waterfall was now much louder and close above them. Towering overhead at the top of a jumble of scree and fallen rocks rose the gullies and buttresses of Black Crag, more impressive in the half-light than they appeared by day. The feeling of being on the threshold of mysteries as old as Time, which comes to all who venture into the mountain fastnesses at nightfall, held them silent for a while as Mr. Lewker laced his ancient nailed boots and rammed his shoes into the rucksack on top of Georgie's tomato sandwiches.

"We'd better start calling, hadn't we?" asked Ted, as the actor-manager stood up. "Though I must say it seems unlikely that she'd leave the path to—"

"Gay would prefer scrambling up rocks to walking up a path," Miss Crump cut him short. "She might have twisted an ankle or broken a leg somewhere here."

Lewker nodded. He was a mountaineer himself and knew the climber's pleasure in gripping rock, even if the rock was only a succession of boulders beside a path.

"Miss Crump, will you take the path?" he boomed. "Mr. Somerset, if you'll go up fifty yards to the left, I'll work over to the right. Remember the girl may be lying unconscious, or too weak to shout. We meet where the path crosses the stream."

The two obeyed without demur, and they began to move slowly up the steepening hillside, shouting at intervals. Mr. Lewker's route took him ever closer to the tumbling stream on his right, which plunged and roared in a miniature canyon between rock walls topped with mountain ash and bilberry. Always, as he mounted over shelving rock and heathery slope, the deeper note of Riggin Spout increased in volume. No reply to his intermittent shouts came to his ear, and presently he realized that between the boom of the waterfall above and the rushing of the stream below him he could not hope to hear anything.

Once he paused for breath, and stood for a moment looking down at the valley. Purple dusk flooded Birkerdale, and the sides of the ravine into which they were climbing shut out much of the outlook; but he could see a section of the track leading up to the lead mines—half a mile away beyond the stream—and made out three figures trudging slowly up it.

The retaining walls of the Riggin Beck began to close in rapidly now. Vera, on the zigzags of the path, was only a few yards away and Ted was being forced closer in by the frowning precipices of Black Crag. Presently Mr. Lewker pulled himself over a damp barrier of mossy rock to find himself on the path with the others waiting for him and the thunder of the waterfall deafening him at short range.

At that darkling hour the place was eerily impressive. The path had zigzagged its way into the maw of the ravine, where Riggin Spout came hurtling down from its upper gorge between the beetling face of Black Crag and the opposite rock wall, equally steep but not so high. The true right side of the fall was a precipice eighty feet high, sheer and unclimbable; and the path, to get itself out of the impasse, crossed the stream below the fall by a wooden footbridge which spanned it where it narrowed after emerging from the dark pool at the foot of the Spout. They were standing now on a rocky hump close above the footbridge, with the pool just below them and the outer spray of the fall touching them with its feathery cold fingers.

"Keep to the path for a little," bellowed Mr. Lewker above the tumult. "Higher up we can—"

He stopped short. His eye had caught a gleam of white below him, at the edge of the pool. Without a word he scrambled down, his boots striking bright sparks from the rock, and stooped to the unquiet water. The thing that floated there had once been a pretty girl with fair hair.

He straightened himself to find Ted and Vera at his side. Their faces were very white in the dusk, and Ted was trembling violently. He put his mouth to the young man's ear.

"Go across and down towards the lead mine track. Get those three men up here."

Ted turned away without a word. Vera gripped Mr. Lewker's arm convulsively.

"Can't we—get her out?" she shouted.

"If you can stand it," he replied.

She nodded, and they bent to the pool. When the limp, sodden body was laid on the water-worn stones Mr. Lewker gestured to the girl and they turned it on its face. He caught sight of Vera's expression and thrust her away in the direction of the path. She obeyed him blindly. Mr. Lewker bent over the body again. The back of the skull had been beaten in as if by a blow against a rock; the wound, he thought, had probably been caused by a fall from Black Crag into the stream above the Spout. Nevertheless—for the remembrance of something heard earlier that evening bothered him— he knelt and made a further examination of the body.

When he had finished, Mr. Lewker sat back on his heels and frowned for a long time at nothing.

CHAPTER III
INDUCTIONS DANGEROUS

IT WAS A SATURDAY WHEN GAY JOHNSON'S BODY WAS FOUND in the pool below Riggin Spout. Next morning Mr. Lewker woke to find the rain prophesied by the landlord of the Herdwick Arms falling steadily and the Birkerdale fells invisible under a Sabbath mantle of dark gray mist. He turned over in his creaking but comfortable bed and went to sleep again—with him an unusual procedure; but it had been long after midnight before the ghoulishly excited Mrs. Crake had shown him up to his room.

There had been much to do. Vera Crump had been sent down to Langthwaite with a message hurriedly scribbled on a leaf of Lewker's notebook; Georgie had driven to Riding Mount (thus meeting her celebrated acquaintance Sir Walter under somewhat difficult circumstances) and the Deputy Chief Constable himself had telephoned the Egremont police station and the ambulance; as a result, ambulance and police car were at Langthwaite within an hour of the bringing down of the body. This last had been no easy matter. Crake, the Langthwaite farmer, was absent at Cockermouth and there were no farm hands available, so that the stretcher-bearing was left to Mr. Lewker, Ted Somerset, and Ben Truby with his two assistants. There are few forms of physical labor more exhausting than carrying a laden stretcher down a mountainside. When there are only five bearers, and the moon is their only light, the toil becomes severe. Fortunately the moon, though its light was diffused through a filmy layer of vapor presaging the rain that was to follow, was up in time to guide their steps; but as the stretcher was of the old-fashioned kind with short handles, the rear man was unable to see his footing. The thousand feet of descent took the little party well over two hours, and even the gaunt shepherd's excited volubility was reduced to an occasional grunt long before they reached the easier valley path and saw the gleam of police torches coming to meet them.

Mr. Lewker, who had taken his full share of the work, flatly refused the police-sergeant's invitation to go down to Egremont and make his report to the inspector there. Over cups of strong sweet tea in Mrs. Crake's lamplit kitchen he and the two Youth Hostelers gave such information as the sergeant required and were bidden to hold themselves ready and at hand in case of further inquiry. Ted Somerset and Vera Crump were then dismissed to make their way once more up the Riggin Beck path to the hostel, and Ben Truby and his friends cadged a lift in the police car as far as the village. Mr. Lewker and his wife went to bed. And it was not until they were breakfasting at the comfortable hour of ten-thirty that either of them felt sufficiently recovered to discuss the events of the previous evening.

Mrs. Crake broached the subject with her first appearance bearing the teapot. She was a little angular woman with a weather-beaten face and an exceedingly limber jaw which continued to move even when she had finished speaking, so that she appeared to be chewing the cud of her last sentence.

"That poor young lass!" she began without preamble. "Not a wink I've slept for thinking, and that's gospel. 'Twas the same when t'other one was brought down, the young man, on the Whitmonday. Not a wink could I sleep that night, and Mr. Crake, he was that short with me for tossing and turning—but I couldn't help myself, and that's gospel. We're fearfully and wonderfully made as the Bible says and that's how I'm made. I dare say you're the same."

As Mr. Lewker appeared fascinated by the action of the good lady's jaw his wife hastened to take advantage of the pause for breath.

"Such a sad happening is bound to affect one, of course," she said, with one eye on the teapot. "But there's nothing like a really good cup of tea for—"

"Just what I said to your gentleman here last night," agreed Mrs. Crake irresistibly. She advanced a step and contrived, in some miraculous manner, to fold her arms while still holding the teapot. "Not but what I was a mite aggravated when I was hustled out of my own kitchen by the police," she added, throwing a reproachful glance at Lewker. "But there, least said soonest mended. When there's deaths about you can't pick and choose, as I told Mr. Crake when he grumbled at them putting Robert Peel's corpse in his barn."

She paused again, but her audience was momentarily too startled to take advantage of it and after a few seconds of cud-chewing she was off again.

" 'Twas the young man's name, Robert Peel. A rock climber, they said, and fell off Black Crag. Maybe the poor lass you found did the same. 'Tis a silly, senseless thing to go clambering on precipices, and if I've said so to Mr. Crake once I've said so a thousand times—and 'twas a mistake to put one of these Youth Hostels on Cauldmoor, which I've told him often enough, though he will have it that they're healthy for young folk. Maybe, I says, but not on Cauldmoor, night to Coffin's Pike and Bent Stones."

Mr. Lewker's little eyes flickered. He was quick enough to forestall Mrs. Crake's next utterance.

"Bent Stones—that is the stone circle on Cauldmoor, I think?" he boomed. "Why do you say that, Mrs. Crake?"

But the farmer's wife apparently discovered at this juncture that she was withholding tea from her guests. Somewhat flustered, she advanced to the table, avoiding Mr. Lewker's eye.

"Bless me if I'm not nursing the teapot while you're thirsting!" she clucked, placing the pot in the midst of the array of toast, butter, bannocks, honey and porridge. "I'm upset, like, and that's gospel. There you are now, and a wee shout will bring me if you want more."

Georgie smiled her thanks. "I'm so sorry we're late breakfasting," she said, "but really we were very tired, and the weather—well, it looks as though it intends to pour all day, doesn't it?"

" 'T will clear tomorrow," nodded Mrs. Crake, glancing at the dripping elms and gray mist framed in the window of her sitting room. "Weeping tears for that poor lass, I reckon." She plodded to the door and paused there. "If 'twas suicide, then you'll find Bent Stones had summut to do with it," she added unexpectedly, and went out.

Georgie, pouring out tea, raised an eyebrow in the direction of her husband.

"What *are* these Stones, and why are they Bent?" she demanded. "And why does Mrs. Crake shy away from the subject and return to it again?"

"A rather unusual stone circle; unusual, that is, in that such a thing is rare in Cumberland." Mr. Lewker laid down his porridge spoon and lectured pontifically. "Archeologists—that is to say some of them, for they never agree—call it a Thing-Stead, which is the Scandinavian name. It may have been a burial place. The Northmen who colonized this part of England probably imported the custom. As to the epithet 'Bent,' that may originate in the fact that most of the standing stones are decidedly out of the vertical. We will walk up and look at it tomorrow if you care to."

"You're positively encyclopedic, darling. But why are people so mysterious about it—that old man yesterday, too?"

"These archeological curiosities generally have some local superstition attached to them. Though it is odd," added Mr. Lewker, resuming his attack on the porridge, "that I heard nothing about the Old Ones when I was last in Birkerdale."

"Chance for you to do a bit of holiday detection, darling," said Georgie flippantly. "The Quest of the Old Ones, or the Remarkable Occurrences on Coffin's Pike. Ben Truby may dance nightly there with Scandinavian witches, or something. By the way, what made Mrs. Crake suggest that poor girl might have committed suicide?"

"I rather fancy she was listening at her kitchen door when Miss Crump poured her intuitions into the ear of the police-sergeant last night." Lewker told her of Vera's remarks about Gay Johnson. "That young lady is as opinionated as Coriolanus."

"Yes—I'm sorry for Ted."

Georgie eyed her husband for a moment in silence.

"Filthy," she said at last, "do *you* think she committed suicide?"

"I am not thinking about it at all," he returned decisively. "Death and porridge do not mix. I wonder why it is that porridge invariably tastes better north of Lancaster."

"Last year," said his wife abstractedly, "you said porridge was only edible north of the Clyde. Filthy, you're shying, like Mrs. Crake. Something's bothering you. I can tell it by the way your hair sticks up. Is it about this dead girl?"

Mr. Lewker pushed away his empty bowl and smoothed his tufts of hair resentfully.

"I do beseech you, madam, be content," he boomed. "The girl was killed by striking her head on a rock, just as we are told young Robert Peel died. She was a rock climber, as was Peel. Her body was found in the same spot—the place where a climber, falling off Black Crag into the Riggin Beck, would eventually land. It is reasonable to assume that she was climbing alone and slipped, quite possibly at the same point at which Peel slipped. Now cast deduction and inductions dangerous behind you, my dear, and un-dishcover the bacon."

Georgie perceived that further pursuit of the subject would annoy him. She dispensed the crisp rashers of Mrs. Crake's home-cured and changed the subject.

"Sir Walter Haythornthwaite was awfully nice, I thought," she said. "I burst in on him with your message just when he was beginning his dinner—all alone, poor man, he's a bachelor—and he remembered meeting me in London at once. He's not my idea of a Chief Constable, though."

"Deputy Chief Constable," corrected her husband. "The C.C. is Colonel Fitzherbert, large, mustached, and military."

"I know, and he's in Europe on holiday. Sir Walter told me. He wants us to dine with him tonight—Sir Walter, I mean."

"Very kind of him. I shall be delighted, the more so that I shall not have to dress."

"Oh, but you will, darling," Georgie said quickly. "Sir Walter was in evening things—black tie and velvet coat, anyway."

Mr. Lewker laid down his knife and fork and regarded her steadily.

"I do not," he said emphatically, "take my dinner jacket into the remoter parts of the Cumberland mountains."

"I know, darling. I packed it with my things. After all, you're a celebrity—"

Mr. Lewker rolled his eyes heavenward and shook both fists in the air.

"Angels and ministers of grace defend us!" he moaned. "By what conceivable right does the female decree the raiment of the male? No sane man would expect me to bring a dinner jacket from London to Birkerdale for the sole purpose of wearing it at his dinner table. Sir Walter will conclude either that I confidently anticipated being invited to dinner, or that I am one of those extraordinary gentlemen who dress for dinner in the African jungle."

"Nonsense!" said Georgie firmly. "He will conclude that you have a charming and thoughtful wife who looks after you properly."

Whatever retort her husband was preparing was forestalled by a knock at the door. Mrs. Crake put her angular face into the room.

"The young gent that helped bring down the poor lass is here," she announced. "He wants a wee word with Mr. Lewker, Privately, he says. I've put him in t' small parlor."

Lewker rose from the table with a sigh.

"Pray excuse me, my dear," he boomed. "And observe that there are six bannocks. I expect to find at least three remaining when I return. I am, of course, thinking of your figure."

Leaving his wife speechless, he followed Mrs. Crake, who ushered him into "t' small parlor" and shut him in.

Ted Somerset, the water dripping from an old oilskin cape and his lank fair hair streaked wetly over his forehead, was staring aimlessly at the array of Sheep Fair certificates that covered the walls of the tiny room. He turned a pale and worried face to Mr. Lewker as the latter entered.

"I hope I'm not troubling you, sir," he began, rushing the words in an excess of embarrassment. "I wanted to thank you for your help last night, and—and there was something I wanted to ask you. I dare say you'll think

I'm an awful nuisance, after all the trouble—"

"Let us be seated," suggested the actor-manager genially. "And, if I may advise it, you had better remove your cape. Mrs. Crake's chairs are genuine horsehair models, but the antimacassars may suffer. So. Now. Good news or bad, that thou comest in so bluntly?"

Mr. Somerset hesitated, twining his fingers nervously.

"It's about—Gay Johnson," he blurted out at last, and came to a full stop.

"Yes?" said Mr. Lewker gently. "I suppose Mr.—Bligh, wasn't it?—is badly shaken up. A sad business."

"Oh, Leonard's very upset, of course. He took it pretty well, though. It's the—the body that worries me, sir."

"Oh. In what way? All the proper arrangements will be made, you know, and the police are informing the poor girl's parents."

"I didn't mean that." Ted Somerset's nervousness was making him oddly defiant. "I mean its—condition."

Lewker looked up sharply. The other saw it, and went on rapidly.

"I think you noticed it too, sir. When we got her on to the stretcher. There wasn't anything but that head wound. Not a scratch on the face— nothing broken. You see, I once had to help bring down the body of a climber who'd fallen off a crag in Wales. It was—well, awfully knocked about. Gay wasn't touched, except for that bash on the head."

He paused, a trifle disconcerted by Lewker's steady regard. The older man rubbed his chin thoughtfully.

"Does it not occur to you," he asked, "that if the girl fell from Black Crag into the water, and so over the fall, she might easily have received no injury besides the fatal blow on the head?"

Ted leaned forward eagerly.

"But she couldn't. Couldn't fall straight into the stream, I mean. I've seen the place, you know, sir, though I haven't climbed on Black Crag. It drops pretty sheer to the gorge where the stream runs, but anyone falling off one of the climbing routes would be certain to hit the ledges where the crag isn't so steep. I'd say a—a falling body would smash pretty badly before it rolled into the water."

Lewker's frown deepened. "Are you suggesting, then, that the girl did in fact commit suicide by jumping into the stream above the fall?"

The young man's jaw set firmly.

"No," he said, "I'm not. She wasn't that kind, and there wasn't enough cause."

"Hum. Have you said anything about this to Miss Crump?"

"Oh, no. She—er—she's always saying I read too many detective stories. I told her I was just going to walk down and thank you for helping us. But look here, sir—don't you think it's a bit funny? About the body?"

Mr. Lewker massaged his chin in silence for a moment without taking his gaze from the thin, rather excited face before him.

"You are suggesting, Mr. Somerset," he said in his deepest voice, "that the girl was the victim of foul play?"

Ted Somerset flinched from this remark, but he replied steadily enough.

"I don't want to go so far as that, sir. I only think it's very odd she should have landed in that pool with just the one wound. And I think the police ought to know about it."

"I see. There is one possibility that may not have occurred to you. Suppose the girl reached a place on her climb from which she could neither advance nor retreat. Suppose she felt herself unable to hold on any longer, and, seeing that her only chance of survival was to fall clear of the rocks at the foot of the crag, jumped for the stream."

Ted's jaw dropped slightly. "I suppose that's just possible," he muttered. "I hadn't thought of it. Even then, though, I doubt if anyone could jump that far, horizontally, from small footholds on an almost vertical rock face."

Lewker nodded slowly. He was beginning to think that young Mr. Somerset, out of the company of his Vera, showed considerably more acumen and determination than was apparent from his rather invertebrate appearance.

"And what do you propose to do about this?" he inquired.

"I—I rather thought you might advise me, sir," replied the young man.

"Yes. Pray tell me one thing more. Have you any other reason, apart from what you so acutely observed about the body, to suppose that Miss Johnson did not die by accident?"

Ted's hesitation before replying, though very brief, did not escape Mr. Lewker.

"No—no reason, sir."

"You are quite sure?"

"Quite." There was no hesitation this time.

"Very well." Mr. Lewker sat back and folded his hands judicially. "I will be frank with you, laddie. The condition of the body did not escape me. Like you, I think it an odd circumstance. But, unless there is some other circumstance pointing to that oddness from another angle, so to speak, it remains merely an odd circumstance. It is odd, but not impossible, that Miss Johnson should have fallen and been killed by a single blow, without further injury. To read into the business any sinister meaning is, if you will forgive me, unjustified by the evidence. I have probably seen a great deal more of violent death, by accident and otherwise, than you have, and I can assure you that accidents, of this type particularly, often present curious details. My advice, in short, is that you should forget the matter."

Ted had listened to this grave diatribe with his gaze lowered to his nervously twisting hands. Now he looked up.

"I see what you mean, sir," he said quietly, "and thanks very much. But I still think I'll go on down to Egremont and mention it to the police. I'll be easier in my mind then, even if they laugh at me."

He got up and picked up his cape. Mr. Lewker rose also.

"You must do what you think right, laddie," he boomed. "One more word. Do not mention your suspicions or conjectures to anyone but the police."

"I won't, sir," promised Ted earnestly. "Er—will there be an inquest?"

"Yes. The sergeant informed me that it would probably be on Tuesday afternoon at the Herdwick Arms. You will no doubt be notified."

Mr. Lewker saw his visitor to the door of Langthwaite and watched him stride away into the gray drizzle. He found five bannocks remaining when he returned to the breakfast table, and having told Georgie that Ted Somerset had walked down from the Hostel to thank them for their help, ate the bannocks one after the other in a somewhat abstracted silence. Georgie forbore to comment; she perceived that the matter of the dinner jacket was superseded in her husband's mind, and like a wise wife let well enough alone.

The cloak of mist and rain showed no sign of lifting from Birkerdale that morning. Georgie succeeded in dragging her husband out for a damp and squelchy walk up the narrowing valley above the farm, where the Birker foamed and tinkled through the dripping mosses under the invisible flanks of Bleaberry Dodd. They returned soaked but with an appetite for Mrs. Crake's roast mutton. The afternoon was equally wet and gloomy. Lewker dozed in an armchair over a yellowed volume of *The Antiquities of Cumberland* while his wife wrote letters. At seven o'clock Mr. Lewker was cajoled and assisted into his dinner jacket and gave it as his honest opinion that his wife, in a dinner gown of clinging russet, looked more charming than any tyrant had a right to look. By half-past seven the ancient Wolseley was splashing through the puddles of the lane on its way to Riding Mount.

Sir Walter Haythornthwaite's house, seen through the gray veil of rain as they drove up the unfenced drive between sodden fields, looked decrepit and uninviting. Mr. Lewker, indeed, was constrained to mutter something about

A slobbery and a dirty farm
In that nook-shotten isle of Albion.

This was unfair, however. The long, low house had never been a farm, and though its gray stonewalls were blotched with lichen where they were not covered with creeper, and its outhouses ruinous, it had an air of decayed grandeur. It stood on a slight rise of ground close under the enfolding slopes of the hills—now darkly invisible in the mists—with a plantation of firs flanking it on the southwest. A few flowering shrubs grew beneath its tall windows, but there was no other garden. Its interior, revealed to them by the neat maid who opened the door, diffused at once a totally different atmosphere. The wide hall was oak-paneled and its oaken chests and chairs shone with polishing. The radiator and the arrangement of pipes that heated the cloakroom where they left their coats showed that Sir Walter had an eye to modern comforts; the almost feminine neatness of the handsome room into which they were shown impressed Georgie as it had done on her previous visit.

Their host came forward smiling to greet them. Lewker, who had not met him before, shook hands with a very tall thin gentleman who (as Georgie had remarked) did not look in the least like a Deputy Chief Constable. Sir Walter Haythornthwaite's silver hair was long enough, and his bow tie large enough, to encourage the conclusion that here was a devotee of one of the Arts. His black velvet jacket supported this impression, as did his long and aquiline features with their surprisingly black brows.   ·

"I saw your *Richard the Third*," he said to Lewker, "but even before that I wanted to meet you. It is a very happy chance that brings you and your wife to my retreat."

He seated them in comfortable tapestry chairs before the fireplace, in which a fire of applewood logs burned brightly, and went to a delicate Chippendale table which bore a decanter and glasses.

"This is a rather delightful Montilla," he said in his slightly mincing tenor voice. "I do hope, Mrs. Lewker, that a dry sherry is to your taste?"

"It is indeed," Georgie replied comfortably. "Sweet sherry always reminds me of funerals."

Sir Walter laughed. Laughter gave his coldly chiseled features a more human cast. He became grave an instant later, however, as he was handing the glasses.

"I cannot forget the unfortunate youngster who fell to her death so recently," he said. "Such a sad business—and how grim a welcome for you, Mrs. Lewker, on your first visit to Birkerdale!"

"It was, rather," admitted Georgie, sipping her sherry. "But we shall forget it when the sun comes out. I suppose it will come out again? There hasn't even been a sky all day."

"I will prophesy a fine day tomorrow, and I have some reputation as a weather prophet. One does not spend most of one's year in Birkerdale without acquiring something of the art of local meteorology." He turned to Lewker. "Though I must admit to failures in the Cumberland springtime— 'the uncertain glory of an April day,' you know."

"Please don't start him quoting Shakespeare, Sir Walter," Georgie begged. "It's a shocking bad habit he's got. And in Filthy's case it's nothing less than talking shop."

"It is my contention," boomed her husband, "that Shakespeare said everything worth saying and said it better than anyone else."

"Nonsense, darling. Shakespeare never said anything about watercolors, for instance—did he, Sir Walter?"

"I cannot recall anything, certainly. Are you interested in watercolor painting, Lewker?"

It was remarkable, thought Mr. Lewker, how the mere mention of watercolors brought life and enthusiasm to Sir Walter's rather effeminate face.

"Very little indeed," he answered.

"Filthy is the original Philistine," said Georgie. *"You* know—'I know nothing about Art, but I know what I like.' "

"Abercrombie Lewker is a very great artist in his own line," said Sir Walter gracefully. "And I only wish I had something in my own line to show him at Riding Mount. Taste is rarely confined to one branch of Art."

"You have no watercolors here, then?" asked Georgie. "I should have thought—"

"Dear lady, here I am a countryman, a farmer. I can indulge my particular passion only when I visit London. And such visits are rare, with the cost of travel what it is—for I am not a rich man, as you will have deduced from the condition of Riding Mount. However, I can sing, with Walton, of 'the sweet contentment the countryman doth find,' and relinquish Art—"

The reverberations of the dinner gong interrupted him. He offered Georgie his arm and Mr. Lewker followed them into a smaller paneled room where shaded candles lit the dinner table.

The dinner, served by the neat maid who had admitted them, was excellent, if plain. Sir Walter talked of Lakeland customs, of fishing, of sheep and shepherds. He talked very well, for he was a conversationalist of an older school and used English in a manner that delighted Mr. Lewker. Nevertheless, the actor-manager could have wished to hear more about watercolors; he was never averse to listening to an expert on his own subject.

The maid, entering to announce that coffee was served in the day room, interrupted a spirited discourse on the trout pools of the Birker stream.

"There's a gentleman waiting to see you, sir," she added. The slight pause before the noun was noticeable. "He says it's important."

"Oh?" Sir Walter frowned. "Who is it?"

"A Mr. Grimmett, sir. He said not to disturb you until you'd finished dinner."

Sir Walter turned to Georgie with a shrug.

"It sounds like police business," he said apologetically. "I do hope you'll excuse me. I shall take as little time as possible."

"Of course." Georgie rose. "I'd almost forgotten you were a Deputy C.C."

"I had quite forgotten," he smiled. "Let me escort you to the day room. I shall have to rely on you to save me some coffee."

They came out into the hall. A sturdy, sandy-mustached man in a weatherstained raincoat rose from the oak settle on which he had been sitting.

"I'll be with you in one moment, Inspector," Sir Walter was beginning, when Lewker broke in.

"Now by two-headed Janus!" he boomed. "If it is not Grimm himself!"

Detective-Inspector Grimmett's round blue eyes gleamed and his brickred face broadened in a smile.

"Mr. Lewker, sir," he returned, "this is a rare chance, so it is."

"You have met before, I take it?" Sir Walter inquired, as the two grasped hands.

"We have indeed," responded Lewker. "Grimm was attached to Department Seven when I was working for them during the War."

"Secret Service," amplified the Inspector with relish. He turned to Sir Walter. "I understand it was Mr. Lewker that found the body of Miss Johnson, sir. If I might suggest it, it'd be an advantage to have him in for our little chat."

"Yes, yes. Very well." Sir Walter looked worried. "I'll take Mrs. Lewker to her coffee and then I will be with you."

Murmuring apologies, he ushered Georgie into the day room. Mr. Lewker grinned at the detective.

" 'Fine apparition! My quaint Ariel!' " he boomed. "What are you doing in these outlandish parts?"

"It's my beat nowadays," replied the other. "Got a transfer. Very quiet here mostly, so it is. Not like old times. D'you remember, sir—"

Sir Walter emerged from the day room and beckoned them to follow him. He led them through a door at the farther end of the hall and switched on the light. The dim radiance (Riding Mount's electricity was provided by a small gasoline-engine) revealed a neat study lined with books on watercoloring, artists, and art collecting. The Deputy Chief Constable closed the door and turned to face Grimmett.

"Now, Inspector," he said sharply. "What is all this about?"

The detective blew through his mustache, a mannerism Mr. Lewker remembered from seven years before.

"Well, Sir Walter," he said slowly, "it might be about—murder."

CHAPTER IV
TO PROVE A VILLAIN

"MURDER?" REPEATED SIR WALTER, EYEING THE INSPECTOR keenly. "Are you suggesting, Grimmett, that this girl Johnson's death was not an accident?"

"I'm suggesting there's a case for investigation, sir," replied Grimmett carefully.

"Oh." Sir Walter glanced dubiously at Mr. Lewker. "Then I really think—"

"Excuse me, sir," interrupted the detective, interpreting the glance correctly, "but by your leave I'd like Mr. Lewker to hear what I've got. As you know, he's helped us more than once, and I've a fancy he might care to help us now. Being a mountaineer, you see, and knowing about rocks and climbers—"

"Very well, Inspector." Sir Walter waved his hand to a couple of leather-backed chairs and produced a box of cigars from a drawer in his desk. "Sit down. We may as well smoke while we talk. I've given Mrs. Lewker a pile of *Connoisseurs* and some cigarettes," he added to Lewker. "I do hope she'll be able to amuse herself for half an hour."

"Georgie can amuse herself anywhere," said her husband with conviction.

Sir Walter nodded and lit his guests' cigars before seating himself in the swivel chair behind his desk.

"Now, Inspector," he said with a briskness quite unlike his manner as an art expert, "let us have your reasons."

Detective-Inspector Grimmett drew once or twice at his cigar, took a leather-bound notebook from his pocket and laid it on his knee, and began.

"I called in at the Egremont station early this morning," he said in his slow, pleasant voice, "in the matter of clearing up the last of the Cockermouth assault case. We've got him, you know, sir—Brimble it was, just as we thought. Well, Sergeant Miles was on duty at that time, and he gave me the tale of this accident on Black Crag. It seems a Miss Gay Johnson was climbing by her lonesome on the Crag, some time after ten o'clock on Friday morning, and fell off the Crag into the Riggin Beck and over Riggin Spout, her body being found on Saturday evening about half-past nine by Mr. Lewker here and two friends of the deceased. Now some of that's conjecture, as you might say. The facts are that Miss Johnson left the Hostel on Friday morning and her body was found in the pool below the Spout on Saturday evening, with a nasty dent in the back of her head. There's no evidence what happened in between."

"The conjecture is reasonable enough, surely," put in Sir Walter. "The girl was a climber and Black Crag is a popular climbing ground. And remember, Grimmett, another unfortunate climber met his death in just the same way at Whitsuntide."

"I'm coming to that, sir," said Grimmett calmly. "I stayed on a bit at the station, having a cup of char with the sergeant, and it so happened that I was there when the doctor's report came in. Doctor Whitmore brought it round himself. That's the police doctor," he added to Lewker. "He's one of these young chaps—always on the lookout for curiosities in the medical line."

Mr. Lewker nodded. He knew the type.

"Well," continued Grimmett, "the report was straightforward enough. When you'd weeded out the sense from a lot of long words it simply said that death was due to a violent crack on the head from something like a jagged lump of rock."

"The girl was not drowned, then?" queried Sir Walter.

"No, sir. She was dead before she fell into the water, or she might"—the detective paused and blew through his mustache "—she might have hit her head on a rock immediately after falling in. The doctor said it was possible, though there was no water in the lungs."

"I don't see—" began the Deputy Chief Constable, as Grimmett paused again.

"One moment, if you please, sir. Doctor Whitmore, he's a stranger to these parts, and he does a good deal of walking on the fells in his spare time. He's no climber, but he's been up the Riggin Beck path more than once, so he tells me, and had a good look at Black Crag. He says to the sergeant, while I was looking at the report, 'Funny thing, sergeant,' he says, 'that these climbers manage to smash their skulls and nothing else, falling off Black Crag.' Sergeant Miles looks sideways at him. 'You mean it's same as young Peel at Whit?' he says. 'Exactly similar,' says the doctor. 'Not a contusion, let alone a broken limb. Only the fracture of the parietal bone in each case. That's odd, you know,' he says, 'because there's some nasty rocks at the foot of that crag.' "

"The parietal bone—that is near the base of the skull, I think?" Sir Walter frowned.

Grimmett drew appreciatively at his cigar, expelled the smoke, and nodded.

"It is, sir. It's a weak spot, so I understand. And if you'll picture to yourself a man falling clear off a precipice and landing on the rocks below so as to smash in the base of his skull—and not to bruise or break himself up in any other place, you'll admit it'd be a funny sort of fall."

"Surely," said his chief, "it is at least possible. And as for the similarity of the wound in each case, that is perfectly natural if one postulates the quite probable circumstance that both climbers fell at the same spot."

"An inspection of the place would give us more on that line, sir. But there's a bit more to come. I didn't pay much attention to the matter at first—after all, it wasn't my pidgin, and I was just sitting in the background, as you might say, drinking char and listening. But after the doctor had gone Sergeant Miles remarks about a young woman, Vera Crump, who told him last night she reckoned Miss Johnson might have committed suicide and mentioned a quarrel the deceased had with her young man the evening before she disappeared. Well, he'd hardly finished telling me before a young chap comes into the station dripping wet. Name of Edward Somerset and one of the Youth Hostel party. It seems he'd borrowed a bike in Birkerdale and rode down." He turned to Lewker. "He was with you, Mr. Lewker, when you found the body?"

"He was."

"Yes. Struck me as being a nervous type, bit excitable. Well, this youngster, he wishes to call the attention of the police to the fact that the girl was found with no obvious wounds or fractures except that bash on the head. I think you also noticed that when you fetched her down, sir?"

Mr. Lewker nodded again.

"Ah. Now this young Somerset, he's got some idea in his head that he won't let out. Miles put him through it gently, as to what he inferred from the matter, why he thought it of interest, and so forth. All he'd say was that he wanted to make sure the police had noticed it. But there's no doubt he had some suspicion or other in his mind."

"I hope Miles did not foster it?" frowned Sir Walter.

"He didn't, sir. Thanked him nicely, told him the matter would be noted, advised him not to worry about it or pass it on, and gave him to understand the police weren't much interested. He went off a bit disappointed in us, I think."

Sir Walter smiled. "Miles does that sort of thing rather well. But look here, Inspector, is this all you have to go on?"

"That's all, sir."

"It isn't much, is it? I can't say I follow your line of thought. Here we have two climbing accidents, one at Whitsuntide, one in late August. Both display exactly similar features, both victims are casual visitors at a Youth Hostel. In the first instance there has been no slightest suggestion of foul play, in the second you have a girl hinting vaguely at suicide and a boy pointing out a not very remarkable circumstance which the police doctor has already noticed as merely odd. There appears to be no connection whatever between the two unfortunate victims. Really, Grimmett, if you are attempting to construct a sinister murderer out of these materials I begin to think you should be writing romances instead of working with the Force."

Grimmett blew forcibly through his mustache and rubbed his head, somewhat abashed.

"It'd be a neat way of bringing off a murder, so it would," he muttered. "Bash your man's head in with a rock, drop him in the place where he'd fall off a rock climb, and everyone assumes he's met with a climbing accident."

Sir Walter wagged his head tolerantly.

"My dear Inspector," he said. "I grant you the neatness of such a method. I grant you—on Doctor Whitmore's evidence—the oddness of the bodies arriving in the Riggin Spout Pool with only the one, fatal, wound. But who would want to kill young Robert Peel, from Derbyshire, at Whitsuntide, *and* Miss Gay Johnson, from Birmingham, in August? And why?"

"We don't know there's no connection between the two," said Grimmett doggedly. "My opinion, sir, is that we ought at least to make a further investigation."

The Deputy Chief Constable shrugged and sighed a trifle impatiently.

"In my opinion you are building mysteries out of thin air," he said. "What do you think, Lewker?"

Mr. Lewker, who had been sitting perfectly still and looking like a cigar-smoking Buddha in evening dress, took the cigar from his mouth and carefully flicked the ash into a tray.

"When I worked with Grimm—I beg his indulgence—Detective-Inspector Grimmett, in Department Seven," he boomed, "we heard a number of what we flippantly called 'Grimm's Fairy Tales.' The odd thing about them was that they always came true."

Sir Walter put out a hand. "Do not imagine," he said quickly, "that I have no respect for the Inspector's opinion. I have always regarded him as possessing remarkable acumen. But the facts of the case, as I put them just now, give no real basis for an investigation."

"The facts as you put them, Sir Walter, constitute the case against investigation," amended Lewker. "As Grimm put them, they make, in my opinion, a reasonable case for at least preliminary inquiry."

"You really think these deaths may have been due to something other than accident?"

"I think there is that possibility, that is all. Here we have two deaths, each displaying the same odd circumstance—odd, that is, until some satisfactory explanation has been found. The second death has the concomitants of a reported quarrel before the event and a suggestion of suicide after it. But," he added rather tardily, "I have of course no right to express an opinion at an official conference."

Sir Walter waved his cigar in courteous dissent.

"Pray do not hesitate, my dear fellow. We may regard you as the gifted amateur of detective fiction tonight, though in fact such gentlemen are rare—eh, Grimmett?"

"Mr. Lewker's helped us more than once, sir," returned the detective defensively.

"Of course, of course. Please go on, Lewker."

Thus encouraged, Mr. Lewker proceeded with his argument. He had at this time no real expectation of unearthing crime. He supported Grimmett's proposition partly because of his old acquaintance's obvious eagerness to investigate and partly because he felt the insidious excitement of detective work in prospect. The thrill of the successful manhunt, once experienced, is not soon forgotten. Like the enthusiastic fisherman, the amateur of detection is impelled to cast his line over any pool, however unpromising.

"The remarkable increase in the number of British rock climbers," he boomed didactically, "and the inevitable increase in fatal accidents, offers an excellent opportunity to a clever murderer, given that his intended victim is an addict of the sport. It so happens that I have personal experience of this. The murderer, concealed at a suitable point on the climb, merely slogged his man with a rock and trusted to the wound being attributed to the effects of the fall—which it would have been, but for a very minor circumstance. The facts of that case were not made public. But I see no reason why someone else should not have thought of the method. As for the lack of connection between the two victims in the present instance, I fancy that if such a connection could be established we should be far on our way to proving a villain in the case."

He sat back in his chair and resumed his cigar. Sir Walter remained silent, frowning thoughtfully.

"There's this, too, sir," put in Grimmett. "If there's been foul play, who's to say it'll stop with two deaths? I reckon we ought to look into it, for our own peace of mind, sir."

The Deputy Chief Constable, with the air of taking a decision, nodded and leaned forward across his desk.

"Very well," he said briskly. "I still think you'll find a mare's nest, but I see, Grimmett, that you're looking for a job. Nothing else on hand?"

"Not now Brimble's arrested, sir."

"Then proceed with your preliminary inquiry. But mark this, Inspector." Sir Walter wagged an emphatic finger. "It will have to be done quietly. We cannot afford to raise a clamor about nothing. You will take charge of the whole thing, of course, and work in your own way. But I fail to see how you can detain the Youth Hostel people for questioning, as you will need to do, without giving some sort of explanation."

"I've thought of that, sir." Grimmett, having won his point, was suddenly apologetic in his manner. "They've all been asked to stay on for the inquest on Tuesday. It's pretty certain the girl will be buried at Birkerdale or Egremont, and we can suggest it'd be a nice gesture if they all attended the funeral, say on Wednesday."

Sir Walter chuckled. "I see. Don't think I'm interfering, Inspector, but just as a matter of interest how do you propose to interrogate the people at the Youth Hostel without appearing in the character of a police detective?"

Grimmett's face deepened its shade of brick-red and his round blue eyes wandered uneasily about the room, finally coming to rest on the ash of his cigar.

"Well, sir," he muttered at last, "I *had* thought of getting Mr. Lewker to help us there."

"Indeed!" His chief's black eyebrows went up. "Mr. Lewker is here on holiday, Grimmett. In any case, he will hardly—"

"My lord, this burden will I undertake," boomed Lewker. "That is, if I can be of assistance. In any case, I intended to have a day's climbing on Black Crag if I can find anyone to climb with. I am still capable of leading a Difficult, provided there are no narrow chimneys."

"That's just it, sir," the Inspector put in quickly. "I'd like someone to have a look at that climb. If I might suggest it, you could stay a couple of nights at the Youth Hostel, Mr. Lewker, and see what you can pick up there."

"I can hardly be described as a youth," objected the actor-manager. "And I presume it is necessary to be a member of the Youth Hostels Association in order to stay at the Cauldmoor Hostel."

"I can fix that, sir. Miles knows Mr. Meirion, the Warden—a queer fish he is, too, so Miles says. You could walk up there casual-like, saying you're keen to see what Youth Hostel life's like. There's no age limit in the Hostels, you know."

Sir Walter, who now that he had given his blessing to the investigation seemed determined to be helpful, nodded eagerly.

"An excellent scheme, Lewker, if your wife will spare you for a day or two," he said. "No doubt the two young people who were with you when you found the body will have told the other Hostelers who you are, but your connection with us will not be known. I think," he added with an impish smile, "that you should wear shorts and a beret. It's in the part—don't you think so?"

"As an intending rock climber," retorted the actor-manager, "knee breeches are both more in character and more suited to my figure. I'll make my entrance tomorrow morning, if that suits your plans, Grimm."

"It's very kind of you, sir, so it is," Grimmett said, beaming. "It'll give me a chance, in the meantime, to find out what I can about Mr. Robert Peel."

"Excellent. You will want me to discover whether any of the present Hostel crowd were staying there at Whitsuntide, naturally. There are not many people there now, I gather."

"No, sir. It's quite a small place—room for eight and the Warden. There were seven staying in the Hostel and now there's six." Grimmett turned the pages of his notebook. "The constable who went up this morning to give notice of the inquest got their names. Four men and two girls—but I'll send you up a note of that with some other matters first thing in the morning. You'll not be leaving before eight?"

"Grimm, I rise with the lark at eight-thirty. Even the prospect of clue-hunting will get me up no earlier."

"All right, sir. I know very well you're itching to get to work. We'll swap results at the inquest."

The two grinned at each other. Sir Walter shook a paternally tolerant head over them.

"Zeal, all zeal, Mr. Easy," he observed whimsically. "I hope, for both your sakes, it is not wasted zeal. For my own comfort, on the other hand, I hope it is."

"To quote the same author, sir," returned Grimmett, "I fancy there'll be a bobbery in the pigsty before long." He pocketed his notebook and rose to his feet. "We can but go ahead and see. I hope you'll apologize to Mrs. Lewker for me, and I'm sorry to have interrupted your evening, sir."

"You did perfectly right, Inspector. If this business does come to any-thing I'll crave your pardon most humbly for my doubts. Meanwhile, you can of course count upon me for any assistance I can give."

"Thank you, sir."

Mr. Grimmett, escorted to the door, sprinted into the dark and rain in search of the small car in which he had driven from Egremont. Sir Walter and Lewker, entering the day room, found Georgie seated on the hearthrug playing with a small Persian kitten.

"Dear lady, how can I apologize?" Sir Walter was effusive; the brisk manner of the Deputy Chief Constable had given place to the mild af-fection of the artist host. "To leave you thus alone, and for so long a time—"

"Oh, but I've been very nicely entertained," she smiled, getting up and smoothing her gown. "This charming member of your household has devoted all his—or should it be her?—time to amusing me."

"Ah, Melisande, naughty one!" Sir Walter shook his finger at the kitten. "You should not be in here! She leaves her hairs everywhere, you know. I shall forgive her, however, since she has entertained you."

He picked up the kitten and put it on his shoulder, where it perched contentedly, digging its claws into the velvet and purring loudly.

"I'm afraid the coffee's cold," said Georgie. "Your visitor must have had a long tale to tell. I hope it was interesting?"

"Interesting, but steep, as Huckleberry Finn remarks," replied Sir Walter. "I shall leave your husband to tell you about it." He sat down. "Let me see—we were talking about trout fishing, were we not?"

"You were," said Georgie frankly. "And I was rather hoping you'd talk about art. It isn't every night one dines with a world-famous expert—"

"Please, Mrs. Lewker!" Sir Walter smiled and raised a hand in protest. "If I were a world famous heart specialist, would you expect me to talk about cardiac peculiarities, here in my retirement? I would far rather talk theater. For instance"—he turned to Lewker—"it has always struck me that this idea of putting Shakespeare into modern dress, merely because the Elizabethans acted the plays in Elizabethan costume, is wholly fallacious. What do you think?"

Mr. Lewker, nothing loath, allowed himself to be drawn into a discussion which lasted until it was time to leave.

The Wolseley was splashing down the drive of Riding Mount some time after eleven o'clock when Mr. Lewker remembered the death of Gay Johnson and his undertaking to become a Youth Hosteler. He told Georgie what had passed in Sir Walter's study, first cautioning her to say nothing of it to Mrs. Crake.

"In short," he finished, "Abercrombie Lewker, the sleuth of a thousand disguises, adopts tomorrow the semblance of a hiker."

"In short, but not I hope in shorts," said his wife flippantly. "Filthy, you're too old for hiking. And I agree with Sir Walter—you're making a fuss about nothing."

"I hope you are right. As for being too old, my dear, I always feel twenty years younger in the mountains. I shall skip like a young ram. I may even disport myself upon a rock climb."

The headlights of the Wolseley picked out the wet gray walls of the Langthwaite barns and he turned the car into the yard.

"Well, don't go playing the goat on a climb and falling off—like that girl," said Georgie seriously.

"My dear," boomed Mr. Lewker reprovingly, "I am the gifted amateur in this piece. I don't fall off. It's not in my part."

CHAPTER V
SHADOW IN THE SUN

MR. ABERCROMBIE LEWKER, GUIDING SPIRIT OF THE WORLD famous Abercrombie Lewker Players and the finest *Lear* since Macready, stumped cheerfully up the Riggin Beck path in the sparkling sunshine of Monday morning. His bald dome was hatless and shining, he wore patched knee breeches of the sort once favored by penny-farthing cyclists, his khaki shirt was open to display a chest furred with grizzled black hair. On the breast of his shirt was pinned a neat badge, a green inverted triangle bearing the letters "Y.H.A." The badge, together with a small booklet, had arrived at Langthwaite early that morning with a note from the efficient Mr. Grimmett informing him that he was now a member of the Youth Hostels Association and that his annual subscription of ten shillings had been paid for the current year; Mr. Grimmett had not forgotten his onetime colleague's insistence on thoroughness in the smallest matters.

The actor-manager appeared to be entering into the spirit of his new part. In spite of the bulging rucksack containing his sleeping gear and three days' food which was slung on his back, he stormed the steep and rugged track at a speed of which his wife would certainly have disapproved. In imagination he had dropped some thirty-odd years from his age and was a youthful hiker engaged on one of those adventurous journeys which the three hundred hostels of England and Wales have made possible for the youth of our country. Mr. Lewker's tendency to adopt unnecessary disguises and to overplay his parts had been much criticized during his meteoric career in the Secret Service, Department Seven; as when, in 1943, he entered Occupied France disguised as an impoverished nobleman from Touraine, with a forked beard, the *Légion d'Honneur* in his buttonhole, and a bottle of Château Lafitte from the cellars of his ancestral home in his suitcase. The invariable success of his dangerous missions had disarmed censure. In the present case—where, to the uninstructed, the playing of a part might appear wholly unnecessary—he would have maintained that if he was to unearth secrets from a collection of young walkers and climbers he must first make himself as much like them in appearance and outlook as possible.

The freshness of the morning aided his attempt at self-rejuvenation. Mountains are always the best renewers of youth for those who love them, and in the morning after heavy rain they give forth the very essence of a world newmade. The sun had topped the shoulder of Coffin's Pike and set every frond of yellowing bracken on the lower slopes flashing with dia-monds. The beck laughed and sparkled over its rocks, the rowans glowed in brilliant reds and greens and golds, the wet gray crags glistened like immense ingots of silver beside the path. The sun, however, was hot as well as bright, and Mr. Lewker was grateful for the cool shadow into which he climbed, the shadow of the solemn rock walls down which Riggin Spout plunged with a roar into its pool. He gained the rocky hump above the footbridge, from which thirty-six hours before he had seen Gay Johnson's body at the pool's edge, and sat down facing the fall with its cool spray freshening his brow.

The Spout was a noble sight this morning, its swollen waters thundering down in a snowy column from the lip far overhead. Higher still, towering above the verge of the fall, the dark facade of Black Crag rose into the washed blue of the sky, its projections and indentations thrown into strong relief by the slanting sunlight. Mr. Lewker surveyed it curiously, with the eye of the mountaineer; the rock was steep but well broken by ledge and gully, and seemed to be more easily angled farther back, where presumably the routes of the rock climbs ran. The spot whence Gay Johnson had fallen to her death would be, he thought, out of sight from his present viewpoint. He shifted his position to look down at Birker-dale. A faint haze, the breath of drenched meadows grateful for the sun, hung like gossamer above the stonewalled fields. The tiny figures of two men were visible tedding the wet hay in one of the fields—that would be Crake, the Langthwaite farmer, and his farmhand. Langthwaite was out of sight, hidden by the rugged lower slope below Black Crag, but Riding Mount was a diminished doll's house on the farther side of the valley floor, with a drift of blue-gray smoke above its chimneys and the high green hills smil-ing above its cluster of trees.

Mr. Lewker sat for some time in dreamy contemplation of the view be-fore he recollected the business upon which he was bent. He sighed and took an envelope from the rucksack beside him. The booklet sent him by Detective-Inspector Grimmett gave him succinct information as to his mode of life as a Hosteler. "The buildings range from farmhouses, water mills and mansions to specially designed hostels, but all provide simple accom-modation including separate dormitories for men and women, washing fa-cilities, a common room and a kitchen where they can cook their own meals. … Every hostel is under the supervision of a Warden. … You will have to help with hostel duties such as sweeping or washing up. … Hostels are closed between 10 a.m. and 5 p.m. Lights Out is at 10.30 p.m." Mr. Lewker frowned dubiously at the mention of cooking; it was an art which he had never thoroughly mastered. He consoled himself with the remembrance that baked beans on toast, eggs, and porridge require no very extensive culinary knowledge, and turned to Grimmett's letter. This was brief and to the point. After informing Lewker of his induction as a Youth Hosteler—effected overnight by string-pulling on the telephone and the lucky discovery that Sergeant Miles' son was a member—it went on to say that the police of Matlock in Derbyshire had been requested to forward information as to the late Robert Peel's character, occupation, and contacts as soon as possible. It concluded with a list of the persons staying at the Cauldmoor Youth Hostel, as follows:

Miss Vera Crump, Handsworth, Birmingham.
Mr. Edward Somerset, Aston, Birmingham.
Miss Janet Macrae, Lockerbie, Dumfriesshire.
Mr. Hamish Macrae, same address (brother and sister).
Mr. Leonard Bligh, Sutton Coldfield, Warwickshire.
Mr. Bodfan Jones, Llandudno, North Wales.

A footnote remarked that the Warden, Mr. Paul Meirion, was filling the post temporarily, in place of the permanent Warden, Mr. Crosby, who was away on a fortnight's holiday. "Crosby away ill from May 10th to June 12th," added Grimmett's neat handwriting. "During this period Meirion was acting warden. Sergeant Miles informs me M.'s home is at Rhyl, Flintshire."

Mr. Lewker scowled thoughtfully at the footnote; Whitsuntide, he remembered, had fallen on the weekend of May 29th to 31st. He noted also that if Y.H.A. rules were followed at the Cauldmoor Hostel it would be closed by the time he arrived there—which meant, he presumed, that all the Hostelers would be abroad walking or scrambling on the fells but that the Warden might be in. The fine spray of the fall was beginning to soak through his shirt. He got up, shouldered his heavy rucksack, and resumed the ascent.

The footbridge was vibrating like a plucked string with the furious passage of the stream beneath it. He crossed it and began the steep scramble up the rocks of the farther side, the thunder of the Spout drowning even the sound of his own nailed boots on the rough track. The slope of mingled rock and heather up which the path now climbed in zigzags was the flank of the rugged hill which formed the southern retaining wall of Riggin Spout, Black Crag being the northern wall. The path led him out of sight of the fall, but not out of earshot of it. The ceaseless drumming of falling water was still bumbling in his ears when he came quite suddenly over a heathery knoll into the full blaze of sunlight. The track led up a little combe of tumbled boulders before climbing steeply out of it and over a high grassy ridge above. Seated close together on a flat rock, absorbed in earnest conversation, were two men, of whom one was Ben Truby, the shepherd. Lewker received the impression that they had been arguing fiercely.

Both men looked up sharply as the sound of Mr. Lewker's approach reached their ears above the muffled booming of the fall. Ben Truby's long bony face expressed no identifiable emotion at sight of the newcomer, but his companion appeared embarrassed. He was a youngish man, prematurely bald and spectacled, clad in rather long corduroy shorts and a smartly cut wind-jacket of bright green suede, a figure as conspicuous among the gray boulders as the old shepherd's was inconspicuous. Mr. Lewker gave them a cheery good morning as he came up to them. The shepherd grunted and nodded and the youngish man stood up with a nervous smile.

"Good morning," he returned in a high voice with an overrefined accent. "I'm not mistaken? You are Mr. Abercrombie Lewker?"

"I am that same," the actor-manager responded.

The other held out a thin hand. "Charmed to meet you, sir. I'm Paul Meirion—at present Warden of Cauldmoor Hostel. What a glorious morning—isn't it?"

"Glorious indeed," replied Mr. Lewker, shaking the hand. It was cold and limp as a dead fish, and he was reminded of a jingle he had once heard—

> No matter how big your brain may be
> You'll never get to the top
> If you've got an eye like a hardboiled egg
> And a hand like a cold pork chop.

Mr. Meirion's eyes behind the thick lenses of his glasses were singularly hard-boiled-egg-like, and his long pointed nose possessed a curious twist or tilt at the end. His manner, however, was ingratiating.

"Decent of you to take an interest in us, sir," he said. "In the Youth Hostels movement, I mean. Miles, the police sergeant—he's an acquaintance of mine, rather an authority on local folklore—sent Truby up with a message this morning to say that you were coming. I gather you're staying at Langthwaite and asked Miles if there was a Hostel you could visit to see how we work things?"

"Just so," nodded Lewker, accepting this convenient explanation. "I fear," he added, "that I have chosen a particularly inconvenient time for my visit."

"You mean the unfortunate accident to Miss Johnson?" Meirion's sallow face expressed grief, deprecation, and dismissal in rapid succession. "That's upset our little family, of course—but you are none the less welcome. The good work goes on, you know. The only snag is that all the young people with me have been told to stay on for the inquest tomorrow, thus overstaying, in some cases, the limit of three nights fixed by the Y.H.A. Luckily I have no bookings for accommodations until next weekend. Otherwise it might have upset things considerably."

A somewhat cold-blooded young man, thought Mr. Lewker. Aloud he said:

"I see. I suppose two fatal accidents within a few months of each other must have caused you a great deal of trouble."

The Warden colored faintly.

"You think I'm callous, sir," he said unexpectedly and with an even more unexpected defiance in his tone. "Perhaps I am, according to your standards. The deaths of two youngsters, when one's seen a hundred young-sters blown into bloody shreds in a day, and others tortured—*et plurima mortis imago*—"

He checked himself quickly and his voice resumed its normal slightly affected accent and lightness of tone.

"I was in Burma, you know, and afterwards in Japanese hands for a long while," he said apologetically. "However—the deaths of two young holi-day-makers must naturally be distressing to all concerned."

"Fules, t' both on 'em!" croaked a voice harshly.

Mr. Lewker had almost forgotten Ben Truby, so motionless had the old man been sitting—like one of the gray boulders that slumbered in the sun-light of the mountainside. Now the shepherd leaned forward, his hoary eyebrows twitching like antennae.

"Askin' for death, 'twas, to go clamberin' on Black Crag on their lee-lane," he added fiercely. "Ye doan't hev to ask t' Old Ones twice, not on Cauldmoor or Coffin's Pike, ye doan't!"

"Yes, yes, Ben," Meirion began hastily, "we know about that—"

"Naw, ye doan't. There's none but me knaws about t' Old Ones. They'll grip ye if they get a chance, d'ye see."

The old man tugged a short clay pipe from the pocket of his velveteen tail-coat and stuffed black tobacco into it with a gnarled forefinger. Mr. Lewker, forestalling some comment of Meirion's, proffered a box of matches.

"Tell me, Mr. Truby," he boomed politely, "what, or who, are these Old Ones?"

The shepherd took the matches, struck one, and held it to his pipe. Through the puffs of blue smoke his watery eyes stared up at the actor-manager. The glinting lights in them, which were totally absent when he was not excited, gave their pale regard an oddly sinister aspect.

"Ye'd like fine to knaw, would ye?" he croaked. "Wull, measter, go ye an' watch by t' Bent Stones, when full moon's oop. Mubbe ye'll see t' Old Ones for yersel'. But mark ye this"—he craned his scrawny neck to stare more closely—"if they see *yew*, measter, ye'll go t' way of t' others."

In spite of the bright sunshine and the air of morning the old man had contrived to make his nonsense sound impressive. Mr. Lewker, who loved a good line properly delivered, nodded appreciatively.

"And what do the Old Ones want with the Bent Stones by moonlight?" he asked.

Ben Truby pushed the box of matches at him and stood up stiffly.

"Ah'm no tellin' ye," he said bluntly. "Mr. Meirion, he've been askin' me, an' Ah'm no tellin' *him*. 'Tes death to tell, d'ye see."

With that he swung on his heel and went striding away up the fellside, his velveteen coat flapping like the wings of some ancient bird of ill omen. Mr. Lewker turned to the Warden.

"A very remarkable character—" he was beginning, when a hoarse cry interrupted him. Ben Truby had halted, balancing easily on the top of a great boulder fifty feet above them.

"Ah'll tell ye this, measter," he cried shrilly. " 'Twas no accident—neither him nor her. They was plucked off t' Black Crag an' flung down. An' 'twas t' Old Ones as done it!"

He turned again and struck up the trackless mountainside, taking rock and heather in his stride with effortless ease, his gray locks flying. In thirty seconds he had disappeared over the crest.

" 'Hell's black intelligencer, fare thee well!' " observed Mr. Lewker mildly. "The old gentleman has an eye to a dramatic exit, however."

"The poor old chap's a bit mental," said Meirion. "Harmless, of course, but inclined to talk a lot of nonsense."

"Yet you were asking him about the Bent Stones, I gather."

"I make rather a hobby of folklore," Meirion said quickly. "One picks up hints where one can, doesn't one?"

"And did you get any hints about the mysterious goings-on at the Stones?" inquired Lewker.

"Oh, nothing much. The usual *mélange* of secondhand legend and superstition." The Warden looked ostentatiously at his wrist watch. "Oh, lord—it's nearly eleven. Look here, sir, I hope you don't mind, but I've got to go down to Langthwaite for eggs and butter, not to mention bread. I was on my way down when I met old Truby. I'll come back with you to the Hostel and let you in—it's only ten minutes from here—and then—"

"Pray do not trouble," Lewker boomed. "I will adhere to the lawful hours."

"No trouble, sir." Meirion was anxious to please. "The youngsters are all out and I always lock the place up, but if you'd like to get in—"

"There is really no need," said the actor-manager firmly. "I shall wander on the fells—lonely as a cloud, like the poet—and eat my lunch in the heather. Tonight you shall welcome me, Mr. Meirion, with no more respect than you would accord to the meanest flower that blows—I mean the meanest hiker that blows in. I shall perform the washing up or the sweeping out, whichever I am allotted, just as any Hosteler would do. In short—no favoritism, no mention of any special reason for my visit. You do not mind, I trust?"

Mr. Meirion smiled rather blankly.

"Oh, not at all. You intend to make a thorough study of hostel life—isn't that so? Of course I shall cooperate."

Mr. Lewker thanked him gravely.

"Well—*auf wiedersehen*," said the Warden, picking up an empty rucksack from the heather and slinging it on one shoulder.

"*Àbientôt*," returned Lewker. He watched Meirion walk away down the path with short jerky strides that betokened a man unused to hills, and turned to continue his own ascent. As he climbed he pondered the peculiarities of Paul Meirion. The man was a queer mixture, on the surface of it, highly strung and unstable; but there was something odd, something less easily defined, beneath the surface. He seemed to be a gentleman and something of a scholar—the quotation from Virgil had not escaped Mr. Lewker—but he did not seem an entirely suitable person to be warden of a Youth Hostel. Of course, he was as it were a locum-tenens, and at least he appeared enthusiastic about the "Movement." It was hard to picture him amid the terrors of jungle warfare; but Mr. Lewker had known too many young men who returned from war and prison-camp mentally and physically changed to wonder at that strange little piece of revelation. It was not that which puzzled him, but the hint of evasion, of anxiety, in Meirion's manner. He had not liked being discovered talking to Ben Truby and he had shied away from mention of the Old Ones and the Bent Stones. Mr. Lewker began to think these esoteric matters required his attention; since he had arrived in Birkerdale, the Bent Stones and the Old Ones had cropped up on three separate occasions, coupled on each with the two fatal accidents.

These meditations and a steady uphill tramp had brought him over the last of the hill, and quite suddenly he was looking at the Hostel, not a quarter of a mile away across almost level moorland.

On any but the sunniest day Cauldmoor is a cheerless place. A wide highland of undulating heather and bog stretches away eastward between the footslopes of Black Crag and the stony flank of Coffin's Pike, rising slightly to a central ridge before dropping away on the farther side to the lonely combes that drain into lower Wasdale. A small tarn, the source of the Riggin Beck, is the only relieving feature of this waste, and by the tarn stands the Cauldmoor Youth Hostel, originally a small stone fishing hut. To stand above Cauldmoor, near the Bent Stones for instance, on a dull and rainy autumn day when the felltops are hidden and the little marshy pools are leaden, is to know the meaning of the word "dreary." No living thing moves in the empty desolation, and the eerie crying of the curlews is the only sound. The curlews were crying as Mr. Lewker surveyed the scene; but he thought it a joyful noise, for the sun was brilliant on golden marsh grass and russet mosses, and the distant peaks of Wasdale—Great Gable and Great End and Scafell itself—rose clear into the pale blue sky beyond the moorland's rim. Solitude was there, but not loneliness. The bees hummed in the heather and the far voices of Sir Walter Haythornthwaite's sheep floated up on the light westerly breeze from the lower slopes of Coffin's Pike. Cauldmoor Tarn was a blue jewel in a setting of green velvet. The Hostel looked a very pleasant lodge in the wilderness, though it was a plain enough building of gray stone no larger than a small cottage. Lewker could see the darker green thread of the path to Wasdale passing close to the Hostel and dwindling in the distance of unfenced marshes.

He hesitated for a moment and then struck off the track to the left, squelching through a patch or two of soft bog to strike the firmer ground of the little hill on the south of Riggin Spout. Contouring round this for a few minutes brought him to the upper reaches of the beck between the tarn and the fall. He turned left above the clear stream and scrambled along its bank on ever-steepening ground until he could go no farther. The beck here entered a miniature box canyon, quite impassable. On the right a bare wall of rock, its upper edge roughly level, supported the rugged screes above which towered the skyscraper height of Black Crag. On the left a vertical and much higher rock face dropped from the heathery crest to the water. This left-hand wall, black and sunless, was cleft by many niches and cracks in which mosses and reedy tufts sprouted luxuriantly, and there were rowans jutting their feathered branches from its overhanging ledges. The chasm twisted, and the outfall of the water at its farther end was invisible; but the distant roar of the Spout came echoing weirdly along the water-worn ravine.

The place was dank and chill, and Mr. Lewker clambered out into the sunlight. His watch told him it was barely noon, but the insistent timekeeper of appetite assured him it was lunch time. He found a comfortable seat in the heather near the crest of the little hill, whence he could gaze over the sunlit width of Cauldmoor, or, by turning his head, survey the face of Black Crag. He munched Mrs. Crake's excellent mutton sandwiches and gave the Crag a close scrutiny.

It needed no more than a glance to tell him two things. First, that the most accomplished jumper could not spring outward from any part of the great rock face and reach the waters of the beck. The scree of moss-grown boulders that fell from the feet of the crag to the verge of the cleft was short and steep, deceiving the eye into the impression that the precipice rose very close overhead; but the horizontal distance from the base of the rock face to a point directly above the stream was at the very least a hundred feet. Anyone falling or jumping from the crag or its summit must inevitably pitch on to the scree before rolling—if indeed a broken body would roll—into the beck. Secondly, it was quite possible for any careless walker to slip and fall into the stream from the edge of the canyon on either side. There had once been a wire fence along the crest on his side, but it was broken in a dozen places and in any case it would not deter an adventurous scrambler from descending to the rim of the chasm if he or she wanted to.

This latter possibility had not previously occurred to Mr. Lewker, and he told himself severely that his detective sense had become atrophied by disuse. Everybody seemed to have assumed that because Gay Johnson was a rock climber she had fallen from a rock climb, whereas she might quite possibly have slipped into the stream from the lip of the canyon—which would account for her only injury being a fractured skull, presumably acquired by being dashed against a rock in the torrent. But if that were so, one had to presume that Robert Peel had met his death in precisely the same way. It had been assumed that he had fallen from Black Crag, apparently; but it was now clear that—barring some sort of ballistic miracle—he could not have done so without receiving terrible injuries. Was it too long a coincidence that two persons should have missed their footing and fallen from that easy slope? Even skilled rock climbers had been known to do such things. Mr. Lewker remembered that Gay Johnson's body had been clad in full climbing kit—windproof trousers and jacket, rope sling round waist, boots nailed with tricounis. Would she have put on all that gear to wander on an August day along the banks of a stream? He wondered how Robert Peel had been dressed when they found him.

The noonday sun was hot in that sheltered place. Mr. Lewker, having taken the edge off his hunger, pocketed the rest of his sandwiches and moved round the hillside into the cooling breeze that blew from the sea. The waters of the tarn by the Hostel looked inviting; if there was water enough for fish, there was enough for a bath, and the Hostel was for the moment deserted. He scrambled down to the level softness of the moor and headed for the tarn.

He had come within a bowshot of the Hostel on his way to the tarn's outlet when a high clear call like a bird's note made him pause and scan the hillside on his left. Down the slopes on the right of Black Crag a small dark figure was speeding, leaping among the boulders like a mountain goat and making for the nearer end of the tarn. Mr. Lewker, who in his time had been a fast mover over rough ground, admired the neat footwork and balance of this fell runner. The small figure danced across the stepping stones at the outlet and came striding up to him, and he saw that it was a short, slim girl in blue trousers and shirt, a girl whose tangle of dark curls framed a face attractive and browned by weather.

"Hello!" she said as she approached. "Sorry I yelled—thought at first you might be the Warden." She halted and surveyed him gravely. "Of course, you're Abercrombie Lewker."

"Such am I called," beamed Mr. Lewker, allowing his gaze to dwell appreciatively on the small heart-shaped face with its charming coloring and candid gray eyes; he was, as his wife was accustomed to point out warningly, extremely susceptible where pretty brunettes were concerned. "You are staying at the Hostel, I take it?"

"Yes," nodded the girl. She pulled out a rather grubby handkerchief and wiped her forehead, regarding him steadily the while. "Grease paint makes an awful difference, doesn't it?" she added ingenuously.

"Is the operative word 'awful'?" inquired the actor-manager solemnly. "I ask in order to know whether I should register Flattered Complacency or Embarrassed Disgruntlement."

The girl smiled at him delightfully.

"Please don't be disgruntled," she begged, and held out a small brown hand. "I'm Janet Macrae, and I didn't miss a single play when the Abercrombie Lewker Players were in Edinburgh."

"I am completely gruntled again," boomed Mr. Lewker, shaking hands. "Which play did you like best?"

"*As You like It*," Janet said promptly. "I always do."

" 'If there be truth in sight, you are my Rosalind,' " he nodded.

"I suppose that's because I 'suit me all points like a man'," she returned composedly. "Very apt—but the line before that says, 'Because that I am more than common tall.' Not so good, Mr. Lewker."

"True. Then you shall be Viola, in your 'masculine usurp'd attire.' "

Janet laughed. "Look," she said, "we can't stand here all day swapping quotations. I see you're a Y.H.A. member. If you're thinking of staying at Cauldmoor I'd better warn you that the Warden isn't taking in anyone else until after the inquest. A bobby came up yesterday and asked us if we'd all attend it—it's tomorrow afternoon. But I expect you know about that. You were with Vera Crump and Ted when they found the—the body, weren't you?"

"I was. But I met Mr. Meirion on my way up and he most kindly agreed to let me stay. It may be," he added gravely, "that he wants my autograph."

She laughed again. "Well, I'd like it too. I've got the Everyman *Comedies* with me—I shall ask you to autograph that. Look—there's something else. Come to the Hostel with me. I've got to break in, since you aren't the Warden."

"And why," demanded Mr. Lewker, as they began to walk along the track towards the Hostel, "does the fact of my non-identity with Mr. Meirion result in burglary?"

"You haven't a key. And it's not burglary. I don't propose to steal anything. It's breaking and entering if you like, and that's because my lunch and Hamish's are inside."

"Hamish is your brother?"

Janet regarded him sharply. "Yes—how did you know? Anyway, we left our lunches behind when we went out this morning with Ted and Vera, and so I've come back for them. Oh mercy! Our windows are all tight shut!"

They had come to the Hostel's end wall, which faced in the direction of Birkerdale. The little one-story building bore signs of recent alteration, including two windows inserted in this wall. Both were of the casement type and were firmly shut. Janet led the way round to the front facing the tarn. The windows here were equally secure, and short of picking the lock of the stout door which stood above two stone steps there was no way in. Janet went up to the door and tried the handle.

"By the way," said Lewker curiously, "why didn't brother Hamish come back for the lunch?"

"I wouldn't let him," said Janet. "You see, Vera Crump, who makes poor Ted do everything for her, said Hamish ought to come back for it. So of course I came."

She gave a final vicious rattle to the door and ran round to the other end of the building. Mr. Lewker followed, admiring the processes of feminine logic. He found Janet standing on tiptoe trying to reach a window whose swollen woodwork had caused it to be imperfectly shut. It was a small window, or part of a window, above the larger casement.

"Here!" she commanded. "If you can give me a hoist up I think I can open this. It's the Warden's quarters, but he needn't know."

"It would be better if I gave a shoulder," observed her companion, examining the position. "It is an A.P. wall with no safe holds."

Miss Macrae shot a quick sideways glance at him. "You a mountaineer?" she said. "So am I—a bit of one. All right then. Let's have the shoulder."

Mr. Lewker stood facing the window, placed a hand on either side of the frame, and waited. Janet placed her hands on his shoulders and swiftly climbed up his body until she was standing with a foot on either shoulder and could begin to tug at the window. The actor-manager, with his nose almost against the glass, found himself looking into a small and plainly furnished room with a camp bed at one end and a tin washbasin on a stand at the other. On the opposite partition wall hung a shelf of books and there was a small table close against the window. There were two books on the table; one of them was a large black notebook with part of a sheet of paper sticking out of the top, and the other was an ancient calf-bound volume whose title was still legible in gold printing on its back—*The Annals of Witchcraft.*

"It's coming," grunted Janet. "Aha—got it! Stand by. I'm going in head first."

There was a light kick, a moment of struggle, and Janet's face appeared upside down inside the window. She winked recklessly at her confederate. Her waving hands pressed the table, her legs whirled in a circle, and she arrived in an ungraceful heap on the floor without upsetting the table. With a wave of the hand she disappeared through the door into the regions beyond.

Mr. Lewker remained scowling through the window. The sheet of paper protruding from the black notebook revealed three lines of handwriting, and almost involuntarily he had deciphered them. The spidery scrawl, with its Greek 'e's' and affected loops, was what might be expected from the hand of Mr. Paul Meirion. Its incomplete message was eerily suggestive:

"… Friday night's failure. Rite requires full moon? Consider casting of virgin into Riggin (Wrykin?) Spout may be …"

CHAPTER VI
INCAPABLE AND SHALLOW INNOCENTS

Mr. LEWKER WAS STILL FROWNING AT THE WARDEN'S TABLE when Janet reappeared inside the room. She had a small haversack, bulging, in her hand. She grinned at him triumphantly as she passed it through the window above.

"I can open one of the big windows if you want to get in," she told him, her voice coming muffled through the glass.

Lewker shook his head and prepared to assist her exit. She climbed lightly on to the table and wriggled head and shoulders through the opening.

"You'll have to catch me," she warned.

"I am ready, yea, and eager."

Janet giggled and wormed her way through. As she emerged, panting, Mr. Lewker caught her beneath the armpits and eased her headlong descent. With a final kick she freed her boots from the sill and landed in his arms.

"Not bad," she said, freeing herself. "I don't think I've left a scratch on the paintwork. Hope I haven't left any on you!"

"None at all. A lightweight in clinker-nailed boots is practically painless. I have had a thirteen-stone guide in crampons trampling on my shoulders for ten minutes while he tried to force a way up an ice wall. That was much less pleasurable, I assure you."

"You've climbed in the Alps, then?" said Janet reverently. "I've only done rock climbing in Scotland and the Lakes. Are you on a climbing holiday now?"

"Not entirely," he told her. "I had thought of trying one of the Black Crag routes, however. Perhaps you would lead me up some climb suited to my age and incompetence tomorrow."

Janet bent to pick up the haversack, frowning slightly.

"Well, we're all feeling a bit off climbing just now—specially on Black Crag. Gay Johnson fell off it, you know. She was climbing solo, apparently. You'd better ask Hamish, if you really want a leader. He's a much better climber than I am. I don't think he'll want to, though. You see—"

She hesitated. The small piquant face looked worried. Mr. Lewker waited.

"Hamish was engaged to Gay once," she finished.

"Ah. Naturally your brother will have a distaste for Black Crag. May I ask if you and he were here when the accident occurred—or rather, when Miss Johnson disappeared?"

"No. We were at Black Sail until Friday—that's the hostel on the pass between Ennerdale and Wasdale. We got here at dusk on Friday night. That was the night she didn't turn up. Then on Saturday there was the search party."

They had begun to walk away from the Hostel in the direction of the stepping stones at the end of the tarn.

"The walk from Black Sail must be a fine one," remarked Lewker casually. "You would come over the summits, I presume, by way of Steeple Fell to Bleaberry Dodd and so to Black Crag and Cauldmoor."

He thought she hesitated before replying.

"We didn't, as a matter of fact. We came down into Wasdale Head and then up the path over the moor."

"I see. And found a sorry business awaiting you. Did you know Miss Johnson well?"

"I didn't. Hamish met her in Skye, on a climbing meet. They climbed together a bit and got engaged—Hamish is an impetuous type. Anyway, it didn't last long. We'd no idea Gay was staying here. But of course, if you're a rock climber you keep rubbing up against the same people wherever there are rocks to climb." She halted on the verge of the stream. "Look—why don't you come and have lunch with the rest of us? We're just idling about in the glen on the other side of Black Crag, sunbathing and sleeping. It's a good place for idling."

"That is a friendly gesture, and I thank you," said the actor-manager. "Nevertheless I shall decline. I propose to do a little sketching."

"Sketching!" Janet was impressed. "I say, you can do a lot of things. You'll get on all right with Leonard Bligh—he's off on his own today, sketching. He plays on a sort of flute, too—at least Ted says so. He hasn't played it since we've been here. Of course, Gay's death must have hit him hard, poor chap, although they weren't engaged or anything."

"He is not with the rest of you this morning, then?"

"No. There's just Ted and Vera and Hamish and me. The other man— Mr. Jones, he's a Welshman and awfully funny—has walked over into Wasdale. You'll meet us all tonight, if you really won't come and have lunch. Look, I must fly. Hamish will be ravenous." She sprang on to the first stepping stone and paused to smile back at him. "Good-bye, and thank you for the shoulder. Don't tell the Warden, will you?"

"Never, upon mine honor!" boomed Mr. Lewker.

He watched her skip over the stream and start up the fellside, moving like a slim blue shadow among the sunlit boulders. Then he walked back to the Hostel and carefully closed the window which Janet had opened and left open. It seemed to him that if a murderer was to be found among the company at the Cauldmoor Hostel it would not be Janet Macrae.

The bowl of moorland shimmered in the afternoon heat and there was no human figure in the wide landscape. Janet was out of sight. Mr. Lewker returned to the tarn, found a projecting rock from which a plunge into five feet of water could be taken, and removed his clothes. The water was the color of light ale and as refreshing as a draught of iced lager. He ate the rest of his sandwiches while the sun dried him and then, shouldering his ruck-sack, set off across the moor in the direction of Coffin's Pike.

Mr. Lewker's assertion that he intended to do some sketching had not been entirely disingenuous. He had a sketching block and pencil in his rucksack and his purpose was to make a general diagram of the Black Crag area from some suitable viewpoint. It had been a habit of his, when he was working with the Secret Service, to make a kind of drawing of the area in which he was about to operate; it had often revealed possibilities and con-junctions which might not otherwise have shown themselves. In the present case, with two dubious deaths that might or might not prove to be murder, with no clues and only a few vague and unsatisfactory hints to go on as yet, he had no great hope that his sketch would help him. All the same, Coffin's

Pike would be a good viewpoint and the Bent Stones were close to Coffin's Pike. Mr. Lewker wanted to have a look at the Bent Stones.

He kept well over to the western rim of Cauldmoor, mounting slowly until he was walking along a rounded undulating ridge with Birkerdale in view below on his right hand. The steepening flank of Coffin's Pike was underfoot when he spied a little stone hut some three or four hundred feet down the hillside at the apex of a stone wall that rambled up and then down. On the farther side of the wall sheep were grazing. He remembered the "la'l bield" old Ben Truby had spoken of in the Herdwick Arms. The stone hut was no doubt the shepherd's bield or shelter. To that hut the three hikers who had found Robert Peel's body had come, at Whitsuntide, to enlist the shepherd's help.

He continued the ascent of Coffin's Pike, perspiring gently and cursing his folly in dragging his rucksack with him instead of leaving it at the Hostel. Halfway up the slope he saw on his left, on the flat top of a subsidiary knoll projecting from the Pike, a circle of gray motionless figures like robed beings turned to stone in the middle of a round dance. He turned across the hillside and came down to them.

The Bent Stones were monoliths of no very impressive size. There were seven of them, all under five feet high and all having a peculiar cant or bend in the upper portion which was unusual in an unhewn rock. They formed a circle of a dozen paces diameter, and whether by accident or ancient labor the space they enclosed was as level as a bowling green. The short grass, sheep-cropped and marked with the droppings of sheep, bore here and there the brown patches which invariably mark the favored spots of those animals; but beneath the tallest of the Stones, a cromlech that to Mr. Lewker's mind resembled a piece of "simplified" modern sculpture (representing Sleep, or Urge, or some similar abstraction), was a larger and darker patch. He went across and examined it. There had undoubtedly been a fire there at no very distant time. He bent and ruffled the ash of the burnt circle with his fingers—wood ash, and two or three inches depth of it. He felt a small hard object and extracted it from the ashes. It was a charred bone.

Scowling thoughtfully, the actor-manager turned again to the ascent. A few minutes brought him to the summit of Coffin's Pike, a pleasantly sharp little hump crowned by a small cairn. It commanded, as he had anticipated, a very wide view of the head of Birkerdale, Black Crag and Cauldmoor, and the high hills beyond. He had taken off his rucksack and was getting out his sketching block when his eye chanced to rest for a moment on the faraway gray dot of Ben Truby's bield, and caught a movement near it. The afternoon sunlight made every detail of that westerly slope plain even at a distance; there was no mistaking the lanky figure that emerged from the hut and began to make up the fellside on a long slant. It was Ben Truby, and he appeared to be heading either for Coffin's Pike or the neighborhood of the Bent Stones.

There are amateurs of the pencil who are pleased to have people looking over their shoulder while they work; Mr. Lewker was not one of these. He was not a good draftsman and he knew it. Nor did he feel in the mood for more oracular utterances from the old shepherd. He hastily packed away his block and slid inconspicuously from the skyline, heading for the high ground farther south. It took him half an hour to find a suitable viewpoint, and by that time he had reached the rough lane coming over from Gosforth, by which he and Georgie had arrived in Birkerdale. It commanded an even wider view than Coffin's Pike and had the advantage of including the Bent Stones. He sat down by the roadside and—untroubled by passersby, for there were none—made his sketch diagram.

The afternoon was well advanced when he had finished. He sat for a while watching the shadows of the peaks lengthen down the hillsides. The distances had taken on the delicate mauve of approaching evening and the farther mountains rose powder blue above the veil of brume. It was very peaceful there. The soothing, age-old melancholy of the hills lapped him round, protesting the futility of man and the infinite power of Nature.

In this Wordsworthian mood the few trifling and unrelated pieces of information he had picked up with regard to the death of Gay Johnson seemed useless—the whole business of his investigation appeared utterly ridiculous. Feeling half inclined to go straight down to Langthwaite and Georgie, he began to walk slowly back towards Cauldmoor Hostel.

He saw nothing of Ben Truby as he crossed the shoulder of Coffin's Pike. A massing of purple clouds in the west had obscured the sinking sun and the Bent Stones looked cold and dour. From behind him a little chill wind began to blow. It quickened his step and woke his appetite, reminding him that baked beans on toast, though a stodgy enough dish in a city, go down very well after a day on the fells. He circled the boggy flats of Cauldmoor and came, a little before six, to the Hostel.

A cheerful sound of voices came to his ears as he approached the door. It was unlocked this time, and he turned the handle and walked in, aware at once of a smell of tea and new woodwork. The three young men who were sitting at the trestle table turned as he entered and Ted Somerset got up and came towards him.

"Hullo, sir," he said shyly. "We heard you were coming. Have you had a good day?"

"Excellent, thank you." Mr. Lewker dumped his rucksack on the floor. "Do I smell tea?"

"Yes. The girls are just brewing up. Er—I'd better introduce you. This is Hamish Macrae and this is Leonard Bligh. Mr. Abercrombie Lewker."

Hamish nodded and grunted amiably. He was short and dark, with his sister's curly hair and gray eyes, but he was twice as broad as Janet and the rolled-up sleeves of his red-and-black shirt revealed his brawny forearms. Leonard Bligh, a willowy youth with a shock of fair hair and a dreamy expression, looked up from his occupation of cutting a loaf into large slices and smiled faintly.

"How do?" he said, with a distinct Birmingham accent.

"If you'd like a wash," Ted said, "the place is through that door, at the end of—"

"It *is* you!" exclaimed the resounding voice of Vera Crump. She emerged beaming from a door on the opposite side of the room and advanced determinedly on the new arrival with large hand outstretched. "Welcome to Cauldmoor, Mr. Lewker. Pardon me if I sound all formal, but it isn't every day we entertain celebrities."

Mr. Lewker murmured polite acknowledgments. Behind Vera he caught sight of Janet peeping round the door of what seemed to be the kitchen. She waved a hand. The actor-manager waved back. Miss Crump's face expressed annoyance, and she turned to Ted Somerset.

"I thought you said you'd mended that small stove, Ted," she said severely.

"It was going all right when I—"

"Well, it's all wrong again. For goodness' sake try and *do* something about it."

"All right," said Ted meekly.

Mr. Lewker thought the young man displayed considerable alacrity in joining Janet in the kitchen. The same idea possibly occurred to Miss Crump, for she turned her prominent blue eyes accusingly on Hamish Macrae.

"You know about Primus stoves, Hamish," she snapped. "Please go and help Ted. I'm sure you're more use than he is."

Hamish heaved himself slowly to his feet.

"Och, I'll take a look at it," he growled, and lounged into the kitchen.

"We're a bit primitive," said Vera, beaming at the actor-manager, "but we manage. Now I'm sure you're ready for a nice cup of—"

"Vera!" Janet's voice called from the kitchen. "You've got the tinned milk. Can we have it, please?"

"Excuse me, won't you?" Miss Crump strode away to the kitchen.

Mr. Lewker sat down on the long bench and looked round at his surroundings. The common room had been formed by partitioning off the two ends of the building, the division on the left being (as he knew) the Warden's quarters and that on the right presumably the dormitories of the Hostelers. At the back, opposite the entrance door, another partition hid the narrow kitchen with sink and cooking apparatus. The partitions had evidently been recently erected and everything was extremely clean.

"Loves doing hostess, does Vera," commented Leonard Bligh with faint derision. He finished cutting the last slice of bread and tossed the knife on the table. "Staying here long?" he added incuriously.

"Two or three nights, I hope," replied Lewker.

He regarded the young man covertly. Bligh's suntanned face, good-looking in an effeminate way, displayed much less grief than might have been expected in a lover violently bereft of his loved one three days ago.

"I feel I should apologize," he said cautiously, "for intruding on the party so soon after your—hum—sad loss. It must have been a great shock to you."

Leonard toyed absently with the bread knife.

"That's all right," he mumbled. "No use in moping, is there?"

"That is quite a reasonable way of looking at it."

The other shifted uneasily on the bench.

"I'm cut up about it—we all are," he said, without looking up. "But—well, she's passed on and there it is. I suppose Vera's told you me and Gay were pretty thick?"

"She did mention it, yes."

"She would. Opens her mouth too wide, that girl. Had a row with her this morning about suggesting Gay committed suicide. Gay never did. She was in the heck of a temper that morning and rushed away to do something energetic to work it off, same as she always did. She tackled Black Crag, bit off more than she could chew, and came off, poor old girl. That's all there is to it."

Despite young Mr. Bligh's creditable attempt to be unemotional and even nonchalant, his voice quavered on the words. Mr. Lewker thought him a mildly unpleasant specimen of the self-centered would-be artistic type, but he was sorry for him. Also he perceived that all these young people were awed, in greater or less degree, by the recent visitation of the stranger, Death; and that each was trying, in his or her way, to shake off that—to them—unusual emotion.

He was about to murmur polite sympathy when the door of the Warden's room opened and Paul Meirion came out.

"Oh—it's you—er—Lewker," he said, with his nervous smile. "Settling in all right? Good, good. I heard you come in, but thought it was Jones returning from his trip to Wasdale. Had a decent day?"

Before Lewker could reply Vera Crump came in from the kitchen bearing a teapot and followed by Ted and the Macraes.

"Tea up!" she announced loudly. "Mr. Meirion, you'll join us in a cupper, I'm sure."

The Warden blinked at her through his glasses.

"No, really, thanks," he said. "I brewed myself a pot before you came in. I suppose you haven't seen anything of our other guest?"

"Mr. Jones? No—he's not come in yet." Vera set the pot on the table. "Come on, Ted! Cups and spoons!"

"Well, if you don't mind, I'll resume my work," said the Warden, and withdrew to his quarters.

"He does a lot of writing," confided Janet to Mr. Lewker. "It's folklore research or something, and he spends—"

"Milk *and* sugar, Mr. Lewker?" demanded Vera, talking Janet down with perfect confidence.

"I have my own sugar, of course," said the actor-manager, suddenly remembering that the ingredients for tea had been carried up in other people's rucksacks, and fumbling with the strings of his own sack.

"Oh, no—I insist," said Miss Crump with refined playfulness. "I want to be able to say I've stirred the tea of the famous Abercrombie Lewker. Both? Splendid!"

Mr. Lewker heaved an inward sigh. Miss Crump, unlike the Warden, was not going to treat him as an ordinary Hosteler. She obviously intended to extract the last ounce of thrill from this fortunate contact with Fame, with a view to retailing every detail to her friends at home. Nevertheless, as he sipped his cup of strong sweet tea and listened to the desultory chatter of the five, interspersed with Vera's unnecessary inquiries as to the satisfactoriness of his tea, he discovered that he was enjoying himself. The life of the theater brought him into contact with few young folk, and those few of a stereotyped kind; these were not old enough to have adopted an effective pose, not adepts in concealing the workings of their minds. There was something refreshing in their youthful frankness and transparency. Even Vera Crump, the schoolmistress (he suspected she was no more than a pupil teacher at some small school) was too obvious to be seriously annoying in her determination to monopolize the celebrated guest's attention.

Their talk was mainly of food. The "cupper," it appeared, was merely an *apéritif* for the meal which was to follow. Mr. Lewker was invited to place his baked beans in the hands of the cooks—Vera and Janet—and informed by Janet (Vera dissenting in a shocked manner) that *all* the men did the washing up. An incautious remark of his, intended to abash Vera, to the effect that he had spent six weeks as a waiter in a German officers' restaurant in Occupied France, was followed by a unanimous request for the full story. He succeeded in postponing this ordeal until after supper; and the conversation turned to the problem of making a pudding.

The actor-manager watched them as they talked. Leonard, fingering his teaspoon and lounging spinelessly across the table, said nothing unless he was directly addressed. He was at the stage when conversation that did not concern himself was mildly boring, thought Mr. Lewker. Hamish Macrae, who had filled and lit an immense pipe of Bulldog shape, grunted sarcastic comments now and then in a very man-of-the-world manner, while his sister, elbows on table and small brown face vividly alive, argued the merits of raisins and rice against Vera Crump's tinned plum-pudding. Mr. Lewker's sharp little eyes noticed that when Janet looked at Ted Somerset, as she did more than once, Ted invariably avoided her glance; and they noticed also, with distaste, the complete domination of Ted by Miss Crump. He caught himself thinking that if one of the five was to prove responsible for Gay Johnson's death he would prefer it to be Vera Crump. And the thought gave him something of a mental shock. What on earth had these children to do with murder? Not one of them was half his own age, and here he was idly looking for a murderer among them. The idea was wholly absurd, viewed in the atmosphere of tea and immature chatter.

"Where's Mr. Jones?" Janet was saying. "I asked him to bring half a dozen eggs back from Wasdale Head—we could make a jam omelette if he gets back in time."

"We've got three eggs," ventured Ted Somerset. "If you like—"

"Not enough," rapped Vera decisively.

"You said you'd get a dozen eggs last Friday, young Janet," growled Hamish Macrae, frowning accusingly at his sister.

"I know. I forgot. Sorry."

Hamish's rejoinder made Mr. Lewker's eyes snap wide open and his bushy brows contract suddenly.

"If I'd had the sense," Hamish growled, "I'd have come through Wasdale on Friday and got 'em myself, instead of tramping over the fells."

CHAPTER VII
WHEREFORE THE WELSHMAN COMES

MR. LEWKER SAW THE INVOLUNTARY SIDEWAYS GLANCE THAT Janet darted at him. She had lied to him about her brother's route to Cauldmoor on Friday; and she knew that he knew she had lied. Why had she thought it necessary to mislead him?

The unpleasant speculations that rushed into his mind were summarily cut short by the sudden opening of the door.

"Back I come from Wasdale Head, wanting food and drink and bed!" announced the newcomer happily. He advanced into the room, beaming. Mr. Lewker assumed, rightly, that this was Mr. Bodfan Jones; he remembered that Janet had described him as "awfully funny." Mr. Jones was a short, neat, stout little man with a round rosy face perpetually smiling. He looked like a middle-aged cherub in plus fours. Over one shoulder of his brightly checked tweed jacket was slung a haversack and he carried a walking stick plastered from handle to ferrule with the little metal badges they sell in Swiss tourist resorts. He put both down on the table and beamed inquiringly at Lewker. Vera was ready.

"This is Abercrombie Lewker—the actor, you know," she announced proudly.

"Actor-manager," corrected Mr. Lewker, and succeeded in silencing Miss Crump at last.

"Delighted, delighted," said Mr. Jones, shaking hands warmly. "I've heard of you, sir, naturally. I am Bodfan Jones, a Welshman of the Welsh and proud I am to say so."

Lewker, with his quick ear for accent and inflection, decided that there was more of Liverpool than of Wales in the spoken English of Mr. Bodfan Jones.

"And a bard, perhaps?" he said innocently.

Bodfan Jones laughed with pleasure, like an overgrown boy.

"You noticed my little rhyme? I do indeed write verse, sir, in my native tongue. On holiday I amuse myself with doggerel—it assists my solitary marches on the hills. The meters of the Cymric bard in Saxon tongue are far too hard." He laughed again, and then with comical abruptness twisted his round face into an expression of grief. "This poor lad," he added in a low voice, laying a hand on Leonard's shoulder, "knows that my fun conceals a very deep sympathy with him in his sad loss."

"That's all right," mumbled Leonard, looking thoroughly embarrassed.

"She is happier far than we are, depend upon it, Leonard," continued Mr. Jones in a grave whisper. "Be of good cheer—this trial will pass."

He administered a final pat to the scowling youth's shoulder and turned away, pulling a handkerchief from his pocket. Mr. Lewker half-expected him to dab his eyes with it, but he merely blew his nose with a trumpeting noise.

"The eggs, Mr. Jones," Janet reminded him. "Did you get them?"

Mr. Jones brightened at once. "The eggs, my dear? Indeed I got them. On these two legs I fetched the eggs. They are in my haversack—intact, I hope."

"Good," said Vera, as he proceeded to unpack them. "We'll have that jam omelette."

"Better get weaving," advised Hamish. "It's past seven already."

"Dinner at eight prompt," she said firmly. "Ted! Mr. Lewker must want to wash and brush up, I'm sure. Do show him round the place."

Bodfan Jones finished handing over the eggs and raised a hand as Ted rose to his feet.

"Allow me," he beamed. "I need a wash myself, indeed. This way, sir."

Mr. Lewker picked up his rucksack and followed the little man through the door into a narrow passageway between weatherboarding partitions, lit by a small window at the far end which framed a view of moorland and a shoulder of Black Crag somber in the evening light. There were three narrow doors, at intervals of a few feet, in either side of the passage.

"Two to each room," explained the Welshman, "and the two end doors are toilet and washbasin respectively." He opened the middle door on the right. "This is unoccupied. It's all yours, sir, as our youthful comrades yonder would say."

The actor-manager found himself in a tiny apartment almost filled by an iron double-tier bedstead and a small chest of drawers. The window looked out upon the leaden waters of Cauldmoor Tarn and the rocky slopes above. He dumped his rucksack on the lower bunk and turned to thank his guide. Mr. Jones was regarding him benevolently.

"I take it," he said, "that you, like myself, are on a solitary walking tour of these delightful parts?"

Mr. Lewker explained that he was staying at Langthwaite with his wife.

As a strong supporter and admirer of the Youth Hostels Association, he added, he had come up to spend a night or two at the Hostel.

"Good, good indeed," said Mr. Jones enthusiastically. "We older ones have much to gain from contact with the young folk. Yes. A great pity, though, that you should find our young friends a little subdued. The sad death of Miss Johnson—you heard of it, of course?"

"Yes. Did you know her, may I ask?"

"Oh, no. I met her for the first time on my arrival here last Thursday evening. A charming and vivacious young lady, yes indeed." Mr. Jones wagged his head sadly. "Such a dreadful thing to happen—so young, so violently cut off from life."

Mr. Lewker agreed. "Leonard Bligh was her—um—boyfriend, I believe," he said. "Were they very strongly attached, do you think?"

Bodfan Jones pursed his lips, reminding Lewker of those cherubs who puff at fleecy clouds in old paintings.

"A boy-and-girl affair, I fancy," he replied. "Leonard feels it, naturally. A nasty shock for the poor lad. Yes. But—a boy-and-girl affair, sir. I don't think it went deeper. He will get over it quite quickly."

Mr. Lewker said he hoped so.

"Depend upon it," said Mr. Jones encouragingly. He lowered his voice. "I understand you and two of our young folk found the unfortunate girl's body."

"That is so."

"The police took charge of it, they tell me. Now I wonder why that was."

Lewker glanced sharply at his interrogator; Bodfan Jones' round face was innocently curious.

"Simply because the girl's disappearance and the search party had been reported to them," he answered. "Also, in a remote place like Birkerdale, the police organization is the only one fitted to deal with such things. They have an ambulance and so forth. They have to be notified, you know."

"Of course, yes," Mr. Jones nodded. "I see now. One gets into the habit of associating the police with crime. The Sunday papers—but I'm keeping you from your wash and brush-up, sir. Gossiping is a national trait of us Welsh, I'm afraid. Oh—the right-hand door at the end is the toilet."

Mr. Lewker, who had picked up a few Welsh phrases during many holidays in the Welsh mountains, thanked him in Welsh.

"*Diolch 'n fawr*," said he.

There was not a great deal of light in the narrow room, but he fancied Mr. Jones' round gray eyes held for an instant an expression quite different from their usual rather childish innocence.

"You have the Cymraeg?" demanded the little man with apparent eagerness.

"About a dozen words," Mr. Lewker admitted.

Bodfan Jones' sigh might have been one of disappointment or of relief.

"A pity," he said. "Our native tongue, as you may know, is meat and drink to us of the true Cymry. I was disappointed to find that the Warden, Mr. Meirion—a Welsh name—has no word of Welsh. However—perhaps you will knock on the door opposite yours when you have finished with the washroom."

He withdrew, and a moment later Lewker could hear him humming *The Ash Grove* to himself in his room across the passage.

The actor-manager, left alone, busied himself with unpacking his kit, arranging the blankets on his bunk, and washing. As he did so his thoughts dwelt curiously on Mr. Bodfan Jones.

He felt quite certain that the little man was playing a part. In such matters Abercrombie Lewker was rarely mistaken; even if Jones' insistence on his Welshness had not been a little too obvious, there were signs, imperceptible to the layman, that told the actor that here was a deliberate cultivated pose. And the hint of his own acquaintance with the Welsh language had certainly disconcerted the other for a moment.

At another time he would have attached little importance to this discovery. Men on holiday alone, especially young men, are not infrequently known to pose as something other than they are, for the impressing of the strangers they meet; it is a form of escapism. Junior clerks become bank cashiers in many a hotel register, salesmen become managing directors, provincial reporters novelists, for the period of their vacation. This harmless form of masquerade is uncommon in Youth Hostels, where the atmosphere does not encourage snobbism, nor do men of forty-odd—and Bodfan Jones was well over forty—often indulge in it. Moreover, however impressive a Welsh bard may be within the borders of his own country, there is little kudos to be got by posing as one in Cumberland. It was possible, of course, that Jones' pose was a mere whimsy; he was certainly a whimsical little man in his way. But Mr. Lewker was not now prepared to accept an easy explanation of any oddnesses he came across. The discovery that Janet Macrae had lied to him had brought his half-awakened instinct for investigation to full alertness. Here were things hidden, the first shadowy outposts of an enemy whose presence was not yet completely ascertained. Whether or not Gay Johnson had met her death by accident or by the hand of a murderer, whether or not these vague hints had anything to do with her death, he was ready to assume the affirmative in both cases and to regard every strange circumstance with suspicion. Until the inquest, when he could exchange news with Detective-Inspector Grimmett and make certain necessary inquiries, there was no point in speculation or the building of theories. For this preliminary stage of investigation his part was to collect facts and impressions.

Mr. Bodfan Jones' rather reedy tenor, muffled and shaken by the vigorous application of a towel, came to his ears from the washroom as he went from the sleeping quarters into the common room. From the kitchen came the smell of baked beans and the loud tones of Vera Crump laying down the rules for making a jam omelette. Hamish was absent. Ted Somerset was laying plates and cutlery on the table, and Leonard was once again cutting bread, slowly and with an abstracted air. His handsome face was devoid of all emotion. Mr. Lewker was reminded of a verse of Thackeray's:

> Charlotte, having seen his body
>> Borne before her on a shutter,
> Like a well-conducted person
>> Went on cutting bread and butter.

Ted abandoned his table-laying rather hurriedly as Lewker entered, and crossed the room to join him.

"Food in twenty minutes," he said in his usual hesitant manner. "Er—come for a breath of air, sir?"

Somewhat surprised, the actor-manager assented, and they went out into the still evening. Cauldmoor looked bleak under the dull sky, where high gray clouds hid all but the faintest glow of sunset. The chill wind that had sprung up in the late afternoon had dropped, but the air was noticeably cold. On the far side of the tarn Hamish Macrae could be seen, pipe in mouth and hands in pockets, gazing into the black waters.

"A change in the wind, I think," observed Mr. Lewker. "Does that mean more rain, I wonder?"

"Northwest, what there is," returned Ted. "It's not a rainy quarter."

They strolled slowly along the green track in the Wasdale direction. The summits of the distant mountains were dark under the gloomy sky to northward, and Lewker recognized Great Gable, an old friend, raising its unmistakable dome above the shouldering ridges. The crags on which he had scrambled in his youth were out of sight on Gable's farther flank.

"Tell me," he said, breaking a short silence. "Is Leonard Bligh a climber?"

"A rock climber? No." Ted hesitated before going on. "That started the quarrel, you know—between him and Gay. She wanted him to climb Black Crag with her. There's a fairly easy route. Leonard just refused. He's a funny chap—won't do anything if he doesn't want to, and says exactly what he thinks. I suppose it's because he's artistic."

Mr. Lewker reflected how easily selfishness was condoned, and even admired, in persons presumed to be "artistic."

"Miss Crump described it 'a fearful quarrel,'" he remarked. "That seems a small thing to quarrel about."

"It led on to—things," Ted explained uncomfortably. "It was at breakfast on the Friday—Mr. Jones and Vera and I were there. Janet—the two Macraes hadn't arrived then, so Gay was the only rock climber in the party."

"You do not climb yourself?"

"No. I'd like to—I've often wanted to. But—well, Vera says it's reckless and dangerous, you see."

Mr. Lewker saw. "A pity," he murmured. "I had hoped you would climb

Black Crag with me tomorrow, before we go down to Birkerdale for the inquest."

Ted glanced sideways at him, quickly and suspiciously. "Hamish might take you up," he muttered.

"Yes. I will ask him. Have you met the Macraes before, by the way?"

"Yes, at Whit. The four of us—Vera, myself, Leonard and Gay—came up to stay at Black Sail Hostel for the Whit weekend. Hamish and Janet stayed there for two nights."

Lewker made a mental note of this information. The Black Sail Hostel, on Black Sail pass, was less than ten mountain miles from Cauldmoor. At approximately the date of Robert Peel's death six of those now staying at Cauldmoor had been within half a day's walk of Black Crag and Riggin Spout.

"I suppose," he said, "that Mr. Bodfan Jones was not at Black Sail?"

"No."

Ted seemed to reach a sudden decision. He came to a halt and turned to face his companion.

"Look here, sir," he said with a kind of apprehensive excitement, "you've come up here to investigate Gay's death, haven't you?"

Mr. Lewker, who had halted also, made haste to dissemble.

"My dear Edward," he boomed. "I am not a policeman. What gave you that idea?"

"Well"—Ted waved an impatient hand—"all these questions you're asking. And when I was down at the police station in Egremont there was a man there—plainclothes man, I think—who showed he recognized your name when I happened to mention it."

Lewker realized that he had been somewhat incautious in his questioning, but he gave young Mr. Somerset credit for this latter piece of observation. He decided to put his cards on the table.

"Let us walk back towards our supper," he suggested. "Now. In the first place, my perspicacious young friend, there must be no mention of this matter to anyone else. Not even to Miss Crump—or to Miss Macrae. Agreed?"

Ted's thin face flushed slightly. "I swear I won't breathe a word, sir," he said fervently.

"Very well. In the second place, there is no evidence whatever that Miss Johnson's death was anything other than an accident. You understand that?"

"But—"

"Because of certain suggestions," pursued Mr. Lewker carefully, "your own remarks to the police-sergeant included, it was decided to make inquiry into the circumstances of the accident. A friend of mine connected with the police suggested that I might do a little preliminary investigation without alarming anyone. This I am attempting to do, but, it seems, not very successfully. That is all."

Ted was silent for a moment. Then he said suddenly: "I'd like to help, sir."

Mr. Lewker was silent in his turn. He rather liked Ted, and suspected that this fervor for detection was in part due to a subconscious desire to do something independently of the overpowering Vera Crump. The phenomenon of a young man helpless in the toils of a determined young woman was sufficiently familiar to the actor-manager to move him to pity rather than contempt. Also, he disliked Vera and felt that the encouragement of Ted's self-assertion would be a salutary check to that young lady's tyranny. But, in his present stage of keeping an open mind, could he safely remove Ted Somerset from a list of suspects as yet unwritten? It seemed unreasonable not to. Had it not been for Ted's persistence in going to the police with his tenuous suspicions there might never have been an investigation. He decided to take the chance, upon a certain condition.

"You can help, Edward," he said, "by telling me the full reason for your suspicion that Gay Johnson was murdered."

Ted flinched visibly from the word. "I haven't—I don't want—" he began.

"Listen to me," boomed Mr. Lewker sternly. "You suspect that the death was not an accident. You have declared that Gay Johnson would never commit suicide. Murder remains. And I am quite certain there is something—some matter at the root of your suspicion—which you are keeping to yourself." Suddenly remembering his companion's youth, he added, more lightly, "If there's to be detection, I shall welcome the assistance of Sherlock Somerset. But my confidence is only given in exchange for yours. As Richard Plantagenet says in Act Two, 'Now, Somerset, where is your argument?' "

Ted hesitated before replying.

"I'm in a bit of a dilemma, sir," he said frankly. "I mean—on the horns of. Can I think it out, and let you know a bit later?"

"Of course. Meanwhile, you were telling me about the quarrel between Leonard and Miss Johnson."

"Oh—there wasn't much more to tell. Gay twitted him with being a funk. She had a quick temper and a sharp tongue, you know. Leonard said if she liked to make a monkey of herself she was welcome, but he wasn't being tied up to one on a crag, or something like that. He's got a lazy, careless way of saying that sort of thing that's pretty maddening. Anyway, Gay lost her temper properly and said a lot of unpleasant things, and Leonard just said if she wanted to wriggle up the beastly crag why didn't she go and do it by herself."

"He said that? And what did Miss Johnson say?"

Ted shrugged uncomfortably. "Told him anyone but an utter fool knew that solo climbing was a mug's game. Leonard made some jeering remark about standing at the bottom to catch her. Then Gay went rather white and said that bit about Eurydice—Vera told you, I think."

" 'You can sign off, Orpheus! This is where Eurydice does her stuff,' " quoted Mr. Lewker softly. "And then?"

"She got up and ran out. We didn't see her again."

"And Leonard? Did he make any comment?"

Ted opened his mouth and then closed it firmly.

"That's all I can tell you until I've thought a bit," he said, frowning at his feet.

They had come within a few yards of the Hostel again. Hamish had left his meditation by the lake and was coming up the short slope towards them. They halted to wait for him.

"Shall I ask him about climbing tomorrow?" Ted inquired diffidently.

"Do, please. Incidentally, his sister thought he would refuse. You know he was once engaged to Miss Johnson, of course."

"Yes," said Ted briefly. He hailed the Scots youth, who came up to them with his slow stride and halted with a look of polite inquiry on his square dark face. Mr. Lewker remembered Janet's description of her brother as "an impetuous type" and covertly studied the very self-possessed young man before him. For all his stolidity, Hamish had a tilt of the head and a jut to his lower lip that might betoken a quick temper and a rash decision. That vertical furrow between the level brows—already deeply cut in spite of his youth—was a sign Lewker had noticed in grown men of a sanguine temperament; dangerous enemies, men quick to love and tenacious in hate, wore, in his experience, that vertical bar. Again he had to remind himself that for all his big pipe and his self-possessed manner Hamish was little more than a boy.

"I say, Hamish," Ted was saying, "Mr. Lewker here wants to do one of the Black Crag routes tomorrow. You've got a rope, haven't you?"

Hamish turned his steady gaze on Lewker.

"We're all going into Birkerdale for the inquest tomorrow," he objected.

"It's not until two," Ted pointed out. "You could easily get it in."

"My visit to Cauldmoor was for the express purpose of climbing Black Crag," said Mr. Lewker mendaciously. "I realize that circumstances have made it—um—unpopular just now, but I shall be exceedingly disappointed if I have to miss my climb. Perhaps," he added, seeing refusal in the young man's face, "your sister would lead for me if you feel—shall I say?—intimidated by the recent sad accident on the Crag."

The lift of Hamish's chin and his quick frown told the actor-manager that he had taken the right line.

"Och, there's no intimidation about it," growled the Scot. "Janet doesn't lead, anyway." He cogitated a moment. "There's two Very Severes and a Difficult on the Crag. You'll not be wanting a lead on a V.S.?"

"A climb of standard Difficult will suit my years and figure," Lewker told him. "I take it that is the easiest route on the Crag? The route poor Miss Johnson would have taken?"

"Ay," said Hamish briefly.

From the Hostel door came an urgent summons to "Come and get it!" in Janet's clear voice.

"If it's fine I'll climb tomorrow," Hamish decided. "We'll start reasonably early, if you're willing."

Mr. Lewker signified that he would be delighted. He thanked Hamish and the three of them went in out of the gathering twilight to find supper ready and a hanging oil-lamp shedding mellow radiance on the common room table.

The meal was a cheerful one, thanks to Bodfan Jones' lighthearted chatter. Mr. Lewker duly played his part in the washing up afterwards, displaying a deftness in the handling of a cloth and three plates at once that won admiration. By permission of the Warden, who emerged from his quarters (where, presumably, he had dined in solitary state) to join them, a small fire had been lit in the common room fireplace and round this the whole party grouped their chairs; for the evening, at fourteen hundred feet above the sea, had a chill that was like a premature breath of winter. Mr. Lewker was made to tell his story of espionage in German-occupied France and was enthusiastically applauded. Mr. Jones displayed skill as a raconteur of stories in Lancashire dialect, which tended to confirm Lewker's impression that the little man's habitat was north of the Dee. Vera Crump related some rather pointless tales of her pupils' misdemeanors, and Janet, assisted by Hamish, told a Scottish ghost-story about kelpies and witches. The shadow of Gay Johnson's death seemed to have lifted, at least for that evening, from Cauldmoor Hostel; though the silent Leonard, who lounged staring into the fire and made no contribution whatever to the conversation, appeared sunk in melancholy.

Mr. Lewker, ever on the alert, found little that was noteworthy in the interchange of talk round the fire. One incident only stuck in his memory, to become significant in the light of later events.

Ted Somerset had been asking Janet whether she had ever seen a witch, and Janet, opening gray eyes wide at him, had replied that she knew an old man in Sanquhar who had been ridden by a witch on Hallowe'en.

"He was an Elder, too," she added solemnly; and turned to Jones. "There are witches in Wales, aren't there, Mr. Jones?"

Bodfan Jones laughed and shook his head.

"Although I'm a true Welshman, Miss Janet," he said, "I've no belief in such things. No, indeed. If you want my opinion, you shall have it in rhyme: 'He who credits witch or gnome, should be safely in a Home.' Don't you agree, Mr. Warden?"

Lewker, who had some inkling of the nature of Mr. Meirion's researches into "folklore," looked quickly at the Warden. He had expected to see some sign of irritation on the sallow features, but he was unprepared for the intensity of emotion—anger combined with something very like terror—that glinted in the eyes behind the strong lenses of the Warden's glasses. That glimpse was fleeting but unmistakable. Meirion lowered his eyes instantly to look at his wrist watch. His bony face looked taut and a shade paler than usual. There was a slight tremor in his voice as he replied.

"Quite so. Very aptly put, sir. I'm afraid I must suggest, however, that the hour for turning-in has come. Lights out in twenty minutes. Well—good night to you all!"

He got up abruptly and disappeared into his room.

The others echoed his good night and began to prepare for bed. Mr. Lewker, having lent a hand to straighten up the common room, retired to his tiny apartment with the candle allotted to him and undressed meditatively. He had another odd item to add to his collection of hints and impressions. Like Bottom the Weaver, however, he had an exposition of sleep come upon him; and he had little difficulty in adhering to his resolve not to try and arrange his collection into a significant pattern. He had placed his candle on the floor for convenience of blowing out and was about to creep into the lower bunk when there was a quick rustle of paper and a small white patch slid under his door. He picked it up. It was a leaf torn from a notebook. A few lines had been scrawled on it in pencil. With some difficulty he deciphered the note by the light of his candle.

After the quarrel, when G had gone [ran the faint scribble], *L said sort of coldly, "I shall kill that girl someday." Only Vera and I heard him. L nearly killed a man in a fit of temper once. Please destroy this note.*

CHAPTER VIII
THEY THAT STAND HIGH

"I'M THINKING YOU SHOULD BE LEADING," SAID HAMISH, knotting one end of the hundred-foot nylon rope round his waist.

He and Mr. Lewker were standing on a glacis of scree at the foot of the topless precipice of Black Crag—topless because its higher steeps thrust upward into the gray mists that veiled the morning sky. It was half-past nine, and though the air was unwontedly chilly there was no rain and the rock was dry.

"Why so?" inquired Lewker as he placed a loop of rope over a convenient rock spike as a belay.

"I didn't know you were an Alpine Club man until Janet told me this morning," Hamish explained. "You'll be the same Lewker that made the new route on the Grépon, I'm thinking. I've read the account in the *Alpine Journal*."

"My dear boy, that was fifteen years ago," said Mr. Lewker deprecatingly.

He was pleased, nevertheless. It had been a trifle disconcerting that all these youngsters had taken it for granted that he was too old to lead a rock climb, though indeed he had invited the assumption. It was gratifying to be remembered as the enterprising cragsman he had once been. And it was very pleasant to be standing here with the mountain-wind cool on his cheek and the mountain-scent keen in his nostrils—with the good gray rock soaring challengingly overhead and the brown moorland spread below. Looking down and back he could see the Hostel beside the silver tarn and one or two figures standing outside its door. Janet's blue shirt was distinguishable, and he thought the figure beside her was Ted Somerset. Ted had sedulously avoided conversation with him this morning; Mr. Lewker guessed that he was regretting the urge of conscience that had led him to the writing of his note last night.

"There goes Mr. Jones," remarked Hamish, pointing to the scree directly below them.

Bodfan Jones had announced his intention of going down to Birkerdale before lunch, "to poke about a bit." His diminished figure could be seen jogging down the narrow green track above the dark cleft of the Riggin Beck. As they watched, it disappeared behind the hillock on the farther side of the stream.

"Well," said Hamish, "stand by. Here we go."

Mr. Lewker, watchful as a good "Second" should be, paid out the rope as his leader stepped up on the first holds of the climb.

Black Crag presented a precipice some five hundred feet from base to summit at its highest part, lower and smooth at its eastern end, high and smooth where it overhung Riggin Spout at its western end. Its middle section showed, to a mountaineer's eye, the most likely route of ascent, where a succession of ledges and chimneys led steeply up into the clouds; but the bottom hundred feet of this obvious route was a wet and mossy face, vertical and impractical. To gain the base of the easiest way, therefore, it was necessary to traverse on an ascending line across the lower part of the cliff—one of those tactical moves in which the rock climber delights. There was a narrow ledge to begin this traverse, and from it started the two other routes, "Very Severes" in the climber's jargon, which only the most skilled of cragsmen could justifiably attempt.

Hamish climbed well, with a leisurely ease of movement that was a pleasure to watch. A mere "Difficult," thought Mr. Lewker, was probably child's play to him. He stepped lightly along the ledge, swung up a short crack, and made a long stride on to the foot-wide platform formed by the top of a half-detached block. Here he belayed himself by making a noose in the rope and dropping it over the natural pillar on which he stood. Then he took in the slack of the rope and called to Lewker to come on.

In the renewal of an almost forgotten joy—that contact with the rough and arching bones of Mother Earth which is to the climber what the crack of willow on leather is to the cricketer—the actor-manager forgot both acting and managing, forgot the hovering shadow of murder, forgot everything but the joy of hoisting himself heavenward by the simple skill of his four limbs. It is this simplification of life, for a brief hour or two, into the all-absorbing problems of hanging on and getting up, that is the chief attraction of rock climbing. There is no room for financial worries or domestic cares when one's life may depend on the correct use of an awkward handhold or the proper placing of a bootnail on a slight rugosity of the rock.

Not that there was much difficulty in holding on here. There were "jughandle" holds for the fingers and solid ledges for the feet. Mr. Lewker climbed the pitch as neatly, if more slowly, than his leader had done and drew himself on to the narrow platform mightily pleased with himself. Their diagonal line of ascent had brought them little more than forty feet above the scree, but already the silver thread of the stream looked twice as far below them.

"Easy enough so far," he observed, breathing rather hard as he secured himself to the belay.

"Aye," grunted Hamish, taking off his own belay and preparing to move on. "There's better stuff ahead. An eighty-foot run-out on the next pitch."

Mr. Lewker saw that between the pillar platform and the next safe halting place, fifty feet higher, a smooth expanse of steep slabs intervened, sweeping down from above to heel over in a vertical wall dropping to the scree. An airy staircase of well scratched footholds led up across this massive boiler plate of rock, heading for a sort of niche at the foot of a steep but broken ridge.

"Ready?" demanded Hamish, poised with one boot on the first hold of the staircase.

Lewker passed the leader's rope over one shoulder and under the other, gripping it firmly in both hands.

> Come one, come all! this rock shall fly
> From its firm base as soon as I!

he boomed in the words of Roderich Dhu; for once, Scott provided him with an apter quotation than his beloved Bard.

Hamish grinned. His reserve was thawing a little under the influence of height and space. He moved up a couple of steps and then paused to speak over his shoulder.

"Halfway across there's the only hard move on this climb," he said. "The peg above it's loose, but it wouldn't pull out when I tested it on Friday."

He moved on up the slab. Mr. Lewker paid out the rope across his shoulder almost automatically. Hamish's words had brought him back into the center of his web of tenuous clues. Hamish had been climbing on Black Crag on Friday; and on Friday Gay Johnson had disappeared after failing to persuade Leonard to climb Black Crag with her.

The distant booming of Riggin Spout, five hundred feet below, made a weird accompaniment to the rhythmic *diminuendo* scraping of Hamish's bootnails. Perhaps it was this and the gray gloom of the precipice that produced grim and fanciful reflections in Mr. Lewker's normally rational mind. Janet had a reason for trying, however inadequately, to hide the fact that her brother had walked over the hills to Cauldmoor on Friday. Could it be that Hamish had met Gay Johnson, and that Janet knew or suspected it? Had Hamish joined Gay in a climb on Black Crag? Might not some smoldering ash of black passion have flared up into—murder? In the mere fact that Hamish and Gay had at one time been engaged there was little enough motive; but there are dark turnings in the channel of human passions, and here was Opportunity revealing itself ...

Another thought insinuated itself. To be alone on a rock-face with a possible murderer was not a pleasant situation, particularly as Hamish (if indeed he had been concerned in Gay's death) must have suspected an ulterior motive in Mr. Lewker's ill-timed insistence on climbing the route from which Gay was thought to have fallen. A jerk of the rope as Lewker crossed that exposed slab would drag him from his holds to dangle helplessly above the scree. The man above could fray the taut rope over a sharp edge until it broke—and swear afterwards that he was powerless to prevent his companion's fall to death. ...

Mr. Lewker shook himself angrily, endangering his balance on his airy platform. This was foolishness. He had resolved not to speculate and here he was building fantastic theories. His job for the present was to amass impressions and facts, to make a comprehensive and unbiased survey of the circumstances surrounding Gay Johnson's death. It was for this purpose, and because he had assured Detective-Inspector Grimmett that it should be done, that he was inspecting this Black Crag route, although he was nearly certain that the girl could not have fallen from it. To fit Hamish into the role of murderer—Hamish, who had so casually given away the information that he had climbed the Crag on Friday—was merely ridiculous. Besides, there had been no broken piece of rope round Gay Johnson's waist when she had been found—

"Right—come on!"

Mr. Lewker started guiltily at that distant shout. He had allowed his attention to stray from his leader, a thing no "Second" should ever do. He hastily untied his belay and looked up and across the expanse of steep slabs. Hamish's black poll projected oddly from the niche eighty feet away, like a gargoyle on the facade of a cathedral. He was in dark silhouette against the mist that swirled across the crags overhead and his expression could not be seen; but his voice sounded cheerful enough.

"It's a pretty wee pitch, for a Diff."

"Here I come," called Lewker.

He stepped off the rock platform on to the sweep of smooth rock.

The holds were well smoothed by the passage of many nailed boots, but they were large—three inches of comfortably angled ledge for toes, convenient cracks for fingers. Exposed though the traverse was, thought Mr. Lewker as he climbed steadily up, a climber would have to be very careless or inexperienced to fall from it. The *mauvais pas* of which Hamish had warned him was a hiatus in the line of good holds, where it was necessary to make a rather long stride to the next high foothold. This Mr. Lewker's short legs might have found it awkward had it not been for a pointed spillikin of rock which projected from a crack in the slab immediately above. This wobbled a little, but appeared to be wedged in such a manner that it would stand a strong downward pull. As he swung across the bad step with a hand hooked over the spillikin he glanced downward. Beyond his poised foot the slabs swept smoothly and dizzily down, curving over on the edge of space some hundred feet below him. His eye passed immediately from the rock to the black gash of the Riggin Beck gorge; it was apparently vertically beneath his bootsoles. He knew that this was an optical illusion, that the horizontal distance between him and a point directly above the gorge was at least a hundred feet and more, probably two or three hundred, with a scree of boulders—invisible because of the slab's angle—filling the space between the gorge and the base of the precipice. Nevertheless, as he climbed slowly up on the large holds beyond the spillikin, he reflected that if that spillikin could be pulled clean out of its natural socket, as he was pretty sure it could, it would leave a place from which a solo climber *might* slip. Particularly if he or she was short in the leg. And Gay Johnson had been rather less than five and a half feet tall.

"Rather pleasant, that," said Hamish's voice in his ear; and Lewker hauled himself into a sheltered nook where a massive block provided a belay that would have held a whole caravan of mountaineers. "It's more spectacular going down," Hamish added.

" 'How fearful,' " panted the actor-manager, " 'and dizzy 'tis, to cast one's eyes so low.' Descent suitable for those with steady heads, as Baedeker would say." He slipped his belaying loop round the block. "I take it you climbed down this route on Friday."

Hamish finished gathering up the coils of rope before he replied.

"Aye," he growled briefly, and turned away to glance up at the next pitch.

A wide square-cut chimney rose above their niche, vertical but with several jammed boulders in its depths.

"Rest of the climb's brute force and bloody knees," Hamish observed.

He clambered agilely into the chimney and by dint of wedging with knees and elbows wriggled slowly up until he could grasp the first of the chock stones. Little by little he rose and finally disappeared on to a stance overhead. Lewker followed with a great deal of grunting, lamenting his lack of training. An easy arête followed, then another chimney. They were climbing into the mist now, and the crag was beginning to lie back at an easier angle. At the foot of a little wall of rock which, Hamish announced, was the final pitch, they halted for a moment.

The gray edges of the mist, drifting just above their heads, veiled the distant view but allowed a downward prospect. Far, far below—for a drop of eight hundred feet looks tremendous from above on a misty day—was the dark cleft of the gorge above the Spout. The fall itself was out of sight, but its giant whisper floated up from the depths, now louder, now fainter as the vagrant mountain wind carried it away. The gorge looked like a miniature Derbyshire dale from this angle. Most of its vertical opposite wall could be seen, and the rowans, rushes and moss that clothed its ledges had the appearance of the clinging woodlands of the Dovedale glen. There was even a cleft like the entrance of Reynard's Cave in Dovedale to strengthen this illusion. Wet-looking gullies interrupted the upper verge and the section near the top of the fall looked unpleasantly loose. It was not a place, reflected Mr. Lewker, where one would expect a climber to go scrambling.

Hamish made quick work of the last pitch. The rock wall narrowed into an easy and almost horizontal ridge leading to the grassy slope of the summit. Here the mist swathed them in its dank folds, still and silent yet with a sense of stealthy swift movements in its viewless opacity.

"Thank you, Mr. Leader," said Lewker punctiliously as he arrived on easy ground and began to untie his waistloop. "That was most enjoyable."

Hamish sat down on a flat rock and coiled his rope.

"The traverse is a nice pitch," he grunted. "How's the hour, please?"

"Ten-forty. We have taken an hour and ten minutes." Mr. Lewker seated himself on a rock.

"Not bad." Hamish pulled out his huge pipe. "Time for a wee smoke before we go down."

Mr. Lewker got out his cigarettes and lit one, passing the matches to Hamish. He puffed for a moment in silence, sending the blue smoke to join the dark vapor of the mist.

"Did you meet Gay Johnson on Friday?" he asked casually but suddenly.

The flare of a match showed, in the gray gloom, the quick sideways flicker of Hamish's eyes. The young man got the tobacco well alight before replying.

"No. I didn't see Gay."

"Your sister tells me you had no idea Miss Johnson was at Cauldmoor."

Hamish's teeth crunched audibly on the stem of his pipe. He scowled sideways at his companion.

"What's the idea?" he growled. "Doing a spot of detection?"

"Why," returned Lewker innocently, "is there anything to detect?"

Hamish said nothing. The actor-manager continued amicably.

"I am a little puzzled, that is all. Miss Macrae informed me that on Friday you walked with her from Black Sail to Cauldmoor by way of Wasdale Head—it sounds rather Chestertonian, does it not? And it seems unlikely that you would arrive at the Hostel at dusk with your sister, walk up Black Crag, and descent the rock face in the dark. I presume, therefore, that you walked over the fells and finished by climbing down the Crag."

"And what's Gay got to do with this?"

"Nothing, possibly."

"See here, sir." Hamish turned to face him squarely. "Was there something phony about Gay's death? Is that why you wanted to climb that route?" He stiffened suddenly, bristling like a terrier. "You're not thinking—you can't be thinking that I——"

"Wait," interrupted Mr. Lewker sharply. "Do not draw hasty inferences, laddie. Miss Johnson's death may have been an accident. I hope it was. One or two little matters, possibly unconnected with it, appear on the surface to be, as you say, slightly phony. One of them is this taradiddle of your sister's. Did she know you were on Black Crag on Friday? By the way, what was the time when you made your descent?"

"You'll be a detective, I'm thinking."

"I am a curious observer, Mr. Macrae. I do not intend to give reasons for my curiosity, and you have a perfect right to resent my questions."

"Och," said Hamish, drawing his black brows together, "there's no mystery, except what young Janet's been making. Here's the facts of the matter for you."

He paused to relight his pipe and then began to speak in short, jerky sentences.

"Gay and I were engaged until last November. There was a lot of unpleasantness about the breaking off. It left me pretty sore. At Black Sail Hostel last Thursday a fellow and a girl passed on their way to Ennerdale. I happened to meet them—Janet wasn't there. We chatted and I found out they'd come from Cauldmoor, where we were going next day. I asked them who was at Cauldmoor and they told me Somerset and Vera and Bligh— and Gay Johnson. They also said Vera had told them all four intended to walk down to Wasdale Head on Friday. I knew Janet wanted to go through Wasdale Head to see some friends of hers at Burnthwaite. I decided I'd take another route. Didn't want to meet Gay."

"You did not tell your sister this?"

"No. I suppose I didn't want Janet to know I was still sore over the engagement business."

"I see. So you walked over the fells and climbed down Black Crag, alone. Did you tell Janet about your climb?"

Hamish nodded. "Nobody else, though—and she kept it quiet."

"May I ask why that was?"

"Aye. It was because Ted Somerset—we met at Black Sail last Whitsuntide—had been asking me about climbing. He's dead keen, only Vera won't let him. I rubbed it in hard how solo climbing wasn't the thing— thought he might wander off on his own and start fooling about on a crag sometime, you see. Well, I lead Very Severes when I'm on form, and climbing solo down a Difficult's safe enough for me. But I didn't wish Ted to know about it."

"Quite so," nodded Mr. Lewker reflectively. "A wise precaution. Can you tell me what time you were on the Crag?"

"Think so, within ten minutes or so. I got in at the Hostel at five-thirty. The Hostel's thirty-five minutes from the bottom of the climb. The climb took me about the same time as we've taken coming up—I went pretty slowly. So I must have started down the Crag at a quarter to four and got to the bottom at four-fifty-five."

"Spoken like a mathematician," approved Mr. Lewker. "Are you one, by the way?"

"Not much of one," said Hamish. "I'm an engineer—leastways, I'm studying engineering. Glasgow University."

"Is your sister at the university, by any chance?"

Hamish grinned. "Not she. Janet's going to get herself blotted out of the family Bible. She's going on the stage. Just started at the Northern Academy of Dramatic Art."

"Has she indeed?" Mr. Lewker nodded satisfaction. "I rather fancy that solves a little problem. Pray tell me one thing more. You reached the Hostel at five-thirty. Did you see the Warden then?"

"Didn't see him. His typewriter was tapping away in his room—he hates being disturbed when he's busy. I brewed some tea, had a smoke, and strolled out to meet the others. When I'd gone about a mile down the path I met Mr. Jones coming up."

"That would be—what time?"

Hamish flashed a glance at him. "This is teckery, I suppose. 'Bout seven when we met."

"He would arrive at the Hostel in the neighborhood of seven-thirty. You went on, met the three coming from Wasdale, and returned with them. Did you see the Warden when you got in?"

Hamish frowned. "No. Bit odd, that. We brewed up some more tea and started talking about Gay's absence. Then we decided we ought to do something about it. It was Bodfan Jones who suggested we'd better ask the Warden. We banged on his door and went in. He wasn't there. Jones said he hadn't spoken to him or seen him go out."

"Hum. What time would that be?"

"Nine-ish. We had some more discussion and then decided we couldn't do anything useful until next day."

"I see." Mr. Lewker got up, rather stiffly. "Well, we had better start down if we are to be in time for the inquest."

The mist thinned as they swung down the broken slopes. Like a colored lantern slide coming into focus on a screen, the landscape grew out of the grayness: the russet and gold of the moor, the tarn steel-blue in a patch of sunlight, the little gray cube of the Hostel. Hamish broke a short silence.

"Look here," he said bluntly. "Am I suspected of chucking poor Gay over the crag?"

"I am inclined to think," responded Lewker slowly, "that you did no chucking."

"Did anyone?"

"Laddie, I am still groping in the mist. As yet, dark night strangles the traveling lamp. To be frank with you, and more colloquial, I haven't a clue."

Yet, had he known it, that morning had shown Mr. Lewker the clue which was to give him the key to the problem of Gay Johnson's death.

CHAPTER IX
IS THERE A MURDERER HERE?

A MOVING PATCHWORK OF SUNLIGHT AND CLOUD-SHADOW crept across the moor as the little party started off for Birkerdale. All of them, including the Warden, carried rucksacks containing lunch. The Warden had suggested that they should lunch on the way down, timing their walk so as to arrive at the Herdwick Arms, where the inquest was to be held, a little before two. Mr. Lewker, who had inevitably been seized upon by the indefatigable Vera Crump and her reluctant young man, stumped along between the two of them and pondered various means of getting rid of Vera so that he could pursue his inquiries with Ted.

It had occurred to him, somewhat belatedly, that he had still some ground to cover if he was to present a reasonably complete report to Detective-Inspector Grimmett. He knew that in thirty-six hours, with the assistance of a telephone and the British police organization, Grimmett would have collected and pieced together much information about Robert Peel's life and death; it was possible that some factor common to both Gay Johnson and Robert Peel would appear from a comparison of the two sets of details. The Gay Johnson set must therefore be as complete as he could make it if it was to be of any use in this odd inquiry. He decided to make the most of Miss Crump's obvious determination to keep up a conversation, and resigning himself to the atmosphere of adulation and excessive perfume set himself to obtain what he wanted.

He was rewarded with a great deal of effusive comment. Oh, yes—Gay had been a keen rock climber. She was a member of several climbing clubs—wasn't she, Ted? The Birmingham Climbers' Club, the Midland Cave and Crag Club—Miss Crump couldn't understand what the attraction was of clambering up rocks like a lot of monkeys. She contrived to suggest that Gay's chief interest in the sport was that it brought her into contact with a lot of men. Mr. Lewker discreetly turned the flow into another channel. Well—you had to admit Gay was excitable and quick-tempered—rather childish in some ways—didn't Ted think so? Miss Crump didn't want to seem catty, she was sure. Gay was fond of childish jokes, too. She liked to keep things secret and then bring them out as a surprise. You could always tell when she had one of these secrets brewing. Well, now Mr. Lewker mentioned it, Vera was pretty sure she'd got something up her sleeve before she disappeared on Friday. The usual childish thing, she expected disdainfully. But, added Vera quickly, she did hope Mr. Lewker wouldn't think her too awful, talking like this about the dead.

Mr. Lewker disclaimed any such thought. "Might this—um—secret have been the idea of climbing Black Crag by herself, and then telling all you non-climbers afterwards?" he wondered.

Both Vera and Ted thought this very unlikely.

"Her secrets were quite infantile," pronounced Vera. "Like discovering some extra pretty spot and then taking us to it. It might have been that—she went pottering off by herself as soon as she got here."

—And discovered an "extra pretty spot" on the verge of the Riggin Spout gorge? wondered Mr. Lewker. Aloud he inquired casually if the weather had been fine when they arrived; and provoked a full account of their journey from the Midlands. The four had come up on the night train, it appeared, reaching Gosforth in the early morning of Wednesday, and had walked from the station to the Hostel, getting there in time for breakfast. They had spent the remainder of the day in exploring the neighborhood of the Hostel or sleeping off the effects of the night journey. Gay had strolled off in the direction of Coffin's Pike; Ted and Vera had got as far as the summit of Black Crag, leaving Leonard to begin a watercolor of Cauldmoor as seen from the eastern slopes of the Crag.

"It's quite a nice picture," said Vera. "He finished it off on Friday—" She stopped quickly. Her prominent eyes flickered towards the silent Ted. "Leonard's not an artist, by profession, you know," she added hastily. "He's apprenticed to an engineering firm, though he doesn't like the job. He's much more of an Orpheus than a Vulcan, if you understand me."

Mr. Lewker indicated gravely that this mixed classical allusion was appreciated. Firmly interrupting an incipient lecture on the artistic temperament, he asked Miss Crump if this was the first time they had visited Cauldmoor Hostel. As he had hoped, this drew forth the details of the Whitsuntide holiday when all four of them had stayed at the Youth Hostel on Black Sail pass. It took very little prompting to obtain a fair idea of their movements. Ted, Vera and Gay had arrived there on the Saturday and had climbed Great Gable together on Sunday; Leonard, who had been unable to leave his work until Saturday midday, had motorcycled to Birkerdale, stayed the night at the Herdwick Arms, and walked over Cauldmoor to Black Sail on the Whitsunday. On Monday all four had walked into Ennerdale and back.

"You met the Macraes at the Black Sail Hostel, I gather." Mr. Lewker was being as casual as he could, but he felt that even Vera must soon begin to suspect that she was being pumped. "A pleasant pair of youngsters, are they not?"

"*Hamish* is a nice boy," she pronounced; and Lewker could feel Ted, walking on his other side, flinch as though he had been reproved. "They were there when we came but left on Sunday. At least, Hamish did—he had to get home before Janet, so he tramped over to Egremont to catch the afternoon train. We didn't see much of them," she added. "In fact, it was rather awkward, meeting them there. Hamish and Gay had only broken off their engagement six months earlier—I'm sure you'll understand that, Mr. Lewker."

"Quite, quite," murmured the actor-manager. "Somewhat embarrassing."

"Yes. Not to Gay, though. She actually wanted to go climbing with Hamish—Leonard doesn't climb, you know. Of course Hamish had more sense of decency."

She went on talking about the innate propriety of the Scots nation— with some difficulty, for the path had left the moorland and was descending steeply, narrowing until they had to scramble down in single file. Birkerdale, lakes of blue cloud-shadow moving across its golden fields, spread itself below them, and the boom of Riggin Spout was increasingly loud out of sight on their right. Mr. Lewker gave up the idea of detaching Ted and looked about him for another victim. The Warden, with the two Macraes, was ahead; Leonard Bligh, striding sulkily with hands in pockets, was a yard or two behind. He slowed his pace, allowing the voluble Vera and the attendant Ted to draw away, and so brought up alongside Leonard.

"This is a wonderful path," he boomed conversationally. "Have you been this way before?"

"No," returned Leonard briefly. He was in a singularly bad temper this morning, judging by the scowl on his good-looking face.

"Ah. I thought perhaps you might have walked over at Whitsuntide," explained Lewker.

Glancing over his shoulder, he thought he detected a fleeting look of suspicion in the other's eyes.

"Went up the lead mines track at Whit," growled Leonard, almost inaudible against the growing noise of the fall. "Why?"

"I just wondered if you had seen anything of the boy who fell from the crag that weekend."

Leonard made no reply. Without apology he pushed rudely past Mr. Lewker and plunged recklessly down the steep track. Lewker, following more slowly and frowning as he went, reflected that for a youth who was reputed to be no mountaineer Leonard was very sure-footed. Sunk in thought, he scrambled down among the boulders and rounded the corner of the steep slope on his right. The full voice of Riggin Spout thundered at him. The waterfall was sparkling snow-white in a burst of sunshine, and a rainbow gleamed in the spray over the footbridge below. Janet Macrae was standing on the hump of rock on the farther side of the bridge with a small camera in her hand. Leonard had already passed her and was hurrying to catch up the others. Janet gesticulated at the actor-manager, making interrogative signs by pointing first at the camera and then at him. Mr. Lewker, pausing in his descent, beamed and nodded, and was photographed as he crossed the bridge.

The girl grinned apologetically at him as he joined her on the path beyond. The thunder of the fall made conversation almost impossible and they moved on down the path.

"Hope you don't think I've gone all Vera-Crumpish," Janet said, when the fall had moderated its voice a little. "It was my last film and I rather wanted a picture of you. You see, I'm sort of interested—professionally—in you."

"Alack!" Mr. Lewker cast up his eyes sadly. "There is one word could well have been omitted."

Janet laughed. "Sorry. I'll say 'professionally as well' if you like. I'm going on the stage, you see. I'm at the Northern Academy of Dramatic Art. I think you know the Principal—Christine Delamere."

"Christine was with me in Ben Frankson's company."

"I know. I went to have tea with her once, and she told me that—and a lot of other things about you. She's a great admirer of yours."

"Hum. Christine was always a great talker. No doubt she told you of my checkered past and of certain occasions when I have assisted the police. Which is why you thought it advisable to lie to me, Viola."

Janet shot him a startled glance and then looked straight in front of her. Her cheeks had reddened.

"I may say," continued Lewker gently, "that your brother has told me about his climb on Black Crag on Friday. Tell me—do you think he might have met Gay Johnson then?"

"No!" cried Janet vehemently. She turned to look at him fiercely. "Hamish had nothing to do with Gay's death—nothing!"

"Then it was foolish of you to lie, my dear. Why did you?"

The girl looked a trifle ashamed of herself. She paused before replying and then spoke more quietly.

"All right. It was silly of me. You see, we'd kept his solo climb quiet—Hamish didn't want to encourage Ted to go climbing on his own. Though," added Janet bitterly, in parenthesis, "he'll never climb at all if Vera Crump has her way. It's too bad, how she—"

She stopped quickly.

"You told no one that Hamish had come over Black Crag on Friday," prompted Mr. Lewker.

"No. And when I met you I began to wonder if you were snooping round in connection with Gay's death—knowing about your detective efforts, you see."

"I never snoop," boomed Mr. Lewker reprovingly. "The word is not Shakespearean. But why should you wonder anything of the kind, pray?"

Janet turned a frowning face to him. "Look," she said. "*Was* there anything queer about Gay's death?"

"I hope not," returned Lewker evasively. "Why should you think so?"

"Well, Vera had been hinting about suicide, you know—and I could see Ted was worried about it, though he kept quiet. So I thought there'd be no harm in letting you think Hamish hadn't been near the Crag. I suppose you don't think—"

"I am not thinking at present," he interrupted firmly. "And you, Viola, are not to suppose. The inquest may clear the whole business up."

Janet was silent for a moment as they clattered down the zigzags of the path.

"Anyway," she said at last, "I'm not worrying. Hamish hadn't anything to do with it, and neither had I. So that's that."

Mr. Lewker said nothing.

The path reached the bottom of the scree and slanted off to the right across grassy slopes dotted with boulders. The rest of the party had halted a little farther on and were settling down to eat their lunch. As they came down to them Janet deserted her companion without a word and went to where her brother was sprawling comfortably on the cropped grass near Leonard Bligh. The Warden had seated himself on a flat boulder some distance from the rest and was peering into his rucksack like a shortsighted vulture. Ignoring the inviting gestures of Vera Crump, who was sitting with Ted close to the path, Mr. Lewker sat down beside the Warden and proceeded to get out his sandwiches. Meirion looked up abstractedly; his thin sallow face looked worried.

"Ah—hello, sir," he said awkwardly. "Glorious day—isn't it?"

Mr. Lewker agreed. He had once again that impression of evasion, of something hidden, that had intrigued him at his first meeting with Mr. Meirion; but today it was intensified. The man was worried, too—and more than worried. He was in a state of nervous excitement. The clawlike fingers fumbling at the sandwich papers were trembling ridiculously. He began to talk rapidly and almost at random.

"I trust you are enjoying your stay at Cauldmoor in spite of the—ah— unfortunate circumstances, sir. You are? Splendid, splendid. The young people are a very decent crowd, I think. Yes." His high affected voice was burdened with forced geniality. "You had a pleasant scramble this morning? I used to do a little climbing myself at one time. I fear my—ah— nerves are not very strong these days. Adventures in the perpendicular are not for me, ha-ha!"

The sudden short laugh sounded peculiarly unnatural. The Warden glanced quickly at his companion and took a hurried bite from his sandwich. The sun, emerging brilliantly from behind a cloud, glinted on his spectacles and showed the pale eyes behind them wide and fixed like a frightened rabbit's.

"Yes—a glorious day," he hurried on. "A pity to spend the afternoon at an inquest, don't you think?"

"Death will have his day," quoted Mr. Lewker sententiously.

Mr. Meirion seemed not to hear him. He seemed to have fallen into a fit of abstraction, and was staring blankly at his half-eaten sandwich as though he suspected it of containing undesirable matter.

"Possibly," observed Lewker, watching him, "you feel that the Dark Angel is rather overdoing it. I suppose you had to attend the other inquest, at Whitsuntide?"

The Warden started and returned from contemplation.

"Oh, yes—yes. Poor young Peel. A sad business."

"No one saw him fall, I gather."

"What? Oh, no. It is rather shocking to think that I could have done. I was alone in my quarters all that day, working. But I never looked out of the window. Very sad. This solitary climbing—one hopes that these two tragedies will prove a warning to others. One certainly hopes that."

"One does indeed," echoed Mr. Lewker drily. "Unless, of course, the Bent Stones accounted for both of them."

The Warden, who had taken a large bite from a fresh sandwich, choked suddenly.

"Wha—what do you mean?" he demanded hastily, with his mouth full.

" 'They was plucked off t' Black Crag an' flung down—an' 'twas t' Old Ones as done it!' " croaked the actor-manager, giving a lifelike rendering of Ben Truby. "The Old Ones," he added in his normal bass, "seem to be closely connected with the Bent Stones—if, indeed, they are not the Stones themselves. Have your studies led you to any conclusion on that point, may I ask?"

"My—my studies?" stammered the Warden.

Mr. Lewker eyed him curiously. The end of Mr. Meirion's crooked nose was positively quivering with nervousness—or was it plain fear?

"Yes—your studies," he repeated patiently. "You are making a study of local folklore, are you not?"

The other gulped. "Oh, that—yes. Yes, of course. I—I'm interested. Research is a hobby of mine. I'm not a Youth Hostel Warden really, you know, sir—only in my vacations, when I do a sort of locum tenens while the official Warden's on holiday." He was talking fast, dragging the conversation away from the Bent Stones, Lewker saw. "I'm Librarian at St. Asaph College," he continued feverishly. "The big Nonconformist training college near Rhyl, you know. I'm very happy there—yes, very happy. It has a fine library, one of the best of its kind, and the Principal is most kind, in fact everyone is most kind—"

He paused, apparently at a loss for further words, and took another large bite of sandwich. Mr. Lewker, feeling experimental, shot a question into the gap.

"May I ask," he boomed casually, "if you often go for long walks at night?"

This time the Warden choked so thoroughly that Lewker was alarmed. He thumped him on the back, to the unrepressed amusement of the Hostelers, until he recovered his wind. Meirion gasped, swallowed, and turned a scarlet face and watering eyes on his companion. He spoke in a kind of tremulous gasp.

"Wh-what are you—ah—implying?"

"Implying?" Mr. Lewker registered apologetic surprise. "Why, nothing, laddie. I merely wondered—as one does, you know—why our young friends could not find you on Friday night. I am told you were not in the Hostel. I find night walks beneficial myself," he added mendaciously, "and thought that perhaps you were of the same mind. I am sorry if you misunderstood me."

"No, no, no—not at all," panted Mr. Meirion rapidly. He drew a deep breath and appeared to pull himself together. "I thought you—but you are quite right, as a matter of fact. I did go for a long walk over the moor and didn't get back until very late. It was a fine night and I felt it would do me good. *In nocte consilium*, you know."

The Latin proverb seemed to complete his recovery. He helped himself to a bun from his bag and began to talk quite intelligently about the geology of the Cauldmoor neighborhood. Mr. Lewker, who had still a question to ask, led him gently to the subject of the types of rock suitable for climbing and thence to rock climbers and their ways. From here it was easy to pass to Gay Johnson and her last climb.

"You were the last to see the poor girl alive, I suppose," he ventured. "The Coroner will probably ask you about her behavior and so forth."

Mr. Meirion did not seem perturbed at this prospect. He had, it appeared, little to tell. Miss Johnson had hurried out immediately after breakfast and had only come in again when all the other Hostelers had gone out. He had been writing in his room and had put his head round the door to see who it was, but had not spoken with her. A few minutes later he had heard her go out again. He had not seen which way she went.

As he finished this brief account the Warden glanced at his wrist watch and stood up.

"We had better be marching, people!" he called. "We mustn't be late, you know."

The party began to repack its rucksacks and get on its feet.

"If we cut straight down the ben," shouted Hamish, "we can cross the burn—there's stepping stones—and get on the road."

Meirion agreed to this route, which cut out the loop of path leading to Langthwaite. Mr. Lewker, who had arranged to call for his wife at the farm, announced that he would take the longer way and catch up with them. Vera Crump, who was having her rucksack adjusted for her by Ted, looked at him appealingly as he went down the path past them, but he had no intention of allowing her to attach herself to him for the ride to Birkerdale. He stumped on, leaving the Hostelers scrambling down the steep hillside towards the road, and arrived at Langthwaite to find Georgie in the barnyard polishing the sides of the Wolseley with a duster.

"Hello, darling," she greeted him. "Had a nice hike with the other boys and girls?"

Mr. Lewker kissed her fondly.

"I have been gathering straws," he boomed, "to see which way the wind blows."

"And which way does it blow?"

"Up, in some cases," he replied gravely. "And what have you been doing in my absence?"

"Oh, moping, of course, darling." Georgie made a face at him. "And cultivating Mrs. Crake. Do you want some lunch? There's a little cold mutton left."

"No, I thank you. The funeral baked meats shall not coldly furnish forth the inquest. We should be on our way." He sat down on the running board and wiped his brow. "I see, however, that you have something to tell me."

Georgie sat down beside him. "Not much," she admitted. "Only I got Mrs. Crake to tell me all she knows about the Bent Stones."

"Excellent. They were the haunt of witches, I presume."

"Filthy, you beast!" exclaimed Georgie indignantly. "You knew about it—and here have I been—"

"The merest guess, my dear," protested Mr. Lewker hastily. "I happened to read in that massive tome on Mrs. Crake's bookshelves—*The Antiquities of Cumberland*, I believe—that Coffin's Pike was a corruption of the original Coven's Pike. A coven is, or was, a collection or gang of witches. Not infrequently there were seven witches to a coven, and there happen to be seven Bent Stones. Hence my guess."

"Well, you're quite right," said Georgie. "Mrs. Crake has a relative named Miles in Egremont, who's a bit of a pundit on local history—"

"That would be Police-Sergeant Miles?"

"It would. You know everything, darling, don't you? Relative Miles told Mrs. Crake, and Mrs. Crake told me, that long ago—in the middle sixteen-hundreds or thereabouts—there used to be regular meetings of witches, Sabbaths and whatnot, at the Bent Stones. They used to raise devils and sacrifice goats and—oh, a lot of weird nonsense."

> Eye of newt and toe of frog,
> Wool of bat and tongue of dog,

chanted Mr. Lewker sepulchrally.

"Yes, and worse. According to Mrs. Crake, they went a bit too far, even for those times, and did human sacrifice. A gentleman named Hopkins—"

"Mathew Hopkins, the witch-finder, no doubt."

"Don't interrupt, darling. This Hopkins was sent for and two of the witches were smelt out and afterwards burned at Carlisle. Horrible! But the point is that they're supposed to haunt the Bent Stones and do harm to anyone who disturbs their privacy. Black Crag and Riggin Spout are haunts of these Old Ones, says Mrs. Crake. I believe she really thinks those two poor children were hurled down by witches. Is all this any help, by the way?"

"Yes," said Mr. Lewker reflectively. "It fills in a corner of the picture. Did Mrs. Crake mention the truck crash that Geo Roughten was telling us about?"

"Oh, yes. Everyone in Birkerdale seems to think it was a mistake to store art treasures so near the Bent Stones. The Old Ones tipped the truck over, of course."

"Hum," said Mr. Lewker. He got up. "Well, my dear, let us go and hear Crowner's Quest law."

"You don't look very respectable," objected his wife.

"The inquest will not be a dressy affair. In you get. It is after a quarter to."

The Wolseley lurched out of the yard and down the sunlit lane between the stone walls. The clouds of morning had given place to hot sunshine and the scent of hay hung heavily in the air. Mr. Lewker, as he drove very slowly and with due regard for his mudwings between the drystone parapets, gave his wife a précis of his activities at Cauldmoor Hostel. Georgie listened attentively.

"I think I shall cast my vote for Mr. Bodfan Jones as the murderer," she remarked, when he had finished.

Mr. Lewker was shocked into apostrophe.

"Angels and ministers of grace defend us!" he boomed, twisting his wheel to avoid a projecting piece of wall. "My dear, murder has yet to be proved. As for Bodfan Jones, there is no evidence that he had either motive or opportunity."

"I know. I'm only going by fictional standards. He's unlikely, a bit mysterious, and a bogus comedian. That adds up to a murderer in a good many detective stories."

Her husband was preparing to condemn this piece of conjecture when the car emerged on to the good surface near the gate leading to Riding Mount. Sir Walter Haythornthwaite, attired elegantly in riding breeches and shiny gaiters, was standing just inside the gate in earnest conference with Ben Truby. He waved a hand and came through the gate as he saw them, leaving the shepherd rubbing his chin and staring at the ground. Lewker pulled the car to a standstill.

"Good afternoon!" called the Deputy Chief Constable. "You're off to the inquest? I fear I shall not be there."

He came up to the car, a slender and extremely neat figure. His ascetic features wore a smile, but his high brow was furrowed.

"Ben has just informed me of a case of liver-fluke among my sheep," he explained. "The only thing to do with these things is to take immediate action. I am going up to investigate now. If it is serious I shall go over to Gosforth tonight and get the necessary chemicals from the vet there."

"Really, Sir Walter, you're a perfect Proteus," said Georgie, smiling at him. "We've seen you as the art expert and the police chief—now you're the careworn farmer."

Sir Walter laughed ruefully. "The last is the most onerous role, dear lady, I assure you." He cast a quick glance over his shoulder at the reflective Truby and lowered his voice. "Grimmett wants a conference after the inquest, Lewker. I shall be back at Riding Mount by then. You will come?"

"Of course," nodded the actor-manager.

"Splendid. How has your Youth Hosteling progressed? Have you brought back any significant results?"

Mr. Lewker had opened his mouth to reply when he caught sight of Ben Truby. The shepherd's pale eyes were fixed upon him with a peculiarly malevolent glare. His scrawny neck was stretched and his head tilted as though he strained every nerve to catch what was said. Finding Lewker's glance upon him, he did not drop his own gaze but continued to stare, twitching his hoary eyebrows up and down rapidly. There was certainly something unearthly—diabolic almost—about the old man, thought Lewker. He answered Sir Walter evasively.

"It has been an instructive visit. I think Grimm will be interested."

Sir Walter nodded gravely. "So. I also shall be interested. By the way, one of your Hostelers—no youth!—called upon me at noon today. He gave his name as Bod something. Bodfan Jones—that was it. A very Welsh gentleman who wanted to know if Riding Mount was an historic mansion. I turned him over to Ben." He swung round. "What did you do with that visitor this morning, Ben?"

The shepherd pursed his lips, worked his gaunt cheeks, and spat expressively.

"Telled him a tale or so an' seed him off," he said scornfully. " 'Twas a fule of a chap. Gave me a saxpence."

Sir Walter laughed and pulled out his watch.

"I've kept you," he exclaimed. "You'll be late—I'm so sorry. Off you go—good-bye, Mrs. Lewker. Will you take tea with me tomorrow? Splendid, splendid!"

The Wolseley snorted and went on its way.

"Does Bodfan Jones' visit to Riding Mount fit into your theory of his guilt, my dear?" inquired Mr. Lewker as they sped more quickly down the straight road to the village.

"Oh, yes," nodded Georgie. "Of course he's in league with Sir Walter—our farmer-baronet-artist is a master criminal—and really came to plan the third murder. What's liver-fluke, Filthy?"

"A bloodthirsty little animal, not unlike yourself, my dear," returned her husband. "Two deaths is ample."

"I'm not bloodthirsty. I only thought it would make it nice and easy for you, darling. A fine fresh corpse, with clues lying about—"

"The jest," said Mr. Lewker, "is in bad taste. The inquest will sober you, I fancy."

The car entered the village street. Between the sharp blue shadows of the few houses half a dozen women were standing, talking busily. They stared at the Wolseley and its occupants with avidity. Outside the Herdwick Arms one or two men in farm clothes lounged, exchanging comments with the police-constable who stood importantly beside the inn door. There were three cars parked near the inn. Mr. Lewker drew in behind the cars and got out. He was escorting Georgie towards the door when he espied Ted Somerset standing uncertainly in the shadow of the cottage next to the inn.

"Will you go in, my dear?" he said. "I will follow you in one moment."

Leaving Georgie to find her own way, he approached Ted. The young man eyed him nervously and began to stammer something about the inquest not yet beginning. Lewker drew him round the corner out of sight of the loungers.

"You have something more to tell me," he boomed. "Let it be the whole truth this time, laddie."

"I didn't want—I don't know anything about inquests," faltered Ted. "I'm not going to tell the police, anyway. I'm dead sure it's not important, or I wouldn't—"

"The point, and quickly," interrupted the actor-manager sternly. "Your note of last night gave part of the reason for your suspicion of Leonard, I know quite well that nine words and an episode of Bligh's past would not lead you to think him a murderer. Your other reason is concerned with Friday morning, I think."

Ted looked up sharply, met his glance, and dropped his eyes quickly.

"I—I meant to tell you," he muttered. "Now—I can't. Leonard isn't—he didn't do it."

"Leonard began a watercolor sketch on Thursday, from the shoulder of Black Crag. On Friday, when you walked over to Wasdale Head, he stayed behind to finish it. Is that right?"

Ted's pale face showed a curious mixture of anxiety and relief.

"I don't know how you guessed, sir," he said slowly, "but it's something like that. We'd gone most of the way across Cauldmoor when Leonard suddenly said he'd catch up with us—the light was just right for finishing his sketch. He turned back and went up the hillside towards the Crag. We went on. He joined us at the pub in Wasdale Head a bit after two."

"How long does it take to walk from where he left you to Wasdale Head?"

"About an hour and a half, I suppose."

"And you parted—when?"

"Must have been something like a quarter to ten." Ted's fingers worked convulsively; he burst out in a sudden panic. "I won't have to tell the Coroner, will I, sir?"

"I fancy not, laddie. But you may have to tell the police later." Mr. Lewker's hand closed on the boy's arm. "Whatever happens, Edward," he said cheerfully, "you have done the right thing in telling me. Come along. We will see what physic this tavern affords."

CHAPTER X
HOYDAY, A RIDDLE!

THE INQUEST ON THE BODY OF PENELOPE GAIA JOHNSON occupied one hour and ten minutes. It was held in the dining room of the Herdwick Arms and was characterized throughout by an air of hushed and hurried informality.

The room, a long low place smelling of Worcester sauce and haunted by the ghosts of past suppers, was rather surprisingly large for so small an inn though hardly spacious enough for the company. Its one window looked out across a patch of scrubby garden to the river and the sunlit fellside beyond and its walls were covered with a shiny paper counterfeiting, with marked unsuccess, dark oak paneling. Mr. Lewker suspected it was used perhaps half a dozen times in a year. The massive rectangular dining table had been turned on its side and pushed up to one end of the room. In front of it, looking uncomfortable or defiant according to their reactions to stage fright, sat the seven jurymen. The Coroner, a cadaverous man in a wing collar, sat at a small table to one side of the center of the room with the superintendent of police from Egremont and Sergeant Miles. Four long benches at the end opposite the jury were occupied by the Youth Hostelers, two journalists, one or two people from the village, and Detective-Inspector Grimmett looking inconspicuous in his old raincoat. The front bench was reserved for witnesses—Leonard Bligh, the Warden, and Vera Crump from the Hostel; Dr. Whitmore, a worried-looking young man; and a small gray-haired gentleman in a clerical collar who was the dead girl's father. The jury had been sworn by the time Mr. Lewker squeezed into a seat on the back bench beside Georgie with Ted Somerset on his other side; he was quickly haled out of this refuge by an apologetic constable and made to sit between Miss Crump and the doctor on the front bench.

After some rapid muttering and sorting of notes the Coroner proceeded with his inquiry. His manner was very nearly informal; it said, in effect, "This is an unpleasant but necessary job and we'll make it as short and pleasant for everybody as we can." The Reverend Hugh Johnson, in an almost inaudible voice, gave evidence of identification. In reply to gentle questioning from the Coroner, he said that his daughter had been a high-spirited girl and fond of all sports, particularly rock climbing, pot holing and walking. She would be the last person, he was certain, to think of taking her own life. Surely there had been no suggestion—? The Coroner was soothing and apologetic; Mr. Johnson would understand that the possibility must be taken into account. Mr. Lewker was then called upon for his account of the search and the finding of the body, which he gave briefly and in a sonorous bass. Miss Vera Crump, unwontedly subdued, confirmed his account and was asked about her suggestion that the dead girl might have committed suicide. She repeated, reluctantly, Gay's last words to Leonard and hastily intimated (with one prominent eye on the bowed shoulders of Gay's father) that perhaps she had attached too much meaning to them. The Coroner looked at her severely and called Mr. Leonard Bligh. Leonard, sulky and monosyllabic, admitted that he and Gay had quarreled on the Friday morning.

"You were very much attached to this unfortunate young lady?" asked the Coroner in his smooth, rapid tones.

"Yes."

"And she, no doubt, was much attached to you?"

"Don't know."

"H'm. Do you think it possible that as a result of this quarrel she may have taken her own life?"

"No. Quarrel was just a silly sort of tiff. Gay wasn't that kind."

"Ah. Thank you, Mr. Bligh."

The Coroner glanced at his notes and called Mr. Paul Meirion. The Warden, who seemed to have recovered from his nervous fit, testified that he had seen Miss Johnson come into the Hostel after the rest had gone and had heard her go out again. His brief glimpse of her had shown him nothing unusual in her manner.

"When you heard her go out," said the Coroner, "could you tell whether she had changed her footgear?"

"Yes. She was wearing nailed boots—climbing boots. She had been wearing rubber shoes when she came in."

Mr. Meirion was asked a few more questions about Gay's demeanor on the evening and morning before her disappearance, the answers to which tended still more against the likelihood of suicide, and then was released. A mutter from the police superintendent led to a short interrogation of Sergeant Miles, a stocky, studious-looking man, about the police procedure after receiving the phone call from Riding Mount. Dr. Frederick Whitmore was then called. Mr. Lewker, watching the young man, thought he appeared a trifle apprehensive. He gave his evidence clearly, describing his examination of the body and the nature of the injury to the skull; he translated his technical language for the benefit of the jury.

"The body was also bruised in several places," he finished, speaking rather quickly. "There was no other fracture."

"The injury to the skull could have been caused by a fall from a height?"

Dr. Whitmore's hesitation was very slight. "Yes. Death would be instantaneous."

"We have heard that the body was found in the pool under Riggin Spout. Could not death have been due to drowning?"

"No, sir. The autopsy showed no water in lungs or air passages. Life was extinct before immersion took place."

"I see. Will you tell us how the body was clothed?"

"Heavy nailed boots, windproof trousers and a jacket of the anorak type. There was a loop of nylon line clipped round the waist with a steel snaplink, like a belt."

"Full rock climbing kit, in fact," nodded the Coroner, with a glance at the jury. "Now, doctor—I know it is difficult to give any exact time of death. Will you give us the best estimate you can, please?"

"I examined the body at 1 a.m. on Sunday. I should say the girl had then been dead between twenty-five and thirty hours. I'm sorry I can't put it any closer. The long immersion has to be allowed for."

"Quite. Thank you, doctor."

The Coroner turned to the jury with an air of having cleared away a good deal of necessary but irrelevant business. Before he could address them a tall young man in much-patched tweeds stood up from one of the benches.

"Please, mister," he said awkwardly, "was this lass as is dead a l'al girl wi' fair hair?"

The Coroner glanced at him sharply.

"If you have any relevant information to give, Darby," he said, "come here to the table and take the oath."

The young man, blushing and muttering something about not knowing whether 'twas any use, complied. He had been over to Nether Wasdale to order some sheep-dip, it appeared, and on the Friday afternoon had walked back by way of the southern skirts of Cauldmoor. He had passed close to the Bent Stones and had seen a girl dressed as the doctor had described sitting near the stone circle eating some food. She had waved to him and shouted "good afternoon." A pretty girl she had been, slim, fresh-colored, with very fair hair. Well—it might be half-past five or thereabouts, he reckoned.

There was some whispering among the Birkerdale folk on the benches at the mention of the Bent Stones and the Coroner frowned repressively at them. Mr. Lewker, turning in his seat, caught Detective-Inspector Grimmett's round blue eye; it was completely expressionless. He noticed also a detail that had escaped him before—Mr. Bodfan Jones was not at the inquest.

The Coroner, having noted Mr. Darby's evidence, dismissed him and turned once more to the jury.

This last piece of information, he pointed out, merely bore out the rest of the evidence before them. At about five-thirty on the day of her death Miss Johnson had been eating her tea by the Bent Stones, very probably after a long walk over the moors to work off the slight mental discomfort resulting from the morning's tiff, and had called a cheerful greeting to this passerby. That did not look like suicide—and it was then eight hours since the quarrel had taken place. The jury had heard that Miss Johnson had changed into climbing kit, presumably with the intention of doing a rock climb. As they knew, Black Crag had lately become a popular place with climbers. It overhung the upper channel of the Riggin Beck and a person falling off Black Crag would in all probability end up in the Beck and be washed over Riggin Spout. It seemed to him a strong probability that Miss Johnson had gone from the Bent Stones to Black Crag and attempted to climb it by herself on Friday evening. A slip had occurred, as might easily happen, and this lamentable tragedy was the result.

The jury conferred for a few seconds only. They returned a verdict of Death by Misadventure, adding a solemn rider condemning solitary rock climbing as a dangerous practice.

Mr. Lewker, making his way through the departing throng to rejoin his wife, caught sight of the Warden with a hand on the arm of the Reverend Hugh Johnson; the old man's face was gently stoical. Georgie linked her arm in her husband's as they passed out of the room.

"You were right about the inquest sobering me, Filthy," she whispered. "That poor old man! If it was murder—"

"Hush!" said Mr. Lewker quickly. Ted Somerset was at his elbow. He spoke in Ted's ear. "Edward, can you tell me the exact time you five arrived at the Hostel on Friday evening?"

"Yes, as it happens," Ted responded. "I timed our walk. It was twenty past eight."

"Bodfan Jones was there?"

"Yes. Been in an hour or more, he said." Ted glanced shrewdly at the actor-manager. "Hamish could give a sort of confirmation," he added. "He met Bodfan Jones before he met us."

"Quite so. Now answer this carefully, laddie. Did any of you go out again after you got in?"

Ted considered for a moment. "No," he said definitely. "Except the Warden, of course. Jones said he hadn't seen him, but we all assumed Mr. Meirion was in his quarters until we looked in. Nobody knew where he'd gone."

They emerged into the sunshine. Detective-Inspector Grimmett was lighting his pipe just outside the inn door. He raised his hat to Georgie and glanced at Ted.

"If you'd care for a lift to Riding Mount, Mr. Lewker," he began.

From the corner of his eye Lewker saw Vera Crump pushing through the little crowd towards him.

"You will not mind driving back, my dear," he said. "I shall be at Langthwaite for tea, I hope. If you can," he added in a hurried whisper, "get Somerset to join us—alone."

He bustled Grimmett to the aged Austin Seven which was the detective's pride and they drove bumpily away up the valley.

"Well, sir," said Grimmett, twisting the wheel in his large capable hands, "what did you think of it?"

"A pretty piece of restraint, Grimm. You have something up your sleeve, I gather."

Mr. Grimmett blew through his mustache and looked bland.

"Wilton, that's the Coroner, he don't like wasting time," he said. "Notice the medical evidence?"

"I had a feeling that the worm of conscience was begnawing the doctor's soul," boomed Lewker.

"Ah. I had a word with Doctor Whitmore. He knows what we're up to, so he does. Reckons he made a bad bloomer in not bringing the fact of the lack of fractures and so on to the notice of the police. No, sir—I meant the time of death."

Lewker nodded. "I did not miss that. Doctor Whitmore's estimate gives us the time as between seven o'clock and midnight."

"Yes, sir. Exactly so. And the doctor told me that although he couldn't safely get it closer he reckoned it was nearer midnight than seven o'clock. Funny time to be rock climbing, eh, sir?"

"Hum," said Mr. Lewker reflectively. "If she was overtaken by darkness on the climb, does not that make a slip more likely?"

Grimmett glanced sideways at him. "Hallo, sir! Found something up there? Think she fell off the climb after all?"

"I am not thinking, Grimm. I am with difficulty preserving an open mind until our coming conference."

The Austin pulled up at the gate of the Riding Mount land. Mr. Lewker had opened the car door to get out when a gaunt figure rose from behind the wall and opened the gate for them. They shouted their thanks as they drove through; Ben Truby, taking the clay pipe from his mouth, nodded and spat.

"Funny old cove," remarked the detective, changing gear as they joggled up the rough drive. "Cracked in places, as you might say, but nowhere near homicidal."

"You have been checking up—dreadful phrase!—on Mr. Truby?"

"Thorough's my motto, sir. I've got tabs on everybody. Ben's all right. Sir Walter vouches for him. He was a sergeant in Sir Walter's regiment in the '14-'18 war and Sir Walter saved his life. Been shepherd to Riding Mount ever since. No trace of connection with Peel or Miss Johnson."

Mr. Lewker looked at his companion with respect.

"Grimm," he boomed, "you are the soul of comprehensiveness. May I ask if you have got—ah—tabs on me?"

Mr. Grimmett laughed genially. "No need, sir. I follow your career in the newspapers. You were in Paris making speeches at the Drama Festival when Peel died, and at your London flat all Friday."

He halted the car in front of the house and they got out. Sir Walter, in breeches and a velveteen coat, opened the door himself.

"The servants have gone to Egremont for the day," he explained as he led them to the study, where a small fire burned in the grate. "I am sorry if you feel the heat. I'm all a-shiver with cold—touch of malaria I picked up in Africa. Sit down."

The visitors obeyed. Mr. Lewker inquired about the liver-fluke.

"It looks like it, I'm afraid," said their host. "I shall drive over and see Bulstrode tonight. They say he has some new treatment for the disease."

"Ah, you can't be too prompt with liver-fluke," nodded Grimmett. "Bulstrode's a first-rate man."

"So I hear. I shall take Truby with me. He says the Herdwick ewes need special care—" He checked himself and grinned apologetically at Mr. Lewker. "We are all sheep experts in these parts, Lewker. Liver-fluke's a worrying business—and I suppose this damned malaria makes it loom larger than it should. However"—he sat down at his desk—"I now perform what your charming wife would call a Protean transformation from farmer to policeman. First of all, the inquest."

He listened very carefully to the detective's concise account of the proceedings. Grimmett ended by quoting Dr. Whitmore's private estimate of the time of death and his own opinion that it was improbable that the girl would have been climbing at that time.

"Perhaps," nodded Sir Walter, his aquiline features intent. "But have you considered that the girl might have reached a spot from which she could neither advance nor retreat, and have remained there for some time until oncoming night impelled her to attempt the fatal step? That would account for the late hour of her death."

Grimmett blew through his mustache and said nothing.

"Grimm thinks she was never on the crag that evening," observed Mr. Lewker.

Sir Walter turned to face him. "And do you think likewise, now that you have seen the spot?"

"I had better give you the fruits of my stewardship," returned the actor-manager. "They are not, I fear, particularly ripe."

He proceeded to recount in full the experiences and impressions of his brief sojourn at the Cauldmoor Hostel. The other two listened in silence; Grimmett made a good many notes in his black notebook, while Sir Walter kept his eyes fixed on Lewker's face.

"The sum of all I have," finished the latter, "I have disclosed. It is incomplete, as I am well aware. The Warden's movements on Friday evening are obscure and so are Bodfan Jones'. However—"

"You have done splendidly, Lewker," cut in the Deputy Chief Constable, a little drily. "To have unearthed so many pointers, even though they all point in different directions, is a positive *tour de force*. I suppose we shall have to go into this matter of young Bligh's murderous assault, or whatever it may have been."

"That," remarked Mr. Grimmett, "brings me into the box, sir." He smoothed the open notebook on the table before him and stared with round blue eyes at his chief. "I've used rather a lot of men on this job, sir, telephoning and whatnot. I hope you'll think it was justified."

"I hope so," returned Sir Walter a little grimly.

Grimmett coughed, blew out his sandy mustache, and began to talk in his slow, agreeable voice, referring now and again to his notebook.

"First, Mr. Robert Peel. Age, 20. Lived at Ashbourne in Derbyshire. A very keen climber. Member of several climbing clubs, including the Midland Cave and Crag Club." He paused and glanced up. "I'd better say at once that Mr. Lewker's mention that Gay Johnson was a member of this same club is the only connecting link between the two I've been able to find."

Sir Walter raised his eyebrows but said nothing.

"That's in their home life, as you might say," Grimmett added. "They'd meet each other at club events and dinners, no doubt."

He turned a page of his notebook and resumed.

"Peel was found dead in the Riggin Spout pool at ten-thirty on the morning of Whitmonday. He was in full climbing rig—boots, breeches and windproof jacket—although both Sunday and Monday were exceptionally warm days. The smashed skull was the only injury bar bruises. At the inquest time of death was given as between ten a.m. and three p.m. on Sunday. So Peel wasn't climbing in the dark. Incidentally, Ashbourne police say he was well known in the town as a skilled cragsman—gritstone they climb on there, it seems, very steep and difficult climbing. And he'd done a lot of what they call pot holing, in Yorkshire. Not the sort who'd fall off a pretty easy climb, same as Mr. Lewker tells us this Black Crag climb is."

"Lewker said there were two much harder routes on the Crag," pointed out Sir Walter. "He might have been attempting one of those."

Mr. Lewker shook his head. "The two Very Severes do not overhang the Riggin Beck. A man would have to fall from the western part of the face to end up in Riggin Spout."

"Perhaps Peel was trying to find a new route there—a variation, as I believe these climbers call it."

The actor-manager leaned forward, his heavy features unusually grave.

"I had better emphasize my considered opinion," he said. "I examined the spot very carefully. A body falling from any part of Black Crag would hit the steep scree beneath with terrible force. It is just possible, though extremely unlikely, that if it fell from the western face it would by some freak of motion roll down into the stream. But it is quite outside the bounds of possibility that a body, falling naturally or even jumping out from the rock face, could escape with no other injury than a fracture of the skull."

Sir Walter looked at him keenly for a moment in silence. "Are you suggesting," he said slowly, "that this body—or these bodies—were somehow *propelled* from the face of the Crag?"

"I am making no conjectures at the moment. Shall we hear the rest of Grimm's findings first?"

Encouraged by a nod from Sir Walter, the detective continued his exposition.

"Peel's movements when he left the Hostel on the morning of Whitsunday

are uncertain—like Gay Johnson's. At the inquest Mr. Meirion, who was
then acting Warden as now, said that Peel left by himself at a little after
nine, leaving his belongings at the Hostel. Nobody saw which way he went.
He didn't appear to know any of the other Hostelers who were staying in
the place. They all went out about an hour later and Meirion saw them go
over the moor towards Wasdale. Peel said nothing to the Warden about
how he intended to spend the day. He may have told the others. We shall
have to get their addresses from the Hostel log and ask them."

Grimmett flicked over a page of his notebook.

"I've made a sort of summary," he said. "It comes out like this. Referring to both cases: bodies received the same form of injury; injuries would
have been very much greater had they fallen naturally from any part of
Black Crag. They were in full climbing kit on a hot day, which strongly
suggests that they intended to climb. Both were good climbers. They were
both members of the same climbing club. In the case of Peel, death took
place on a bright day within an hour or two of noon. In that of Gay Johnson
the time of death was probably after dusk." He glanced up at his listeners.
"By the way, old Ben was up on the fells by Coffin's Pike on Whitsunday,
and also during most of last Friday, until well after dark."

"He spends a large part of his life there," put in Sir Walter, "either on the
hillside or in his bield. You can't be suggesting that poor old Ben had anything to do with either death, Grimmett."

"Course not, sir. The point is, he saw and heard nothing of any climber
on the Crag either day. He'd be some distance away, no doubt, and in any
case he'd be out of earshot. It's probably not much of a point. Anyway—
that's all I've got on the deaths."

Sir Walter remained for a moment apparently absorbed in contemplation of his fingernails.

"It is not a great deal, Inspector, is it?" he said at last. "The connection
between the two is slight and fortuitous. Admitting Lewker's contention
that they could not have fallen from the crag, why should they not have
fallen from the same place on the edge of the gorge, say?"

"It'd be a bit of a coincidence, sir, wouldn't it?" said Grimmett.

Sir Walter sighed. "We seem to be back at the old stage—the thing is
odd but not impossible. I am inclined to be thankful that none of this was
brought out at the inquest."

Grimmett's round face took on a stubborn expression.

"We kept it quiet, as you know, sir, so as not to scare our criminal," he
muttered.

"If there is a criminal. I have not heard any evidence that suggests that
these young people were murdered by someone who hit them on the head
with a lump of rock. You have some information about the people at the
Hostel?"

"Yes, sir." The Inspector assumed his normal placid manner. "I've been
lucky, especially with the Birmingham police. I suggest that Mr. Lewker

tacks on his little piece for each one, so we can get an idea of possibilities."
He began to read from his notes. "Vera Crump. Teacher at Aston Street
Infant School, Birmingham. Not known to police, was with Mr. Lewker
when body was found."

He stopped and nodded at Lewker.

"An irritating young lady," continued that gentleman, "but with no ap-
parent motive and no opportunity for committing murder in either case.
She, Edward Somerset and Janet Macrae give each other alibis for
Whitsunday and last Friday."

"Aye. That knocks them out, on the face of it. Leonard Bligh. The Special Branch at Birmingham got hold of something here. Bligh works at the
Fosdyke Engineering Works and they saw the manager. He says Bligh went
for one of his fellow apprentices with an iron bar, tried to kill him. It was in
a fit of temper and his mates managed to get hold of him before he could do
any damage. That was last February. The firm hushed the matter up. Nothing else against Bligh except that he behaves oddly at times."

Mr. Lewker took up the tale.

"Our Leonard was more or less in love with Gay. Quarreled with her on
Friday morning. Was heard to say thereafter 'I shall kill that girl some day.'
Was alone on the slopes of Black Crag on Friday morning, sketching, but
both the medical evidence and the statement of Mr. Darby at the inquest
give him an alibi, for he was with four other people from two o'clock on-
wards. At Whitsuntide he walked alone from Birkerdale to Wasdale over
Cauldmoor on Sunday morning. Says he went via the lead mines track, not
by Riggin Spout."

"Gives him opportunity for the Peel business," remarked Grimmett
thoughtfully, "but there's no link between him and Peel so far. Now for
Hamish Macrae, of Dumfries. Engineering student at Glasgow University.
Member of Scottish Junior Climbers' Club. Nothing else from me, Mr.
Lewker, but I believe your end's suggestive."

"Perhaps. Hamish was engaged to the dead girl until November of last
year. He admits to climbing alone down Black Crag on Friday, between
three forty-five and five o'clock. He says he saw nothing of Gay Johnson.
He arrived at the Hostel at five-thirty, according to his own account, so that
the medical evidence appears to give him an alibi. According to Vera Crump,
he walked from the Black Sail Hostel to Egremont on Whitsunday, which
may have taken him past Cauldmoor."

Sir Walter, frowning, interrupted. "Your information is incomplete in
this case, Lewker. I take it you have no confirmation of Macrae's movements on Friday evening?"

"Not as yet, it is true. Bodfan Jones could confirm Hamish's story that
he met him on the Wasdale track at seven or thereabouts."

"That would give him an alibi of a sort. He returned with the rest of the
party at twenty past eight and, I take it, was with them for the rest of the
evening." Sir Walter tapped impatiently on his desk. "If we are going to

take this up, we must get all these times established where possible. Macrae's movements on Whitsunday must be inquired into. He appears to have no alibi for the time of Peel's death. Go on, Inspector, please."

"Bodfan Jones," Grimmett read from his notebook. He emphasized the next sentences. "Gave his address as 47 Wilton Avenue, Llandudno. Llandudno police inform us the address is nonexistent. There are seven hundred Joneses in the town but they know of no Bodfan Jones. Don't like the look of that, sir."

"This was the little man who came poking round here this morning," nodded Sir Walter. "I was rather short with him, I fear. Why, I wonder, should he give a false address?"

Mr. Lewker rubbed his chin thoughtfully. "He had no reason to expect that the police would need to confirm it," he pointed out. "His name and address were taken in case his evidence was needed at the inquest."

"It means he's got something to hide, all the same," said the Inspector.

"Possibly, or even probably, that is so," Lewker agreed. "And he is certainly a little too Welsh to be true. I wonder if, under some other name, he is known to the police."

"There seems to be no suggestion of motive," Sir Walter remarked.

"No. Nor is there any evidence that he was anywhere in this neighborhood at Whitsuntide."

Grimmett frowned at his open notebook and wagged his head.

"There's a deal to be done yet," he said. "I'd like to have ten minutes' official interrogation of each and all in this case. Jones' alibi for the second death is a bit thin, so it is."

"He met Hamish at seven," observed Mr. Lewker, "and presumably went on to the Hostel, where he was when the others got in at eight-twenty. Unless the Warden heard or saw him within that period of an hour and twenty minutes, he cannot be said to have a complete alibi for the period assigned to Gay Johnson's death."

"Another point for confirmation," remarked Sir Walter. "Whitmore's evidence," he added with an impish look, "seems to have put your more likely suspects out of court, Lewker."

"Perhaps. However, Bodfan Jones impressed me as a man of strong character acting a part. He also succeeded in frightening Mr. Paul Meirion with a piece of doggerel that went like this:

> He who credits witch or gnome
> Should be safely in a Home.

The joints of Mr. Meirion's knees were unloos'd, if I am not much mistaken."

"Ah," said Grimmett quickly, "this Mr. Paul Meirion, seems he's a queer bird. The police at Rhyl didn't get me much—he's librarian at St. Asaph College, was badly shell-shocked in Burma, nothing more. But he's been down at Police-Sergeant Miles' place a couple of times, so Miles tells me, asking questions. Miles is a bit of an authority on olden times in these parts, folklore and what-have-you."

"Miles is a scholar in his way," Sir Walter nodded; his dark eyes were troubled. "Some time ago I gave him an old volume from Riding Mount library dealing with ancient practices in Cumberland. I dare say he told you."

"Aye, sir, he did. It's this book Mr. Meirion's very interested in, it seems. Miles tells me the last time he was there, about a fortnight ago, he got all wrapped up in it. Absorbed, you might say. It's called *A True Record Of Wizardrie In The North*." Grimmett turned to Lewker. "That links up with your little piece all right, sir."

"Yes," said Mr. Lewker slowly. "There is that odd bit of writing about casting a virgin into Riggin Spout. There is the fact that he has no alibi for the time of either death. There is his mysterious disappearance—for a long walk in the dark—on Friday night. And there is his undoubted fear of Bodfan Jones."

The Inspector glanced sharply at his old colleague.

"Fear," he repeated. "You and I know what lengths fear will drive a man to, Mr. Lewker. What's this about a Home, now? We'll have to get after that."

The Deputy Chief Constable rose suddenly to his feet and walked to the window.

"I hoped this wouldn't have to come out," he said, speaking without turning round. "I happen to know what Bodfan Jones meant—if indeed he knew what he meant. I'd better tell you. Paul Meirion is the son of a man who was in my regiment during the first world war. I've helped him a little. He came to me for references when he was applying for the post of librarian at St. Asaph College, and I recommended him for this temporary warden's job. He has been quite frank with me, but I saw no reason to pass on what he told me."

He swung round and came back to the table to stand looking down at them earnestly.

"You see, Paul's mind was affected by his experiences in the last war. He had been interested in research into the supernatural when he was at Oxford, and the mental illness turned that interest into dark channels—or so I suppose. Anyway, there was a horrid scandal. Four centuries ago Paul would have been burnt by law. As it was, he was sent to a Mental Home. He was released as cured in 1948. It was then that I helped him to get his post."

"And what," asked Grimmett, "did Mr. Meirion do that caused this scandal, sir?"

"He practiced witchcraft," replied Sir Walter gravely.

CHAPTER XI
OF DAMN'D WITCHCRAFT

"WITCHCRAFT?" REPEATED DETECTIVE-INSPECTOR GRIMMETT, his round brick-red face incredulous. "You're not telling me, sir, that there's any such thing?"

Sir Walter made an impatient gesture. "Sorcery, witchcraft, attempts to communicate with demons and gain power from them—of course there's such a thing and always has been. Whether there are any results nowadays is another matter. There used to be, if one can trust the mass of evidence."

"But—well, broomsticks and that, sir!" Mr. Grimmett was clearly shocked at his superior's credulity. "Mr. Meirion wouldn't ride a broomstick, now?"

"Paul Meirion came out of the army a psychoneurotic—they'd have called it a shell-shock case in 1918. You can call his eccentricity an obsession if you wish. The facts that we are concerned with are that he was in a Mental Home during '47 and '48 and that he is dabbling in the same dangerous pool again."

"The revelation of either fact," said Mr. Lewker slowly, "would mean the loss of his situation as librarian, I take it?"

"Indubitably," nodded Sir Walter. He strode heavily to the window and back again, twisting his thin fingers nervously. "This is extremely painful to me," he said in a low voice. "I see only too well where it is leading."

Mr. Grimmett wagged his head sympathetically.

"Ah," he murmured. "We can't blink it, sir. If it was found he was—um—practicing witchcraft again, it'd mean more than losing his job, I dare say. He'd be for the loony-bin again."

A spasm of pain crossed the ascetic features of the Deputy Chief Constable. He inclined his head.

"So if anyone happened to see him at his jiggery-pokery," continued the detective, "they'd be best out of the way, from Mr. Meirion's point of view." He leaned back and puffed strongly through his mustache. "I reckon we've got a strong motive there, sir. *And* opportunity—*and* means." He snapped his notebook shut and leaned forward, his blue eyes gleaming. "How's this? Meirion finds out Peel has spotted his tricks. He gets him down to the edge of the beck on some pretext, slugs him with a rock, and tips him in. Over he goes, into the pool under the Spout, and—as Meirion expects—we all think he's fallen off Black Crag. When Gay Johnson finds him out again two months later he does the job in just the same way. You know how it is with them—Smith and the brides in the bath—same method over and over again—"

"Wait!" Sir Walter spoke so sharply that Grimmett jumped. "This is all speculation, Inspector."

"Circumstantial, sir. But it'll stand as a theory," said Grimmett stubbornly.

Sir Walter was silent for several seconds.

"I must admit," he said at last, slowly, "that an official investigation seems indicated. What do you propose?"

"Get going right away, sir. I'll want a search warrant for the Hostel, and a couple of men."

"Yes. I should go up there first thing tomorrow. The Warden cannot have any suspicion that the police are interested, as yet. The young people at the Hostel—what about them?"

"I shall want to interrogate some of them, sir—but that's all right. They're all staying on, until tomorrow afternoon at any rate." The detective turned to Mr. Lewker. "Will you be at the Hostel tonight, sir?"

"I think I had better," said the actor-manager slowly. "It may be as well to keep an eye on Mr. Bodfan Jones."

Grimmett whistled. "Lord, yes. I'd forgotten him. He knows about Meirion's spell in the Home—and took good care to let him know it. What was his game, I wonder?"

Mr. Lewker said nothing. He was still rather silent when, five minutes later, Grimmett's Austin Seven was jolting the two of them down the Riding Mount drive.

"Well, sir," the detective said with a sidelong glance, "we're for it now. Meirion's my bet. At a guess, you've something else in mind. Eh?"

"There are other things in my mind," acknowledged Lewker. "Including—for example—the loose spike on Black Crag."

"Aha!" Mr. Grimmett was amused. "Someone fixed up a booby trap that'd catapult a climber off the precipice into the beck. Someone with a good alibi, I suppose, because the trick would work on its own."

The Austin pulled up at the gate leading to the lane. Ben Truby was not there to open it this time.

"Remember, Grimm," boomed Mr. Lewker as he got out, "both Hamish and Leonard are engineers."

He opened the gate, firmly refused the Inspector's offer to drive him up to Langthwaite, and having assured him that he would contrive to keep the

Hostel inmates handy until the arrival of the police in the morning, set off up the lane to Langthwaite. The late afternoon sunshine was delightfully warm, yet with that hint of abatement or satiety which is the herald of autumn. The night, thought Mr. Lewker, would probably be chilly on Cauldmoor; and he congratulated himself on having a spare bunk with its attendant blankets in his sleeping quarters there. Beneath these surface thoughts his mind was working steadily but with no very clear idea of its objective, like a man feeling his way through a dark labyrinth, seeking the light but unsure of the turning that would lead him to it. The most obvious passage of the labyrinth might be the true one—and yet his mind refused to enter it without exploring the others.

He stumped on thoughtfully between the mossy stone walls, pleasantly aware of the sun on his bald head, and turned up past the barn to the door of Langthwaite. In the sitting room he found his wife pouring out tea while Mrs. Crake, in full spate of gossip, stood in the center of the room holding a jug. Sitting at the table opposite Georgie was Ted Somerset.

"And here's your good gentleman in time for a cupper," Mrs. Crake declared without so much as pausing for breath at Lewker's entrance. "I was just telling Mrs. Lewker how Sir Walter helped us tide over the bad winter three year ago, not but what it's just like him, a rare good landlord he is, and kind to all us Birkerdale folk as George Roughten could tell you if he liked though I reckon he doesn't like, though its common knowledge enough as he was nigh bankrupt and would have been too if Sir Walter hadn't aided him, and that's gospel."

She drew a long breath, champing her bony jaws.

"You would say, with Salarino, 'A kinder gentleman treads not the earth,' " said Mr. Lewker, accepting a cup of tea from his wife. "Thank you, my dear. I see you have kidnaped Mr. Somerset."

"And that's gospel too," recommenced Mrs. Crake, presumably referring to the quotation. " 'Tisn't as though Sir Walter's a rich man, neither. Spends all his money on pictures, I've heard tell, a foolish thing to my way of thinking, but every man to his taste as the Bible says, though he'd do better to marry a wife 'stead of being wed to a lot of paintings, which is a mite like going after strange gods as we heard in Birkerdale church Sunday before last, or it may have been the one before that, parson being taken with a croup last Wednesday fortnit—"

A stentorian bellow from the farm kitchen put a period to a sentence that looked like attaining record length.

"There's Mr. Crake crying for his tea," she finished. "I'm away. Let a wee shout if you want anything."

She hurried out.

"There goes a lovely character part," sighed Georgie. "I could have played it beautifully, Filthy."

"So you could, my dear." Mr. Lewker winked at Ted, who was plainly not at his ease. "My wife was something of a witch on the stage, Edward.

Now she practices her arts off the boards."

"Yes—I've noticed it," said Ted unexpectedly.

Georgie smiled at him charmingly. "Mr. Somerset was very kind," she said. "The car was running very badly, you see, darling, and I happened to catch up the Youth Hostel people and asked Mr. Somerset if he could help me with it. I told the others to go on and he'd catch up with them, but it took rather a long time so I asked him to take tea with us."

"I looked at a lot of things before I discovered that two plug connections had pulled out of the commutator," explained Ted.

Mr. Lewker hid a smile in his cup. His wife told him to take his rucksack off and sit down properly.

"Edward and I can walk up together tonight," he said as he obeyed. "Before that, however, I want you to run us into Egremont, my dear. It is only nine miles, and a good road once we are past Birkerdale village."

"All right," agreed Georgie. "More cake, Mr. Somerset? We'd better not ask him why," she added. "I expect he's been sworn to secrecy at this conference."

Mr. Lewker helped himself to a piece of shortbread. "There was no swearing of any kind," he responded. "I have no doubt that in telling you what passed I am incurring the possible wrath of the Deputy Chief Constable of this county, not to mention a Detective-Inspector who is an old friend of mine. None the less, I will the tale unfold."

Ted Somerset began to get up.

"If—er—perhaps you'd rather I didn't hear it," he said diffidently.

Lewker waved a hand imperiously at him.

"I particularly wish you to hear," he boomed. "Sit down, I beg." He turned to his wife. "Edward has had to make a very difficult decision, my dear. He was possessed of evidence, both of motive and of opportunity, which—slight though it was—tended to incriminate someone he knew. Very rightly and sensibly, he told me."

Ted looked embarrassed and more than a little uneasy.

"And you have told the police?" frowned Georgie.

"The information is now in the hands of Detective-Inspector Grimmett, who has charge of the case."

"There's going to be a case, then?" asked Ted apprehensively.

"There is. The police are taking over tomorrow. I, however, am not thrown out of my part. I am still sustaining the role of Gifted Amateur, and I shall require you, Edward, to assist me."

"He means he wants someone to listen to his maunderings," explained Georgie.

Ted smiled halfheartedly; his youthful face looked worried.

"Thanks very much, sir," he said hesitantly, "but if it's—going to be Leonard, I'd rather not—"

"At the moment," said the actor-manager carefully, "the eye of the Law is not focused on Mr. Bligh. That, of course, does not mean that he is freed from suspicion. Consider, laddie. There is going to be no mistake. If an arrest is made, it will be the person who brutally murdered your friend Gay Johnson."

"All right," said Ted suddenly. "I'm on."

"You will Watson for me? Excellent. You realize that I am trusting you with police secrets, which I should not do?"

"You can rely on me, sir."

"I believe I can. My dear, another cup—and let it be the color of yonder mahogany sideboard, or thereabouts. Have I your ears, good gentles? Then attend."

Moderating his sonorous tones so that they should not penetrate to the other side of the sitting room door, he summarized the discussion that had taken place at Riding Mount that afternoon. The others listened intently. Ted, whose eyes never left the actor-manager's face, showed signs of excitement as the narrative progressed.

"Then it's all right!" he cried, as soon as Mr. Lewker had ended. "Leonard's got an alibi after all!"

"So have the Misses Macrae and Crump," added Georgie, "and it rather looks as though Hamish Macrae will produce one—and Bodfan Jones too. I rather fancied Mr. Jones."

"I fancy," said Lewker thoughtfully, "that proving two satisfactory alibis for every possible suspect is going to be difficult. Something tells me this case may not depend upon alibis."

"It's pretty clear against the Warden, isn't it?" said Ted. "I suppose he's off his rocker—this witchcraft touch, and so on—but, you know, I'd have said he hadn't the guts to bump off two people like that."

Mr. Lewker glanced at him sharply.

"That is not in your part, laddie," he boomed. "Watson should back the obvious suspect."

"Meaning," frowned Georgie, "that you don't think the Warden did it."

"The case against him is not proved," her husband pointed out. "Furthermore, if he is bloody, bold, and resolute enough to eliminate two persons because they happened to discover his secret passion for necromancy, why did he not have the sense to inflict some different kind of injury on his second victim? Or to provide himself with some sort of alibi?"

"He nearly got away with it, darling, didn't he? If it hadn't been for Mr. Somerset—but I'm forgetting my favorite suspect. Bodfan Jones wasn't at the inquest, I noticed."

"True," nodded Lewker, frowning. "I wonder why. He struck me as the type of gentleman who would rather enjoy an inquest. Especially an inquest held at a pub. I have an idea Mr. Jones is fond of his glass."

The entrance of Mrs. Crake with a large tray put an end to the conversation. Georgie, with a glance at Ted, reminded her that she had promised that young man some eggs and butter to take up to the Youth Hostel.

"Ay, he shall have 'em," nodded Mrs. Crake, collecting tea things on to the tray. "What's more, he shall have a twig of rowan to keep in his pocket. 'Tis a sure guard against witches, is rowan, and I reckon he needs it up at yon place."

"Mrs. Crake," said Lewker suddenly. "You were born and brought up in this valley, were you not?"

"I was that, sir." She straightened up with the loaded tray in her hands and visibly unlimbered her formidable jaw. "Well do I remember in those days how the price of mutton—"

"Do you remember," Mr. Lewker boomed determinedly, "whether there was any talk of witches at the Bent Stones, or the Old Ones, or anything of that kind?"

"Well, now, sir," said Mrs. Crake slowly. "Now you mention it, we didn't hear nowt much about them when I was a girl. But 'tis an ill place up there, and that's gospel. Old Ben Truby, he's seen terrible goings-on by Bent Stones—too terrible to tell of—he being the only one as'll go up by the old mines to Coffin's Pike after sundown, being as he's to look after the sheep, and these young folk from the Hostel they don't know the danger, nor the Liverpool folk as sent those vallyble pictures there in the War, and look what happened to 'em when George Roughten was driving 'em away in his truck, not that we knew till afterwards as 'twas the Old Ones as did it—"

"Mrs. Crake." interrupted Lewker quickly. "Am I right in saying that this evil activity on the part of the Old Ones has only been suspected during the last five years or so?"

"I suppose 'tis true what you say, sir," she responded reluctantly. "Though 'tis plain enough," she hastened to add, "as they've been at it since olden times, as you'd see if you read a book my cousin Daniel Miles has got."

"Ah, yes. I would very much like to see that book. In fact, I thought of going into Egremont this evening. Do you think he would be kind enough to show it to me?"

"I'm certain sure he would, sir. And if he's on duty you ask Aggie—that's his wife—and tell her I told you." Mrs. Crake turned to the door. "Come along, young master. I'll get your eggs and you can choose 'em yourself."

She went out, followed by Ted. Georgie turned an accusing eye on her husband.

"Filthy," she said, "you're up to something. What is it?"

"Possibly I am merely drawing the net a little closer round our friend the Warden. Incidentally, my dear, you did very well to produce Edward without his Vera."

"It was a bit of a job. Filthy, I'm sorry for Ted. He's a nice boy, and she treats him like a naughty child. If she marries him he'll develop into one of those poor silent downtrodden breadwinners whose only conversation is 'Yes, dear.' "

"Yes, dear," said Mr. Lewker submissively.

Georgie threw a cushion at him. "I'm serious, darling," she said. "She's got him where she wants him—she's the type who grab the quiet inoffensive boys before they know where they are. He deserves a better fate."

"I fancy," said Mr. Lewker thoughtfully, "that Miss Janet Macrae thinks the same. Are they engaged, do you know?"

"Ted told me Vera wants to announce their engagement after this holiday. He's very reluctant to talk about it. I think—" She sat up suddenly. "Filthy, I do believe you're setting up as a matchmaker! You be careful!"

"I will let my discretion be my tutor. Now, my dear, get your bonnet and we will go clue-hunting. I think, since it is nearly six o'clock, a call at the Herdwick Arms should be paid on our way to Egremont. We may find something there."

"No doubt," said his wife. "In a glass, darkly."

Ten minutes later the Wolseley pulled up at the door of the Birkerdale inn. Mr. Roughten, beaming and rosy as ever, greeted them as they entered the dark little bar. There were two other customers seated at the table with pint mugs in front of them; one was old Ben Truby, the other the young farmer who had testified at the inquest to meeting Gay Johnson by the Bent Stones on Friday afternoon. They returned Mr. Lewker's salutation briefly and went on with their talk, in the Cumbrian dialect that, to a southerner, is a foreign and incomprehensible tongue. Lewker had scarcely ordered a beer for himself and cider for his wife and Ted Somerset, however, before the gaunt shepherd rose to his feet and picking up his blackthorn staff went out into the evening sunlight.

"Old Ben's off early this evening," observed Mr. Roughten. "Where's he bound for, Mr. Darby?"

"Motorin' to Gosforth wi' Sir Walter to see Bulstrode," returned the farmer. "Rackons t' liver-fluke's got among t' sheep."

He picked up a copy of the *Farmer's Gazette* from the table and began to turn its pages. The landlord shook his head gravely.

" 'Tes right nasty to get rid of, liver-fluke," he said, and turned to Mr. Lewker. "I couldn't get in to inquest this afternoon, sir. Nothin' exciting, I hear."

Mr. Lewker confirmed this impression. "I was rather expecting," he added, "to meet an acquaintance of mine there. He is staying at the Hostel—a short, plump middle-aged gentleman in a red-and-gray tweed jacket. Rosy face, cheerful manner, has a Welsh accent. I wondered if by any chance he had called in for a drink during the morning."

The landlord's own rosy face had undergone a slight but curious change during this speech. He bent down quickly and shifted some bottles under the bar. When he reappeared his sharp gray eyes refused to meet Lewker's gaze.

"Don't recall anyone o' that description," he said shortly.

Mr. Darby looked up from his paper.

"Why, you've a short memory for customers, George," he said. " 'Twas about eleven, an' I was takin' my t'other half-pint, a chap like as this gentleman says comed in. Don't ye remember, after he'd gone I says to you 'twas the same chap as was in here on t' Whitmonday an' knocked over a full pint mug?"

"Must ha' forgotten," said Mr. Roughten. " 'Scuse me a minute."

He ducked through the low doorway behind the bar and disappeared.

"You have a better memory than our friend, sir," boomed Mr. Lewker conversationally. "I should say, from your evidence at the inquest, that you are unusually observant also."

Mr. Darby looked pleased. "Never forget a face, sir. 'Twas your pal, right enough. Heard him say he was goin' up to call at Riding Mount."

"And he was in here on Whitmonday last? What time would that be, I wonder?"

" 'Bout half-past ten, I rackon. Quite a crowd in here, there was. Old Ben—him as just went out—he was tellin' your pal all about t' Bent Stones an' t' Old Ones, an' the rest of it."

"You don't believe in such things yourself, Mr. Darby?" remarked Georgie, finishing her cider.

"Naw, ma'am, I doan't." The young farmer was contemptuous. "Bairn's tales, they are. Wasn't any talk of 'em till old Ben started seeing ghosties up by his l'al bield yonder. Means no harm, he don't, but folk did ought to see as how he's a mite cracked."

Mr. Lewker agreed. They lingered a few minutes longer; and then, as Mr. Roughten had not reappeared, Lewker shouted a "good night" and the three went out to the car.

"And now," said Georgie when they were bowling smoothly down the valley towards the sunset, "what was all that about?"

She was driving, with Ted beside her. Lewker leaned over from his seat behind.

"What did you gather from the conversation, Edward?" he boomed.

Ted paused for a moment before replying.

"The landlord didn't want to admit that Jones had been in this morning," he said slowly. "He was lying when he said he didn't remember."

"That was odd, wasn't it?" Georgie put in. "I don't see how he fits into anything. But the odds are shortening on my outsider."

"That's right," said Ted. "Bodfan Jones was in Birkerdale the day after Peel was killed, at any rate. And we're not certain about his alibi for Gay's—the other death. If Hamish got back to the Hostel at five-thirty, as he says, he must have been there when Jones arrived. We got in at eight-twenty and he was there then." He twisted round to look at Mr. Lewker. "Did you expect to find that he'd been at the Herdwick Arms on Whitmonday, sir?"

"I must confess, laddie, that that was a stroke of luck. But if Bodfan Jones is our man, where is his motive?"

"You said yourself you got the idea he was hiding something," said Ted.

"Or at any rate pretending to be something he wasn't. And he gave a phony address. Suppose both Peel and Gay found out this something, and he followed them up here to bump them off."

"Ingenious," commented Mr. Lewker. "But if we are to follow it up we—or the police—have a great deal more work to do."

"What do you think yourself, Filthy?" inquired his wife.

"I think, my dear," returned the actor-manager, "that Mr. Bodfan Jones is going to tell us a little more about this case."

Wherein he was literally wrong and figuratively right.

The mountains were left behind. The car had passed through the wide and forested lower valley, and now it emerged into the coastal plain. Houses, small and dingy, became more frequent; the marks of industrialism soiled the fields and hedges. Street lamps, already lit, began to flicker past them and mounds of refuse from the iron mines rose blackly against the smoky crimson of the western sky. Egremont proved to be an unimpressive little mining town dominated, incongruously, by the ruin of a medieval castle. Lewker had obtained Sergeant Miles' address from Mrs. Crake and they had no difficulty in finding the neat semidetached house.

Mrs. Miles, a comfortable body in a gaily colored frock, received them hospitably. Her husband was on duty, but she was sure he wouldn't mind their looking at his book. It was very valuable, she'd been told. Yes—a present from Sir Walter Haythornthwaite. He knew Dan was interested in such things. As she talked she led them into a snug and very tidy sitting room and switched on the light. The book was produced from a glass-fronted bookcase. Dan took care of his books, said Mrs. Miles proudly. He wouldn't lend this one, not even to Mr. Meirion from the Youth Hostel, who was a bit of an authority, like, and had wanted to borrow it. She handed it to Mr. Lewker, who was seated on a sofa with Ted beside him, and sat down opposite Georgie. While his wife exchanged politenesses with their hostess Lewker examined the book.

It was a large volume bound in black leather and very well preserved. *A True Record Of Wizardrie In The North*, announced its faded and elaborately engraved title page, *Written in the Time of the LATE WARS, by Mr. Burton. Adorn'd with a new Set of Cuts.* He turned the brown pages of uneven print. The "Cuts" were Hogarthian in character and portrayed, in somewhat bloodcurdling detail, Witches' Sabbaths, the conjuring of demons, and various unfortunates who had been burnt for practising these things. After a little search he found the passage he wanted. He and Ted read it together.

Antiquaries will have it that thofe Rites, which are yet remember'd in Birker-dale, have their Origins in the practices of the Norfe Ancients. In the laft Century, as it appears, Sabaths and the Worfhip of Demons had their place upon the Coven's Peak, hard by the Hamlet in Birkerdale; when, as Robert Baflow the Exorcift tells us with every Circumftance of Truth,

*the Demon MAHU in particular did feveral times appear before thefe Con-
jurors. For the Conjuring of this MAHU, a Demon of great Power, the
sacrificing of a He-goat, Raven, Hedgehog or Hare is necefsary, likewife
the Burning of the fame in a Fire and the defcribing of the Pentagon as
aforemention'd. The Cabaliftic Word is TETRAGRAMMATON. The prefent
Author has vifited the Place, call'd the Bent Stones, where thefe Rites were
Perform'd. Anciently, fays Legend, it was the Cuftom of Sorcerers to caft a
Young Virgin into the Torrent call'd the Wrykin Spout for that their Invocations of MAHU might be the more Succefsful. As with the Ceremonies
we have notic'd elfewhere, thefe muft be perform'd at the Full of the Moon.*

The learned writer went on to discourse of witchcraft elsewhere in Cumberland. Mr. Lewker reread the Birkerdale passage, while Ted muttered
"Good Lord!" several times under his breath. He then returned the *True
Record* to Mrs. Miles, with his thanks, and made haste to bring her gossip
with Georgie to an end. They were not allowed to go, however, without
tasting a glass of Mrs. Miles' elderberry wine, which—contrary to expectation—proved to be excellent.

"You'll have a nice ride back," she said as she saw them go out in the
gloaming. "It's full moon tonight, you know."

Mr. Lewker was not very talkative as Georgie drove them back up the
dark length of the dale. It was when the shapes of the mountains swam into
sight against the night sky, phantasmal and lovely, faintly silvered by the
rising moon, that he leaned forward to speak to Ted.

"Did Mrs. Crake give you that twig of rowan, Edward?"

Ted laughed. "She did, actually. Why?"

"We may need it," said Mr. Lewker darkly.

CHAPTER XII
WHAT BLACK MAGICIAN

"They're different at night, somehow," said Ted, looking up, as he plodded
along the track, at the gigantic humped shape of Black Crag. "In the daytime they're just mountains, but at night they're—they're living things
asleep."

"One feels them as presences," Mr. Lewker agreed. "Friendly presences.
You know that thing of Lascelles Abercrombie's—'And the great natures
of the Hills round me friendly were.' "

"That's it, exactly," said Ted eagerly.

They passed out of the faint radiance of the new risen moon into the
black shadow of the Crag and began to mount the slopes towards Riggin
Spout. Mrs. Crake had provided them with a glass of hot milk and biscuits
before they left Langthwaite. While he dealt with this Mr. Lewker had
been busy with a fountain pen and a sheet of paper. Georgie, reminding

him that as a Youth Hosteler he was supposed to be in his Hostel before ten-thirty, had hustled them off before he had quite completed his writing. The night was very still and beautiful; mist lay whitely along the hayfields of the valley, the hills above Riding Mount shone like mounds of pale gold against the night-blue gauze of the sky, the deep note of the waterfall above seemed hushed. The moon had not yet reached her full height, but her light, reflected from the fells across the valley, was sufficient to show the glimmer of the path, and they climbed steadily.

"I'd give anything," said Ted suddenly, "to climb a really big peak, like the Matterhorn or Mont Blanc. I don't suppose I ever shall."

"Why not?" Mr. Lewker spoke over his shoulder from a few paces ahead. "Most of the great climbers, like Mallory of Everest, learned the essentials on British hills, you know."

Ted tramped on in silence for a moment. Then he spoke half to himself.

"It's no good. Vera would never hear of it—she's dead against rock climbing."

"If and when this case is brought to a successful conclusion," observed Lewker, slowing his pace in order to gain breath for speech, "I propose to celebrate by climbing Napes Needle. It is a charming little climb, and we can reach it easily from Cauldmoor. I shall ask you to come on my rope, Edward."

"That's jolly nice of you, sir. But—" Ted paused and sighed resignedly. "Well, there it is. I'm sorry."

"Hum," said Mr. Lewker, and said no more for a while.

The steepening ascent made conversation difficult, as did the loudening roar of the Spout. They toiled up the zigzags to the footbridge below the waterfall. Riggin Spout was a ghostly wall of white dropping out of the dark sky; its giant voice filled the night for a minute or two, until they had passed the bridge and were scrambling up the rough path round the corner of the mountainside. When they reached the little combe where Lewker had first met Paul Meirion he shot a question at his companion.

"Hamish Macrae met the three of you on your way back from Wasdale on Friday evening. What time would that be, Edward?"

"What? Oh!" Ted's thoughts had gone far away from detection. "It would be something like seven-forty-five. Yes—we were half an hour from the Hostel when he met us."

"You got in at eight-twenty. Let us call it seven-fifty when you met. You are quite certain none of you heard the Warden moving or typing in his room after you reached the Hostel?"

"Well, pretty certain. When we found he wasn't in we thought he must have gone out between the time Hamish left to meet us and the time Bodfan Jones arrived."

"Yes."

Mr. Lewker relapsed into thoughtful silence. They plodded on slowly, came to easier ground, and emerged quite suddenly into the silver radiance of moonlight. Cauldmoor lay before them, its undulations black and pale gold. Half a mile away the tarn gleamed like a disc of polished jet; a pinpoint of yellow light showed in the square shape of the Hostel. Here and there on the moor wreaths of mist lay in weirdly curling forms. It was very still and not yet too cold to sit down. Mr. Lewker sat down on a flat rock.

"That I am fat and scant of breath," he boomed, "would be a gross misstatement. I am, however, a little tired. Let us rest awhile and contemplate that wat'ry star."

"Not so wat'ry," remarked Ted, sitting down beside him and regarding the great moon that sailed clear above the far eastward fells. "You could see to read a book by her tonight."

Mr. Lewker took a fountain pen and a folded sheet of paper from his pocket. He unfolded the paper, made a careful addition to its contents, and passed it to Ted.

"Perhaps you can decipher that," he said. "It is the sort of thing we Gifted Amateurs always produce at this stage of a case, except that this effort is decidedly unsatisfactory. Let me have your comments."

Ted spread the paper on his knee; the bold writing was easily read. He looked up almost at once.

"Janet went over into Ennerdale with two climbers on Whitsunday," he said with a touch of defiance. "They did a climb on Pillar Rock. They'd give her an alibi—not that she needs one."

"Very well," boomed Mr. Lewker pacifically, handing over his pen. "Make a note of it, if you please."

Ted complied and resumed his study of the document. It was headed, in capital letters, "TELL'ST THOU ME OF 'IFS'?" and subtitled "*My tables; meet it is I set it down*. Hamlet, Act 1, Sc. 5."

1. EDWARD SOMERSET, VERA CRUMP, JANET MACRAE.—*Opportunity*: These three give each other alibis for the Gay Johnson affair (hereinafter termed G. J.). Edward and Vera give each other alibis for Peel (R. P.). Has Janet an alibi for R. P.? (Yes. Climbing with Mr. & Mrs. Weston on Pillar Rock. E. S.) *Motive*: None apparent. *Notes*: The lump of rock which is assumed to have been the murderer's weapon scarcely suggests a girl as our murderer.

2. BEN TRUBY.—*Opportunity*: Yes, for both murders, IF he cannot prove alibi. Was on fells near Coffin's Pike during crucial period for G. J. and R. P. (Grimmett). *Motive*: None, unless he was acting on behalf of "T' Old Ones" whose sanctuary R. P. and G. J. had profaned. *Notes*: Regarded locally as "a mite cracked" but displays no signs of homicidal mania.

3. LEONARD BLIGH.—*Opportunity*: For R. P., yes, IF he crossed Cauldmoor by Riggin Beck path on Whitsunday instead of via the lead mines track as he states. For G. J., no; alibi given by Somerset, Crump, Janet Macrae. *Motive*: For R. P., none apparent. For G. J., fit of anger after quarrel in

morning (weak, IF there is no deeper cause of quarrel). *Notes*: Record of previous assault on fellow apprentice in fit of temper. *N.B.* Link between Gay and Peel is membership of same climbing club. Find out IF there was anything between the two and IF Leonard knew of it.

4. HAMISH MACRAE.—*Opportunity*: For R. P., yes, IF he can prove no alibi, which is probable; was walking alone over fells from Black Sail to Egremont (passing near Cauldmoor) on Whitsunday. For G. J., an alibi but only just, IF Jones confirms statement that H. met him at 7 (outside limit for G. J. death). Met Somerset and others about 7.50, yet it took them only half an hour to reach Hostel. *Motive*: for R. P., none apparent. See Notes on Bligh. For G. J., had been engaged to her. Jealousy? (A weak motive.) *Notes*: Descended Black Crag alone on Friday evening before G. J.'s death; could have done the same on White-Sunday. *N.B.* Loose spike? Both Hamish and Leonard are engineers.

5. BODFAN JONES.—*Opportunity*: For R. P., possibly. Was seen in Birkerdale on Whitmonday. For G. J., again possibly. Was at Hostel alone— though Warden may have been in his room—from about 7.20 to 8.20; may not have entered Hostel until just before the rest returned. *Motive*: None apparent. *Notes*: Gave false address. Manner suggests a pose, possibly to conceal his true identity or purpose. Too many IFS here.

6. PAUL MEIRION.—*Opportunity*: For R. P., yes. On his own statement was alone at Hostel all Whitsunday. For G. J., yes; left Hostel some time before 8:20 p.m. and returned at time unknown. *Motive*: IF R. P. and G. J. both discovered his addiction to witchcraft he has a sufficient motive. *Notes*: There is probably no way of proving whether they did in fact discover this, unless Meirion can be made to admit it. The practicing of witchcraft by M. is so far a matter of surmise.

For Attention

(*a*) Where is the weapon? Probably it was flung into the stream, but it MAY have been hidden elsewhere.

(*b*) Tackle Bligh again about his route over Cauldmoor on Whitsunday. Also sound him as to possible connection between Peel and Gay Johnson. *N.B.* Grimmett to try getting information from Midland Cave and Crag Club.

(*c*) Find out if Hamish can produce alibi for Whitsunday—people seen on route, etc. Get Bodfan Jones to confirm time of meeting him on Wasdale path on Friday evening. Did Hamish climb down Black Crag on Whitsunday?

(*d*) Get Bodfan Jones' statement about movements at Whitsuntide and confirm if possible. Why did he give false address?

(*e*) *Tonight.*—Attempt to obtain confirmation of Meirion's secret activities.

"Well, Edward?" demanded Mr. Lewker, as Ted laid down the paper.

In the cold light of the moon the boy's face looked pale and anxious.

"Janet's clear, anyway," he said slowly. "As for the rest, it doesn't really look as though any of them had both motive and opportunity except the Warden, does it?"

"Even in his case motive is not proved," Lewker pointed out.

"I suppose not. Look here, sir—what's the idea about the loose spike on the climb, and Hamish and Leonard both being engineers? D'you think either of them could have fixed up a booby trap of some kind on the Crag— something that flung the—the bodies clear into the beck?"

"A little far-fetched, is it not? Detective-Inspector Grimmett thought the same."

"Anyway," said Ted firmly, "Leonard can't climb and Hamish—I'm dead sure he wouldn't do a thing like that."

"Do not think of them as people you know, laddie," advised Mr. Lewker gently. "Think of them as L and H, possible murderers."

Ted took this literally. "Well," he said uncomfortably, "I suppose the scheme would be the fixing of this spike so that a climber would be sure to fall at that spot. It sounds ridiculous, somehow. Why should it throw them out into space? Anyway, if it *was* done like that, Hamish could have fixed the contraption when he climbed down the Crag on Friday afternoon. Don't see how he could know that Gay intended to climb it later—if she did. Then he would have to dismantle the thing again, of course. He might have done that on Saturday—he and the others were on this search party and they wouldn't stick together. But there was the chance that he'd be seen on the rock face. Could he have done it when he was leading you up the climb this morning, sir?"

"It would have had to be a very small and simple arrangement if he did," replied Lewker thoughtfully. "However, let us consider Mr. Bligh."

"Leonard's not a climber—I told you."

"That is, he has told you he is not a climber. That does not prove that he is unable to get up a fairly simple climb."

"Oh, well," said Ted, a little taken aback, "if he *could* climb, he could have arranged the trap on Friday morning when he left us to finish his sketch. Same as with Hamish, he might have found a chance to dismantle it on Saturday. But—"

"But, as you have said, it sounds ridiculous. Consider Mr. Bodfan Jones, for a change."

Ted leaned back on his rock and frowned at the Sphinx-like face of the moon.

"That brings us back to the idea that the murders were done by lamming the victims with a rock and shoving them into the stream," he observed. "Well, it looks as though Jones might have had the opportunity. The motive might have been the same as the one we're taping Meirion with— both Gay and Peel found out something about Jones and had to be silenced at all costs. There's something odd about Jones. And why did he give a false address? It seems a silly sort of thing to do—the police were bound to spot it."

"Not necessarily," said Mr. Lewker. "Jones thought, quite reasonably, that his address was being taken as a matter of routine. Had there been nothing but an inquest on a fatal accident in hand the police would not have checked that address. No, laddie. I suggest that Mr. Jones thought there was a chance that his real address might strike a chord of memory in official minds. I have a strong suspicion that his real name, which is not Bodfan Jones, is known to the police."

"But look here," objected Ted. "Doesn't all that point to his not knowing that Gay was murdered?"

"Nicely reasoned, young Edward. So it does. All the same, I could bear to know a little more about our little pseudo-Welshman. And remember, if he was the murderer he might have felt so safe—having heard nothing of police activity in the matter—that he considered it a fair risk to give a false address. Incidentally, if both Peel and Miss Johnson had discovered this fatal secret of his, it is surely a remarkable coincidence that both of them came here to be killed by Jones, who—presumably—followed them. And why didn't one or both of them give the secret away?"

"The secret might be connected in some way with this club they were both members of," said Ted slowly. "I don't know why they didn't split. But Jones might have some link with the club—found out from another member—oh, I don't know. It's all pretty complicated, guessing like this."

"True. Nonetheless, laddie, I think you have hit the right line. The key to this business lies in the link between the two victims, slender as it is."

Ted sat up suddenly. "I say," he said. "Has it occurred to you that perhaps Peel's death was an accident—gave someone the idea of doing in Gay Johnson in the same way?"

"It has. But consider. Peel's death had certain odd circumstances about it, had it not? And would a murderer be fool enough to repeat those exact oddnesses, the very things that aroused suspicion in the mind of the astute Mr. Somerset and, later, in that of Inspector Grimmett?"

"No, I suppose he wouldn't—unless he was mad. I notice you've put Ben Truby in your list, sir."

Mr. Lewker nodded. "There is no really tenable motive, I know. But he was one of the few people who had opportunity. I wonder, by the way, whether he saw Gay Johnson on Friday afternoon. Darby said she was at the Bent Stones at half-past five, and old Ben was somewhere up there then, probably brewing tea in his bield. However, his madness seems to be limited to spreading eerie tales about t' Old Ones."

"That brings us back to the Warden, then," remarked Ted.

"Yes. Does anything strike you about the case against Mr. Meirion?"

"Well," said Ted reflectively, "as you say, it's going to be a tough job to prove Peel and Gay saw him at his games, unless he confesses. And there's this, too. If he went out some time between half-past five, when Hamish heard him typing, and eight-twenty, to kill Gay, what was she doing then, and where was she?"

"Good," approved Mr. Lewker. "I can see I shall have to undertake the part of Watson myself and recast you as the Great Detective. That is a point. But we may conjecture a little. Suppose Gay was lingering on the moor, not intending to come in until after dark. Suppose she saw Meirion starting on his magic and crept up on him to watch. He discovers her, and kills her as he killed Peel."

"That fills the bill," agreed Ted enthusiastically. "I'm beginning to think he's the man, all right."

Mr. Lewker held up a hand. "But wait. You should have put your finger on two flaws. First, he threw the body into Riggin Spout. There would be a lot of blood, you know. Did he drag it all the way across the moor to the beck?"

"He might have been doing his witchcraft right on the bank of the stream."

"I am almost certain that his ceremonies are performed nearly a mile away from the stream, laddie."

"Oh. Then say he pretended to be friendly, got her to the stream on some pretext, and then did his stuff."

"That is better. But here is the second flaw. Peel was killed between ten o'clock and three, in broad daylight. It is most unlikely that Meirion would perform his sorceries in the daytime."

"Well, then—say Peel spotted his goings-on during the previous night, and let him know it. Mr. Meirion got him down to the stream next day, same as with Gay, and finished him off."

Lewker wagged his head. "Yes, but Meirion could not know whether Peel had kept it to himself. I looked at the Hostel logbook last night. There were seven other Hostelers staying at Cauldmoor on the night of Whit-Saturday. Peel might have told any of them what he had seen—indeed, I can see no reason why he should keep the Warden's secret."

"There are snags about Mr. Meirion being the murderer, then," frowned Ted.

"There are a few. And I can see this, laddie. If he turns out not to be our man there is going to be a great deal more work to be done on this case." He heaved himself to his feet with a groan. "Unless, of course," he added, "you and I can bring off our brilliant coup and hand the real murderer to the police with our compliments."

"Gosh, that'd be great," said Ted. "How do we go about it, sir?"

"We do the job that's nearest, laddie. We investigate the sorceries of Mr. Meirion—tonight."

"How d'you know he'll be operating tonight?"

"My dear Edward! I have told you what was written in the Warden's notebook. You have read the passage in Sergeant Miles' book——"

"Lord, yes! And tonight's full moon. How shall we work it, sir?"

As they walked together towards the light of the Hostel Mr. Lewker told him.

The wreaths of mist had swollen and spread even in the short time they had been talking. Cauldmoor Tarn was hidden under a white blanket whose surface was silvered by moonlight, and all over the moor the milky vapor was filling and overflowing the marshy hollows. They reached the Hostel through a belt of mist that came up to their waists.

The Warden and Vera Crump were sitting by the living room fire, the latter talking and the former looking slightly bored. Both looked up as Ted and Mr. Lewker came in, and Vera sprang to her feet.

"I thought we'd lost our celebrity, I'm sure," she shouted. "All the others have turned in, but I stayed up to be a reception party."

"I am sorry we are a little late, Warden," boomed the actor-manager, taking off his rucksack.

"I'm sure we don't mind waiting for the great Abercrombie Lewker, do we, Warden?" said Vera archly, forestalling Mr. Meirion's reply. "Lots of audiences must have waited for you to come in, I should think. It must be just grand to hear the applause and cheers."

The Warden saved Lewker the trouble of replying to this by looking at his watch and announcing that it was just ten-thirty.

"Mr. Jones hasn't come in yet," he added. "I think I shall leave the door for him."

Vera had turned on Ted with an asperity markedly different from her greeting of Lewker.

"I do think you might have told me *you* were going to be late, Ted," she snapped. "You never seem to think. I don't like it, I can tell you."

Ted shuffled his feet and felt sheepish. Mr. Lewker felt uncomfortable and also that he was being obliquely rebuked. Both sensations annoyed him.

"Now, Mr. Lewker," Vera said brightly, "you'll just sit down and drink a nice hot cup of cocoa. I've got it all ready and you need it after your night walk."

"Miss Crump," boomed the actor-manager, "there is an excellent proverb which says 'Never take the antidote before the poison.' Thank you, but I shall go to bed."

"I also," murmured the Warden. "Good night, all."

He went quickly into his room. Vera, recovering from her "celebrity's" rudeness, vented her wrath on the unfortunate Ted. As he went through into the sleeping quarters Mr. Lewker could hear his Watson being bullied into drinking hot cocoa.

He took off his boots and lay down fully dressed. His rucksack he had placed on the floor beside him; it contained, among other oddments, a flashlight, a compass, and a loaded .32 revolver. He heard the voice of Miss Crump grating unceasingly. It continued through the faint sounds of washing up and fell to a whisper as the two tiptoed into the sleeping quarters, ceasing only with the closing of Miss Crump's door. He heard Ted's door close. Ted occupied the bottom bunk in the cubicle opposite, which he shared with Bodfan Jones; it would be annoying if the belated Jones turned up just when the night's operations were beginning.

The muffled sounds of movement ceased. The Hostel was perfectly quiet. Mr. Lewker lay staring at the window, where the silver flood of mist, risen now about the building, hid the dark shapes of the fells. He wondered which of the occupants of the Hostel were asleep and which awake. He wondered whether one of them was lying staring at blankness, as he was—but seeing there the bloodstained faces of two murdered youngsters. He wondered why Bodfan Jones had not come in ...

He woke with a start. It had been a tiring day and in spite of his resolve to keep awake he had dropped off into a deep slumber. His watch told him it was twenty minutes to midnight. He got up cautiously and very carefully opened his door. The door of Ted's room opened simultaneously and Ted's face revealed itself as a white oval in the gloom. Mr. Lewker gestured and nodded and the face withdrew. A moment later they were both creeping in stockinged feet towards the outer door. It was unlocked and opened noiselessly, letting in a drift of white mist. Lewker closed it gently behind them and they sat down on the step to put on their boots. The night was clammily chill.

"Heard something five minutes ago," whispered Ted. "Think it was him going out. Mr. Jones hasn't come in yet."

"Right," Mr. Lewker whispered back. "No more talking. Stick close to me."

He stood up and shouldered his rucksack. In his hand he held the compass; so strong was the diffused moonlight in the mist that the luminous dial scarcely shone. They set off, their footsteps noiseless on the soft ground, Ted close behind his leader. They must, reflected Mr. Lewker, look rather like Wenceslaus and the page. He steered by continual glancing at the compass—Bent Stones lay south-southwest from the Hostel—but peered ahead at intervals into the thick folds of the mist. It was like walking on a treadmill. The walls of the mist kept the same distance in front and behind; they seemed to be making no progress. Only the changing ground underfoot, a marshy bit, then heather, then a slight rise and a few small rocks, told that they were moving across Cauldmoor. The silence was profound, and eerie. They moved in a white radiance like that of a spotlight, yet there was nothing to see beyond a foot or two of rough ground.

They had been walking at a steady pace for more than ten minutes when Mr. Lewker halted suddenly and Ted cannoned into him. The actor-manager pointed. Straight ahead of them a faint rosy glow shone through the greenish-white of the mist. They moved forward more slowly, and now the sound of a man's voice raised in a high monotone came to their ears. The glow became red and more concentrated; it wavered like a flame, and began to seem brighter than the screened moonlight. Suddenly a vast shadow, like a djinn, hovered between them and the glow, and Ted gasped. Mr. Lewker halted again and grasped the boy's arm.

"Round to the left," he whispered. "Steady, now, and quietly."

They began to bear away, rounding the glow. The monotone continued; the words were indistinguishable—a kind of gibberish—but now quite close. Lewker started to close in. Great shapes wavered in the mist, and he knew they were the shadows of the Bent Stones. The glow took form as a small fire, and they could make out a thin figure that was no shadow standing above it. The monotone rose sharply and there was a horrible squawking, instantly checked. Ted stifled a startled exclamation and Mr. Lewker gripped him and placed his lips close to his ear.

"Raven, probably," he whispered. "Remember? The sacrifice. Truby gets them for him, I expect." He went down on hands and knees and began to crawl towards the nucleus of fiery radiance. When he was a dozen feet from the uncertain bulk of the nearest Stone he could see, as through a semi-opaque glass, the lean figure and writhen features of the Warden, Paul Meirion.

Meirion was standing erect, with a long white wand in his hand. He moved the wand as though he were drawing with its tip on the cropped turf within the circle of the Stones, and Lewker could see that he was tracing a pentagon. The high chanting had ceased, but at each gesture of the wand the man muttered a word. It might have been "*Tetragrammaton*." Mr. Lewker crept a little nearer; behind him Ted's strangled breathing was audible.

Quite suddenly, and without warning, the wizard flung his arms high and gave vent to a cry, fierce, intense, imploring: "*Mahu! Mahu! Mahu!*" The last syllable died away and left a silence. Lewker had time to notice the stink of burning feathers and flesh that hung in the mist before a fearful yell, a few feet from his left ear, made him jump and swear.

It made the wizard jump also. He jumped to the fire, scattered it with a wild kick, and took to his heels. The thud of his flying steps sounded for a brief instant and then was gone.

"My dear Edward," expostulated Mr. Lewker, struggling to his feet, "if you cannot control—"

"I—put my hand on it!" jittered Ted. He was on his feet, and Mr. Lewker, stretching out a hand, felt him trembling violently. "I put my hand on it!" he repeated.

"On what, laddie?"

"A—a body, I think."

Mr. Lewker pulled out his torch. The narrow beam cut the white veil of mist. It fell on a huddled figure lying close to the shadowy finger of stone; it moved to the round white face, the staring eyes, the bared teeth.

It was Mr. Bodfan Jones, and he was quite dead.

CHAPTER XIII
MORE DIREFUL HAP

MR. LEWKER SWITCHED OFF HIS TORCH AND THE THING THAT had been Bodfan Jones became a shapeless dark mass under the luminous wall of the mist. He stood for a moment quite still, thinking, while Ted Somerset gulped convulsively at his side. Lewker had not been serious when he had hinted to Inspector Grimmett that Jones might be in danger; he had felt then that in spite of the net of circumstantial evidence that appeared to be closing round Meirion, the Warden was not the murderer. Now he began to wonder if, after all, he had been at fault. He turned to his companion.

"One of us will have to go down to Riding Mount and ring the police, laddie," he said. "For my part, I should like to take a look around. Do you feel equal to acting the messenger's part?"

Ted swallowed hard. "I—I'm all right," he replied rather shakily. "Sorry about—that yell. I was startled."

"Naturally enough, laddie. We had learned as much as we needed about Mr. Meirion's little act, however. Now we are presented with what my wife called 'a fine fresh corpse,' and I intend that it shall tell me a thing or two."

He glanced shrewdly at the dark figure of the young man. "I take it you will be happier putting the miles between you and this poor dead shell of man?"

His matter-of-fact voice and words had their effect. Ted drew a deep breath and spoke steadily enough.

"If I could help at all, sir," he said, "I'd like to see what you're going to do."

"That is the Watson spirit, Edward. Ten minutes, then—we must not delay longer."

"Suppose Mr. Meirion comes back?" Ted suggested a trifle apprehensively, peering round into the blank obscurity of pearly vapor. Those moon-spun curtains, tenuous and intangible, would serve to hide a hundred sorcerers—or murderers—even though they were crouching a few yards away.

"He will not come back, laddie," boomed Mr. Lewker. "If I mistake not, he will fly swifter than an arrow from the Tartar's bow to the Hostel and bundle in through his window—it was ajar when we passed it." He switched on his torch again. "Do not look if it upsets you."

He ran the bright beam slowly round the silent thing on the ground. The coarse grass, laden with dew from the mist, showed the darker patch where

Ted had crept up unawares to touch the body. There were no other signs. Mr. Lewker knelt down and placed his hand on Jones' red-and-gray tweed coat; it was drenched with moisture.

"Will you hold the torch, Edward?" he said without looking up. "I am going to turn him over."

Ted complied. Lewker took hold of the shoulders and gently lifted the body, turning it on its side for a moment. It was as stiff as iron. The flashlight beam jerked a little, and there was the sound of a gasp from behind him. The back of Bodfan Jones' skull was an unsymmetrical mess, dark and sticky.

"Shine your beam where the head was lying," commanded Mr. Lewker sharply.

The light showed a flattened patch of grass very slightly discolored by dark stains. Lewker lowered the body carefully into its original position and sat back on his heels.

"The plot thickens," he boomed with some satisfaction. "Edward, I fear Inspector Grimmett will swear, but I must go farther into this matter."

"Need I shine the light on his—its face?" Ted asked in a low voice.

"No. Just illumine the waist. Thank you."

Without disarranging the clothing Lewker inserted his fingers into the pockets, first of the jacket, then of the plus fours. The articles he extracted he replaced when he had examined them: a handkerchief, a penknife, seven-and-six in half-crowns, a pocket compass, and a tin of throat pastilles. He tried the inside breast pocket of the jacket last. There was a worn leather wallet containing eight pounds in notes and a folded paper which seemed to have been there some time and had one or two figures—bus or train times, by the look of them—jotted in pencil on its margins. It was the catalogue of a sale of pictures at an art dealer's in Shaftesbury Avenue, and one or two items had been ticked in pencil; one of them caught Mr. Lewker's eye: "Ramsgate Sands, by Thomas Girtin." Against this had been scribbled the word "fake." He replaced the wallet and the catalogue and bade Ted hand over the light. With meticulous care he ran the beam slowly from neck to foot of the dead man. Then he took hold of the left foot and lifted it slightly—with difficulty, for it was very stiff. He was replacing it on the ground when a small object dropped from the shoe. It was like a grayish irregularly-shaped pebble, and appeared to have been lodged between the leather and the stockinged foot. Mr. Lewker stared at it for a full ten seconds before dropping it into his pocket. Then he rose to his feet and— telling Ted to follow closely in his footsteps—walked away from the body and made a wide circle round it, shining the torch on the ground. Outside the area enclosed by the Bent Stones the moisture-laden grass showed no sign of anyone having passed. Lewker came to a halt in front of the glowing ashes of the sorcerer's fire, which had burned at the foot of the largest of the Stones. A stench of burnt flesh rose from it and the light showed some small charred bones. With the motionless pillars of the mist closing it in on every hand it was an eerie place, and the knowledge of what lay just outside the unholy circle of the seven Stones, its grinning face upturned to the peering moon, made it—for Ted Somerset at least—a place of horror. Mr. Lewker guessed his companion's state of mind and was at pains to remedy it.

"The great Holmes would call this a three-pipe problem,' " he boomed, squatting down and warming his hands at the embers of Meirion's fire. "Unhappily, I have only cigarettes with me." He held out his case. "I recommend one, Edward."

Ted accepted and Mr. Lewker lit both their cigarettes with a glowing stick from the fire.

"Not everyone," he remarked, "can boast of having lit their tobacco with a brand from hell fire, or—to put it more mildly—from the sacrificial fire of the demon Mahu. That raven hath a very ancient and fishlike smell, but it is becoming less potent. I wonder, Edward, whether Meirion took your vocal effort for the preliminary to the apparition of Mahu, and found himself unable to face it."

Ted managed a chuckle, and puffed strongly at his cigarette. "We certainly scared him," he said after a moment. "No doubt about his witchcraft now, is there, sir? But what about—Mr. Jones?"

"Ah. I see you are ready for some deductions. Go ahead, laddie—what do you make of the unexpected presence of the late Jones?"

Ted hesitated. "I suppose," he said slowly after a moment, "that he knew Mr. Meirion was going to—to perform here tonight. He sneaked up here and waited for him. Mr. Meirion spotted him and—killed him."

Mr. Lewker clucked his tongue gently. "Edward, Edward, this is overplaying your part. I must suppose that your observation has been so sicklied o'er with the pale cast of care that it is atrophied. We are to believe, then, that the Warden, who had no more than ten minutes' start of us—by the way, are you sure it was he you heard leaving the Hostel?"

"I think so—yes, I am sure. I lay awake listening all the time, and the only noise came from his side of the Hostel, and it was definitely a window being pushed open. At least," added Ted quickly, "I'm sure it was the Warden's window that opened. It might have been someone else getting out or in."

"You are warming to the work, laddie. We will assume that it was the Warden getting out. In the ten minutes before we sighted his fire, then, he had met Jones, smashed his head in without any outcry from his victim— we should have heard it, I think—lit his fire and begun his incantations."

"He might have done just that, all the same, sir."

"Very well. But he could hardly have arranged for rigor mortis to have attacked the body so quickly that it is already totally rigid. Furthermore, the jacket was soaked with moisture."

"He'd have got wet if he'd been waiting here in the mist," objected Ted.

"I will grant you that. But you noticed, or I hope you did, that the wet grass round the body bore no footprints or marks except those we made; that in spite of that ugly wound in the back of the head there was very little blood beneath it, and none to be seen near the body or in this circle of stones. Take that in conjunction with the state of rigor, and—"

"I say!" exclaimed Ted eagerly, obviously forgetting his horrors in the excitement of detection. "He wasn't killed here at all. He must have been put there, dead, some time before the grass began to get wet with mist."

Mr. Lewker waved his cigarette encouragingly. "Excellent, laddie. Go on."

"Well, I can't think of much else—except that Mr. Meirion didn't kill him after all."

"That does not follow. I am no doctor, but I can tell you that rigor mortis begins to set in from two to three hours after death, affecting the upper parts first and the lower limbs last. Until the proper medical examination has been made, we may assume that Jones had been dead at least five hours. If Meirion, or anyone else, left the Hostel for any considerable period between the time they got back from the valley and, say, seven o'clock, they might have killed Jones somewhere near here and deposited him where he is."

"They'd have had to carry him," Ted remarked.

"Yes. And this ground is too firm and rough to retain impressions. Moreover, we have no time for a search."

Lewker flung the stub of his cigarette into the almost dead fire and stood up.

"There's one thing, sir," said Ted, following his example. "What was that bit of stuff you put into your pocket—the bit out of his shoe?"

In silence Mr. Lewker took out the fragment, placed it in Ted's palm, and shone his light on it.

"It looks like coke," said Ted after peering at it for a moment.

"So it does." Mr. Lewker returned it to his pocket. "It suggests a singular train of thought, laddie, which for the moment I shall leave you to follow. The present need is to get the police—and the police doctor—up here as soon as possible. You will go down as fast as you can to Riding Mount and knock up Sir Walter Haythornthwaite, the Deputy Chief Constable, who will—as they say in commercial circles—do the necessary."

He produced a compass and a one-inch ordnance map from his rucksack and laid them on the grass. Ted knelt beside him holding the light while he set the map by compass.

"In this mist," continued the actor-manager, "your best route is to make for Ben Truby's bield and strike down to the lead mines track. Truby seems to visit his bield very frequently, so we may find a beaten track thence to the lead mines."

Ted squinted at the compass, which Mr. Lewker had placed immediately over the spot on the map representing the Bent Stones.

"The bield's about west-nor'west from here," he remarked, "if this black dot's the building."

"I think it is." Lewker stood up and shouldered his sack. "I will accompany you as link-boy as far as the bield, Edward. I shall then return and keep my watch beside the late Jones until the arrival of Inspector Grimmett and his pards. I shall be cold and deucedly irritable by then, I doubt not, but my martyrdom may atone for our meddling with the body."

They left the Bent Stones and plunged into the blank whiteness of the mist, Mr. Lewker going first with light and compass as before. The luminous walls of vapor had a spurious appearance of transparency as long as the light-beam was directed on to the ground, but if Lewker shone his light straight ahead or to either side they became solid, impenetrable, almost menacing in their unyielding opacity. Ted, blindly following the squat form of his leader, felt sure they had turned right-handed and were heading back to the Stones; although he knew they were following a compass course, that perverse and treacherous "sense of direction" received an illogical shock when the stony ground began to drop away in front of them. Lewker, remarking that the eye of faith might discern a sort of track here, headed a little to the right. In another two minutes a square shape loomed out of the mist and resolved itself into a small but stoutly built stone hovel.

"Mr. Truby's bield is a considerable mansion," observed Lewker, halting a few paces from the hovel and playing his light-beam over it. "He has even a chimney, I see. I wonder if he is at home."

He advanced to the door, a rather ramshackle affair of weatherworn planks, and tried it. It opened at once. He went in, with Ted at his heels.

The hovel was untenanted—so much could be seen at a glance, for its single room was no more than twelve feet square and very sparsely furnished. A wooden pallet stood against the right-hand wall with a few tattered blankets heaped upon it, a rough stone fireplace occupied the end opposite the door, and a crudely made wooden bench stood beneath the tiny window on the left. A couple of stout hazel-wood crooks leaned in a corner and there was a heap of firewood near the hearth. The stone floor was unexpectedly clean. Mr. Lewker went at once to the fireplace. It contained an untidy heap of ash, in which he poked about for some time, examining various fragments minutely with his light.

"No coke, sir?" said Ted behind him, suddenly.

Mr. Lewker looked up. "Art thou there, truepenny?" he boomed. "No, there is no coke. Nor has this fire been lit today, or for some days, I should say. These are the only items, besides wood ash, that present any problem." He held up two thin strips of brass, about half an inch wide and two inches long, and flashed his light on them. "What do you make of them?"

"They might be the terminals of a flashlamp battery—a cycle-lamp, perhaps," pronounced Ted after a brief scrutiny.

"Yes, I think so. A large dry battery has been burned here." Mr. Lewker got up and dusted his knees. "Perhaps Mr. Truby lights his bield with electricity."

"Look here, sir," Ted frowned. "You're not suspecting Ben Truby, are you?"

"I suspect Mr. Jones was killed somewhere handy to the Bent Stones and carried there afterwards, laddie. But, as you see, there is no gore on these stones. I fancy, however, that this floor has lately been cleaned." The light-beam swept along the walls and reached the bed, glinting on a jumble of empty bottles and rusty tins. "What have we here? The remains of past orgies? Baked beans, mostly, and the bottles are sheep medicine and liniment."

He stooped and pulled at a piece of rubber-covered wire that protruded from beneath the pallet. There was about three feet of it, and its other end was attached to a flashlamp bulb-holder and reflector mounted on a piece of stout leather four inches long and two inches broad. The ends of the leather strip seemed to have been cut with a knife.

"Well, there's his lamp," remarked Ted.

"Yes."

Lewker's monosyllable was almost whispered; he seemed to be replying, not to Ted's comment, but to some question that had presented itself to his own mind. He stood perfectly motionless, holding the lamp and flex in the brilliant beam and staring fixedly at them, for so long that Ted was moved to inquiry.

"Is it a clue, sir? I say—is it something to do with Gay Johnson being killed in the dark?"

Mr. Lewker carefully replaced his find beneath the pallet before replying.

"Edward," he boomed as he straightened himself, "I see, as in a map, the end of it all—as the Queen says in *Richard the Third*, and with good reason. Yes, I believe it is something to do with Gay Johnson being killed in the dark. But thought and action both must ensue before we can prove it."

He led the way out of the hovel and closed its rotting door. A plain track, showing the marks of hobnailed boots, led up to it from the invisible hillsides below. Lewker shone his light on it.

"That will almost certainly be your best way down to the lead mines track, laddie. Off with you now."

"What shall I tell Sir Walter?" demanded Ted.

"The facts," returned Mr. Lewker. "We followed Meirion, scared him away from his sorcery, and stumbled on the body of Bodfan Jones who had been murdered. There is no need to mention our efforts at Holmesery. You will have to get Sir Walter out of bed, and he may be annoyed at first. He had a touch of malaria upon him this afternoon. Come, come, dispatch!"

Ted turned and strode swiftly away down the narrow track. The mist swallowed him almost at once, and his quick footfalls were lost in the all-pervading silence.

Mr. Lewker, after a moment's hesitation, went once more into Ben Truby's bield. This time he went over every inch of floor and furniture, scrutinizing it by flashlight. Some fragments of bread and a good deal of dirty wool was all that this search produced. He spent some time removing all signs of his visit and then retraced his way up the fellside to the Bent Stones.

He found them without difficulty; their ghostly shapes, looking twice their actual size in the strange half-light diffused through the mist, impressed even Mr. Lewker with a sense of old forgotten sorceries and the ancient evil that once dwelt there. He crossed the circle, passing the now dead fire beneath the largest Stone, and shone his light for an instant on the dead man. Then he removed himself to the farther side of the ring of monoliths and made himself a dry seat with a few loose flat stones at the base of a conveniently leaning Stone. Having donned a woolen sweater from his rucksack and provided himself with cigarettes and chocolate from the same source, he settled himself to wait for dawn and to think.

He passed in review all the events of the past four days. Easily, now, some of them fell into place to form an astonishing but irrefutable pattern. Mr. Lewker, not liking that pattern, strove to form his clues into another shape, taking new incidents from the few he had rejected as irrelevant. It was useless; speculation and conjecture might build possibilities, but the facts refused to make more than the one picture. He knew, beyond doubt, why and where Robert Peel and Gay Johnson had been killed. He felt reasonably certain who had killed them. He was less certain about the reason for Bodfan Jones' murder, but he would have wagered fifty pounds that his inferences on that point were correct. The more he turned the matter over in his mind the more certain he became that here was no mistake, no chance coincidences of facts, but a case strong and damning, needing only the final proof. And the key clue to this padlocked chain of reasoning was a thing he had noticed on his climb with Hamish Macrae.

The moon sank behind her mist curtains and left a thick darkness. A little wind rose and, wraith by wraith, the mists trailed their threadbare robes away from the moor, leaving it cold and black against a graying sky. Mr. Lewker sat there motionless under his rock. Not until a pale streak low down above the eastern fells showed that the long night was ending did he stir, rising stiffly to his feet and walking to a little hump from which he could survey the gray slopes falling away into Birkerdale.

Five hundred feet down the fellside a dozen men were plodding slowly up towards the Bent Stones.

CHAPTER XIV
THIS PALPABLE DEVICE

"WELL, IT BEATS ME, SO IT DOES," SAID DETECTIVE-INSPECTOR Grimmett for the fourth time in two hours.

He sat at the small table in the Warden's room at the Cauldmoor Youth

Hostel. The sunshine of midmorning fell obliquely on his red good-humored face; it was unshaven and puckered with unaccustomed perplexity. Opposite to him, conning the pages of a large notebook, sat Police-Sergeant Miles, thickset, pale-faced, and spectacled. A uniformed constable stood woodenly against the door. The three of them made the tiny room look even smaller.

Inspector Grimmett had moved with all possible speed when the message from Riding Mount, reaching him by way of Egremont police station, had dragged him from a bed he had only just got into after a heavy day's work. He had roped in Sergeant Miles, two constables, Dr. Whitmore, and three men to help with the body; he had collected five local men from Birkerdale (among them Ben Truby, who informed him that t' Old Ones didn't like policemen) and had toiled with his little company up nearly fifteen hundred feet of steep hillside; he had listened to Mr. Lewker's terse account of the finding of the body and his confession to the moving of it, and had reluctantly agreed to the actor-manager's contention that Ted Somerset could tell him anything else he wanted to know while he, Mr. Lewker, descended to Langthwaite for breakfast and a shave. He had then seen the doctor and the stretcher bearers start on their slow journey down to the waiting ambulance and had led his remaining forces to invest the Hostel, confident that a thorough interrogation of the Hostelers would throw a great deal of light on Bodfan Jones' murder. It was disconcerting to find that everyone was present, and that everyone—including the Inspector's pet suspect, Mr. Meirion—had what appeared to be a solid alibi for this third murder.

Vera Crump had been up when the police came down like the Assyrian on the Hostel, but the rest had been in various stages of dressing or washing. Vera, disturbed in the making of porridge, had treated Inspector Grimmett and his assistants to her impression of a society hostess making the best of a difficult situation and had offered them tea, which they accepted gratefully. By this time the Warden, pale and shaky, had emerged from his quarters and the others began to arrive in the common room. Grimmett, who knew the virtues of informality in certain circumstances, was bluff and fatherly, explaining with heavy tact the reason for his visit, while his round blue eyes missed nothing. At the news of Bodfan Jones' death, and that it had been a violent one, the reactions of all were natural enough. Paul Meirion sank down on a chair and covered his face with twitching hands; Leonard Bligh said "God!" and poured himself a strong cup of tea; Hamish whistled and rested a hand on the shoulder of his sister, who looked pale and frightened; Vera, after exclaiming loudly that she had felt in her bones that something had happened to poor Mr. Jones, started to cross-question Ted Somerset, who had arrived a little after the police, in irritating whispers. The Inspector had then requested everyone to remain in the common room, displayed his search warrant to the Warden, placed one of his two constables on watch outside the Hostel, and politely requisitioned the Warden's room as an office. He had interrogated Ted, who—though very tired and considerably awed at having his statement taken down in the police-sergeant's notebook—had managed to give a fairly clear and comprehensive account of his night's doings with Mr. Lewker. Vera Crump, Janet, Hamish, and Leonard had been interrogated next, in that order. Now, at half-past ten of this brilliantly sunny morning, there remained only the Warden to be questioned.

Sergeant Miles, who had frowned at his notebook in silence for a moment or two after Grimmett's remark, tapped it thoughtfully with the butt of his pencil.

"This young Bligh's a sulky customer," he observed.

"Bad witness. Thinks we're aiming every question to trap him."

"That's so," nodded the Inspector absently. "The type's common enough—and it don't signify, you know, sergeant. Vera Crump's statement gives us all we want in the way of facts. Just run over it, will you?"

Miles flicked over the pages. "Vera Crump. Yes. The party—all those staying at the Hostel, with the exception of Edward Somerset—returned together from Birkerdale at ten minutes to five." He looked up over his glasses at Grimmett. "H. Macrae says 'about five' and his sister says 'between four-thirty and five.' "

"All right. Go on."

"Yes. Crump continues that she and J. Macrae got tea for the party, of which all partook including the Warden. The Warden went into his room and did some typing. She is positive the typing continued, irregularly, until seven, at which time she went in to ask him whether he would take supper with the party or eat in his own room. The only person to go outside the Hostel between the time they got in and the time they retired to bed—ten o'clock for everyone but herself and the Warden—was H. Macrae, who walked down to the tarn and back. He was out about twenty minutes and she saw him from the window strolling by the tarn. The Warden had supper with the others and stayed up talking to her until ten-thirty, at which time Mr. Lewker and Edward Somerset arrived having walked up from Langthwaite. That's all, sir."

Mr. Grimmett puffed air through his mustache and shook his head. "It's enough, too, sergeant. The others confirm all of that, between them—which boils down to the fact that between noon and ten-thirty p.m. none of these five people was out of sight of the rest for more than a few minutes, and Bodfan Jones was seen alive at noon. Yet the doc says the temperature of the body shows he was killed somewhere between four and nine p.m."

"Doctor Whitmore was a bit puzzled about the rigor," observed Miles. "He made a point of telling us it was funny the rigor was so far advanced."

"Yes, but he explained that rigor sometimes comes on quickly if the corpse has been exerting himself a lot just before death. Might have been that Jones was chased over the moor for a mile or two before the murderer got him. Besides, Whitmore's being pretty cautious since I let out we reckoned the other two deaths were murders. We can take it that four and nine are the limits."

Miles sucked his pencil thoughtfully. "Mr. Lewker seemed sort of as if he'd got something up his sleeve, I thought," he ventured.

"So he did, sergeant." Grimmett screwed up his face until his blue eyes were almost hidden by wrinkles. "He's no fool, you can take it from me. I'd have skinned anyone else for touching the body—aye, and for taking that young Somerset into partnership without authority." He opened his eyes in a sudden stare at the sergeant. "What did you make of that bit of coke in Jones' shoe?"

Miles pursed his lips, looking rather like a barn owl in a blue tunic. "Your Mr. Lewker attached importance to that. Means Jones had been somewhere where there was coke lying about, far as I can see."

"And you've noticed the small Ideal boiler in the kitchen? There's been coke burned in that not long ago—and see there." He stabbed a finger at the small fireplace. "No fire there for months, but there's fragments of coke in the hearth."

"They had a small fire going in the common room last night," pointed out the sergeant.

"I know. Bits of coke in the ash there, too. But how's it help us? You can't get past these alibis, sergeant."

"Not if they've all told the truth, sir—no," said Miles slowly. "But we have it that this Crump girl and the Warden stayed up for half an hour after the others turned in. Suppose they were in it together—"

"Jones arrives, is bashed on the head with a rock, and they hide the body—all while the rest are in a room a few feet away? Won't do. Besides, Jones was dead before that half-hour."

"Well, sir, we might get something else out of Mr. Meirion. He's the only one we haven't interrogated."

Grimmett heaved a sigh and rubbed the back of his head. "Yes. I left him till last—give him time to get worried. He's pretty shaken, I reckon, though that may not mean anything." He spoke to the constable at the door. "Greaves, ask Mr. Meirion if he will kindly come in."

The constable turned to obey, but was forestalled by a knock on the door. The constable who had been on guard outside came in.

"It's that bald-'eaded little bloke, sir," he announced. "Bloke as was with the body this morning. Says he'd like a word with you."

"Let Mr. Abercrombie Lewker come in, Willis," said the Inspector reprovingly, and the man withdrew.

A few seconds later Mr. Lewker's sonorous voice was heard in the common room giving a cheerful good morning to the assembled Hostelers, and immediately afterwards the actor-manager himself rolled into the little room, which now began to look overcrowded. His freshly shaven jowls and sprightly air suggested that he had made good use of his visit to Langthwaite.

"How now, my hardy, stout, resolved mates!" he boomed. "A lovely morning sergeant! Well, Grimm, is the problem solved? No—do not disturb yourself, I beg. I will sit here, if I am not intruding."

He sat down on the Warden's bed and beamed at them. The Inspector grinned reluctantly.

"All very well, sir, for you to be chirpy. You may as well know that Whitmore gives between four p.m. and nine as the time of Jones' death. All the folk here have alibis for that period."

"I had anticipated it, Grimm." Mr. Lewker nodded serenely. "Have you questioned them all?"

"All except Meirion. I was just going to put him through it when you arrived."

"Oh, Then perhaps I had better—"

"You stay, sir, if you like. Greaves, call Mr. Meirion."

The constable opened the door and spoke through it. Paul Meirion came in. He cast a glance, frightened and resentful, at Mr. Lewker and then addressed Grimmett in a high strained voice.

"I cannot think why I and these young folk should be subjected to this ordeal, Inspector. It is perfectly clear that we could have had nothing to do with this unhappy business." His glance fell on the neat pile of papers on the table. "My papers! I must protest—"

"Now, now, sir," interrupted Grimmett, raising his eyebrows and looking like a study of Frustrated Benevolence, "you must realize that we have our duty to do. We rely upon you to help us if you can. Please sit down."

He got up and sat beside Mr. Lewker on the bed, leaving the chair for the Warden, who lowered himself into it slowly and with rapid and apprehensive glances at the uniformed police.

"We just want a friendly chat," continued the Inspector genially, "and we shan't keep you long. All the same, I'll have to go a bit formal-like and call your attention to Sergeant Miles and his notebook, with the reminder that anything you say will be taken down and may be used in evidence. That's just—"

"It's monstrous!" Meirion's voice cracked on the word and he beat both hands on the table. "Of what am I accused? You can't imagine I—I killed Bodfan Jones! Why, man, I was sickened of killing in Burma—I couldn't, literally couldn't, kill now—"

"Except the sacrificial raven?" boomed Mr. Lewker unexpectedly.

Paul Meirion seemed to shrink into himself. His pale eyes, enormous behind their glasses, stared at Lewker as though the actor-manager had hypnotized him. He made little gulping noises in his throat.

"Come now, sir," said Inspector Grimmett comfortably. "We don't want a fuss. If you'd rather not answer my questions until there's your lawyer standing by—"

"Oh, no—no," interrupted Meirion hoarsely, tearing his gaze away from Lewker. "I've nothing to hide—nothing criminal."

"Very well. Now, Mr. Meirion, you returned with the rest of the Hostel party after the inquest yesterday?"

Grimmett extracted from him a story of his movements up to ten-thirty on the previous evening that tallied with all the other accounts. The Warden answered his questions in a low, nervous voice; obviously he was expecting to hear more about his "sacrificial raven." He was not disappointed.

"Yes," purred Grimmett. "That's all quite clear, so it is." He leaned forward suddenly, his round blue eyes steady on Meirion's face. "I understand you left the Hostel shortly before midnight. Mr. Meirion. Why was that?"

Meirion darted a swift glance at Mr. Lewker's benign countenance.

"Yes," he muttered. "I—wanted a walk."

"In a thick mist?"

"There was a moon. I could see all right. I tell you I wanted fresh air. I—"

Mr. Lewker interrupted quietly. "I think, Inspector," he said, "that Mr. Meirion should be told that he was followed on this walk of his."

The Warden went very pale.

"It was you, then," he whispered.

"Your movements were observed, sir," said Grimmett tranquilly. "It would be best to tell the truth."

"It—it has no possible bearing on this murder you're supposed to be investigating. Look here, Inspector—my activities last night might be—ah—misunderstood by certain persons who—well, who—"

"If they prove to be irrelevant, sir," said Grimmett, "we may find it possible to avoid making them public."

Meirion glanced from one to another of them and then seemed to make up his mind.

"All right, then," he said with a certain defiance. "I make a hobby of investigating supernatural phenomena. I went out last night to make certain experiments."

"At the Bent Stones?"

"Yes."

"These—um—experiments involved the killing and burning of a raven?"

"Well—yes." Meirion swung round to face Lewker, a sneer on his trembling lips. "I suppose you told your friends the police all this."

"Certainly," returned Mr. Lewker. "I have also told them of the book, given by Sir Walter Haythornthwaite to Sergeant Miles, from which you took the spells used for the invocation of Mahu."

Grimmett resumed his questioning.

"How long were you at the Bent Stones, Mr. Meirion?"

"I got there about a quarter to twelve. I was there perhaps twenty minutes."

"Did you see any other person near the Stones?"

Meirion hesitated. "I heard a yell," he muttered. "It startled me and I abandoned my experiment."

"You saw nobody—alive or dead?" persisted the detective.

"Nobody. I—" The Warden's jaw dropped ludicrously. 'Dead? You don't mean—was *he* found there?'

"The body of the late Bodfan Jones," said Grimmett evenly, "was found at the foot of one of the Bent Stones, Mr. Meirion. Can you suggest how it came to be there?"

"How should I know? You don't—you can't—" The Warden faltered into silence; his face was ghastly.

"Did Bodfan Jones know of these—experiments of yours?" Grimmett inquired quickly.

"I don't know—no! How could he?"

"He didn't hint to you that he knew?"

"I—I—" Meirion scrambled to his feet, his eyes wild. "I refuse to say anything more! I refuse—do you understand?"

Grimmett stood up. "Certainly, Mr. Meirion. We'll make that the lot for the moment. I'm sorry to have—"

But Mr. Meirion was already outside the door.

Grimmett looked at Mr. Lewker and shrugged. "Scared as a rabbit," he remarked. "He hasn't helped us, though."

"A very natural performance," agreed the actor-manager. "The impression conveyed was that he did not realize what you were getting at until you asked whether Bodfan Jones had hinted that he knew of his activities."

"Ah," nodded the sergeant. "He spotted we'd seen his motive then."

"Quite so," said Mr. Lewker. He looked thoughtfully at Sergeant Miles. "By the way, sergeant, when Mr. Meirion came to examine that book of yours—the *True Record of Wizardrie*, you know—did he tell you how he came to know that you possessed it?"

The sergeant took his glasses off and polished them, frowning. "Why," he said at last, "so far as I recall, he said Ben Truby told him."

There was a knock at the door. Constable Greaves opened it and Vera Crump put her head inside the room. Her face was paler than usual, but her voice, though slightly less stentorian, retained its schoolmistressly command.

"I'm sure you could all do with a cup of tea," she announced. "There's one ready in the common room."

Grimmett thanked her cordially and she withdrew.

"That's a very self-possessed young woman," remarked Sergeant Miles.

Grimmett grinned at him. "Like to put her on the suspect list, sergeant? She's got no motive, means, or opportunity, you know."

The sergeant scratched his head. "Well," said he, "there's a cool one at work in this business, to my way of thinking."

"Look out she doesn't poison your tea, then," said the Inspector flippantly. "You and Greaves carry on and get your cup of char. Tell Willis to come in and get his. Mr. Lewker and I will be out in a moment."

As the two went out he turned to Mr. Lewker. His blue eyes were troubled.

"Miles is right," he said. "There's a cool hand behind these murders."

"Less cool than it has been, I fancy," returned Lewker, getting up and taking the chair vacated by Miles. "This Bodfan Jones business was bungled. I see traces of flurry in it. Our murderous friend has overstepped himself and also, I think, stumbled into our arms."

"You've got a theory?" said Grimmett quickly.

"I have a theory, Grimm. If you will indulge me so far, I hope to prove it this afternoon."

The Inspector flung himself back in his chair and blew noisily through his mustache.

"It's not like you to hold things back, sir," he growled. "If you've anything relevant—"

"My dear Grimm! I have told all I have seen, and the rest you know already." He ticked the items off on his fingers. "Gay Johnson's parting words to Leonard, the overturned truck of Geo Roughten—you knew about that? I thought you would—Ben Truby's hints about t' Old Ones, the electric lamp in the bield, the *True Record of Wizardrie*, the evidence of Vera Crump and company, the way the bodies of Gay Johnson and Robert Peel were clad, the—"

"Hold hard, sir!" begged the Inspector. "You mean all these things point one way?"

"To put it fancifully, one might say that if they are placed so that their edges fit snugly together they form the shape of an accusing finger."

"And that bite of coke, too?"

"Ah," said Mr. Lewker reflectively, "there we trench upon a matter of a different color."

"You mean Bodfan Jones' death was the work of someone else?"

"No, no. The same hand or hands is or are at work throughout this business, Grimm. I meant that I think Jones was killed for a slightly different reason and in a different fashion. By the way, have you set your hounds on the trail of the *soi-disant* Bodfan?"

Grimmett nodded. "I have that. Description's gone out by now to the main police stations on the North Wales coast and to Liverpool. I remembered your idea he might have been a Liverpool man. And I've got a man telephoning. Waking up Llandudno and Liverpool. We'll find out who he was, all right. They're going to check up on his prints, too."

"You found nothing helpful in Meirion's papers?"

Mr. Lewker pointed to the neat pile of notebooks and manuscript on the Warden's table.

"Nothing about Bodfan Jones," replied Grimmett. He took a black notebook in which several loose sheets had been placed from the pile, and passed it to Lewker. "Meirion was writing a book on witchcraft, it seems. Made his notes on odd papers and then wrote a fair copy into the book."

Mr. Lewker glanced through the loose sheets and selected two. A rough diary had been kept by the Warden and the two pages recorded the last three days. The second sheet was the one whose top portion he had seen through the Hostel window when Janet Macrae had made her burglarious entry. Mr. Lewker read the notes aloud, beginning at the foot of the first sheet.

"*SUNDAY.—Seeking for reasons to account for Friday night's failure. Rite requires full moon? Consider casting of virgin into Riggin (Wrykin?) Spout may be conducive to success, being a part of the more ancient ritual, though in this case accident.*

MONDAY.—T. provided another Sacrifice but demanded quite disproportionate payment, which I refused. T. became abusive. Fear I cannot rely on him again.

TUESDAY.—Full moon tonight. Prosper my invocations!"

The writing ended halfway down the sheet. Mr. Lewker looked up and cocked a bushy eyebrow at the Inspector.

"This is interesting, Grimm," he boomed. "You notice Meirion had quarreled with Ben Truby?"

"I don't see how that bears on the matter in hand, and that's a fact," returned Grimmett. "He writes about Gay Johnson's death—she's the virgin he refers to, I reckon—as if it was accident, all right, and there's nothing about Jones. But that's how it would be if he thought his notes might be read by anyone else."

"Yes." Mr. Lewker replaced the notes in the book and the book on the pile. "Well, Grimm, my conjectures about Bodfan Jones' murder—for so I must modestly term them—are confirmed by those entries."

The Inspector looked very hard at the actor-manager for a moment. Then he relaxed and sent a long and expressive expiration whistling through his mustache.

"If it was anyone but you, sir," he said, "I'd be annoyed, so I would. Are you getting at Meirion again? He's got an unbreakable alibi—"

"Are you sure of that, Grimm?" interrupted Lewker gently. "Remember the piece of coke. A man would hardly walk about with that in his shoe. It got there after he was dead, then. It is suggestive. And so, you may think, is an expressive if vulgar phrase that occurred to me when I saw the Warden's face just now. He looked, in modern idiom, 'like death warmed up.' "

"By golly!" Grimmett said slowly. "You think Jones' body was kept heated up, to confuse the time of death, until it could be got to where it was found. The coke—there's plenty in this place. That might blow Meirion's alibi, and the others, sky-high, so it might. But it piles up a lot of other problems. Why—"

"Oh, excuse me!" Vera Crump's head had appeared round the door. "Would you like your tea in here?"

"Thank you, no," replied Mr. Lewker before Grimmett could reply. "We shall be with you anon."

"There's a—a policeman coming up the path," added Vera, with a certain apprehension in her loud voice.

"It's a messenger from Egremont, likely," said the Inspector. "Thank you, miss."

Vera showed her teeth and withdrew.

"Told them to send word if they got anything on Jones," explained Grimmett. He got up rather wearily and leaned on the back of his chair. "Now, sir, I know it's the thing to keep the poor copper in the dark when you've worked out a theory that fits the facts, but I tell you straight I could do with a bit more from you. If it's Meirion, why did he cart the body out to the Bent Stones? How did he hide it here? When did he kill Jones, anyway?" He rubbed the back of his neck violently. "Seems to me you're wrapping this business up in red herrings."

"A very nice metaphor." Mr. Lewker beamed; and then, observing the Inspector's expression, became instantly contrite. "I am sorry, Grimm. I can find an answer to all the hows and whens and whys, it is true. And I will confess that there is one small thing—something I observed when I was climbing with Hamish Macrae—that gave me the key to the rest. But you will understand that my theory is based very largely on circumstantial evidence and, in part, on something very like guesswork. It can be proved or disproved this afternoon, and until then I would rather like to keep it to myself." He paused, and then added gravely, "It is not a nice theory."

Grimmett frowned at him for a moment. "All right, sir," he said at last. "What's the drill for this afternoon?"

"I suggest we start as soon as we have had our cup of tea. You could leave Miles in charge here. I would like to take young Somerset with us, if you agree."

"You're the boss," said Grimmett resignedly. "Where are we going—or is that a secret?"

"I think we will call first at Ben Truby's bield," said Mr. Lewker. "And here," he added, "is your messenger."

A confused sound of footsteps and voices came from the common room. Grimmett opened the door and admitted a young constable, very hot in his bulging uniform. He saluted and held out an envelope.

"Super sent me up with this, sir. Came on me motorcycle from Egremont and walked up, sir. Terrible hot, it is—"

"Get a cup of tea outside," said Grimmett, dismissing him. He tore open the envelope and scanned its contents eagerly. "Ah—this tapes him. Phone from Liverpool."

"Bodfan Jones?"

"Yes. Description fits a man named Bertram Jarrett—initials the same, too. Jarrett did time for attempted blackmail, 1947 and 1948. They're sending photo and prints to confirm." He stared at Lewker. "Your hunch about him being known to the police turned up nicely, sir."

"It did, didn't it?" responded Mr. Lewker blandly. "Now shall we go and take tea with the suspects?"

CHAPTER XV
BY PROOF WE SEE

THE ATMOSPHERE IN THE COMMON ROOM WAS FAR FROM comfortable. At one end of the trestle table sat Hamish, Janet and Leonard, silent and subdued. At the other the three uniformed constables sat, talking in undertones and sipping their cups of tea. Sergeant Miles was standing before the fireplace cup in hand and the Warden, with his back to the room, gazed moodily out of the window. All of them looked up, apprehensively or inquiringly, as Lewker and the Inspector came in. Vera Crump bustled out of the kitchen and paused to shout angrily over her shoulder.

"Ted! Hurry up and wash those cups!" She advanced on Mr. Lewker with her toothy smile. "We're rather short of cups—you don't mind waiting one moment, I'm sure."

Lewker, in spite of his dislike for the girl, found himself admiring her. It must be clear to her as to the rest of them, he reflected, that this was a murder case—that one of her fellow Hostelers had been brutally killed a few hours ago and that suspicion rested on persons in this room. Yet she succeeded in behaving as though this was an informal tea party at which a number of unexpected and rather distinguished guests had turned up. Nonetheless, he discerned in Vera Crump's prominent eyes a lesser reflection of that look which could be seen more plainly on the faces of the others: the stealthy look, inimical and apprehensive, that marks the hunted. He saw it in Janet Macrae's swift glance at him and the hasty dropping of her gaze. He had ranged himself with the hunters of men, and the fear that the quarry might be someone of her own circle had set her among the hunted. Mr. Lewker, not for the first time, felt a hearty distaste for the task he had tackled so lightheartedly.

While Grimmett held a low-voiced discussion with the sergeant he drank his cup of scalding hot tea as quickly as might be and replied absently to Vera's ridiculously inapposite remarks about the proportions of milk and sugar. The Inspector concluded his conversation with Miles and cleared his throat preparatory to addressing the Hostelers.

"I must ask you all to remain here, ladies and gentlemen," he said mildly, "until I have concluded certain investigations in this neighborhood. I hope—"

"See here," interrupted Leonard Bligh, scowling fiercely at him, "I've got to get back to Birmingham sometime."

"I hope," continued Grimmett, as though he had not spoken, "to return in an hour or two. I assure you that you will not be detained longer than is absolutely necessary." He turned to Lewker. "I shall require your assistance, sir, and I think we should ask Mr. Somerset to come with us."

Ted rose to his feet with alacrity. Vera, her face red, stepped in front of him, facing the Inspector.

"You've no business to ask him," she said loudly, dropping her hostess manner at once. "You're treating us all like suspects—why's Ted any different from the rest of us? He refuses to come with you, and he's a perfect right to refuse."

Ted, his color a shade or two deeper than Vera's, shuffled his feet and looked at the floor. Mr. Lewker noticed Janet's swift glance at Ted: her own face was flushed and angry.

"Well now," said Grimmett, somewhat disconcerted, "there's been no suggestion of forcing Mr. Somerset to come, miss. I think if you'll let the young gentleman speak for himself—"

"Ted's place is with me," declared the girl, glaring at him. "I need his protection and I won't have him running off on police errands. You understand that, don't you, Ted?"

The young man raised troubled eyes to Mr. Lewker's inexpressive countenance; then his gaze, as though drawn by a magnet, turned to Vera.

"I'll stay, of course," he mumbled.

"Very well, sir," said Grimmett cheerfully. "Come along then, Mr. Lewker."

They went outside into the sunshine and began to walk away from the Hostel in the direction of the Bent Stones.

"Needs his protection, eh?" commented the Inspector. "I reckon it's him that needs protecting. The female of the species—"

"—is more possessive than the male," finished Lewker. "I am sorry for Edward."

"You've got to be pretty determined if you're going to get away from that sort," nodded Grimmett. "She's got him by the short hairs. However, I suppose we can do whatever we're going to do without Mr. Downtrodden Somerset. What *are* we going to do, sir, by the way?"

Mr. Lewker did not at once reply. The two tramped over the heather and squelched across the patches of red and ocher moss in silence.

"Grimm," said the actor-manager at last, "if I am right, you are going to receive something of a surprise. I would rather you surprised yourself, as it were. Let me play the amateur know-all a little longer, releasing my astounding discoveries in progressive doses. I may yet be wrong—and if I am, by two-headed Janus, I shall fall—

> Like a bright exhalation in the evening,
> And no man see me more."

Grimmett chuckled. "Well, it's your party, sir," he said amiably. "You know I was never one to resent someone else using his brains. I'll own this case is about as clear as pig swill to me. If you've seen your way through it you're a better 'tec than I am, though I reckon that's not saying much."

"It's saying a good deal of nonsense, my friend," rejoined Mr. Lewker with some heat. "If you had had my chances of observation, and perhaps one little piece of specialized knowledge—"

He stopped and looked round. Ted Somerset came running over the little knoll they had just crossed and caught them up.

"Changed my mind," he panted, falling into step beside Lewker. "Hope it's okay."

"Excellent, laddie," said Mr. Lewker briefly.

Grimmett was less tactful. "How'd you manage to slip the chain, young feller?" he demanded.

Ted reddened. "She had to—she went into the—anyway, I cleared out. Where are we bound for?" he added hurriedly.

Mr. Lewker, who a few minutes ago had given up hope of saving Ted from his fate, took heart again; the subtle process of stiffening Ted's spine with injections of the crime-investigation virus might yet bear results.

"For the last chapter, where all shall be made plain," he boomed in answer. "Your coming, Edward, falls out passing well. Here be we three, the Astute Amateur, his Watson, and the inevitable Policeman, marching down together to what may be the final proof. We will head down hill for yonder rock, I think, and then contour round the fellside."

They began to descend on the flank of hillside overlooking Birkerdale. The valley smiled in the sun. The river, a chain of irregular silver links laid across green meadows, flashed far below them. A thin spiral of blue smoke, clearly seen against the yellowing bracken of the lower slopes across the dale, rose from the chimney of Riding Mount and suggested that the Deputy Chief Constable was still nursing his malaria. Mr. Lewker, in the lead with Ted close behind him, turned across to the left on a line that took them just above the ruined stone buildings of the old lead mines. He kept a sharp lookout on the wide sweep of hillside as he walked. Once he thought he saw a figure moving among the rocks lower down the slope, but a second glance showed the pastures deserted except for grazing sheep.

"Edward," he said suddenly, speaking over his shoulder, "Inspector Grimmett has discovered that Bodfan Jones—which was not his real name—had served a period of imprisonment for attempted blackmail. I feel that with that piece of information to add to the rest we have garnered you should be able to formulate a theory."

"Blackmail?" repeated Ted. "Then doesn't it look as though—wait a bit! Suppose Gay found out—or knew beforehand—that Jones was a jail-bird going under an assumed name. Suppose Jones had a big game on and didn't dare risk being given away. Gosh, yes! He was on the blackmail again—Meirion, it must have been. Peel must have spotted him at it, too." He paused and then added excitedly: "Jones killed Peel and Gay because they knew who and what he was. He went on blackmailing Mr. Meirion, went too far, and got done in. It fits!"

"Done in by the Warden?"

"Yes. It fits, doesn't it, sir? Jones had the opportunity—at least, it looks as though he had—"

" 'Looks'," cut in Grimmett. "And there's your snag, young feller. It's a pretty story, so it is, but if it's true we've a devil of a way to go before we get proof. How're we to prove that both Peel and Gay Johnson knew? How did they get to know? Why did they both turn up here, and why should they go and tell Jones they knew about him? The whole thing's full of holes, and I can't see how we'd fill 'em up."

Ted looked crestfallen. "Well, what's your theory, anyway?" he threw over his shoulder.

"Seems as if Mr. Lewker's going to spring something on us," said the Inspector, "but whatever it is, I don't see how we can get away from Paul Meirion. I'll go with you, Mr. Somerset, as far as saying Bodfan Jones had a go at blackmailing him, or at least hinted that he was heading that way. And I'll accept Mr. Lewker's idea that Jones' body was kept heated up, to confuse the time of death, in some place or other—say the Warden's quarters."

Ted gave vent to a loud ejaculation.

"The coke, laddie," boomed Mr. Lewker, from in front. "But, Grimm, there had been no fire in Meirion's room."

"Well, he managed it somehow. We're theorizing, and I'll assume he worked it—dare say we'll find out how in time. Anyway, Meirion had the motive. He's as good as admitted he knew Jones knew about his 'experiments,' and he's scared stiff he'll lose his job and be put back in the loony bin. He had clear opportunity for both the other murders. Miss Crump tells us Gay Johnson appeared to be holding on to a secret—say it was that Meirion, knowing she had spotted his little game, had kidded her he'd let her in on one of his witchcraft parties. She was waiting by the Bent Stones at five-thirty, remember. He nips out after dusk and meets her, spins her a yarn about muttering spells over the gorge or something, and away they go and she's shoved in. He couldn't kid Bodfan Jones the same way as he did Peel and the girl, but he got him all the same. There's a lot to fill in, I know," he finished somewhat defiantly, "but I don't see a likelier theory, and that's a fact."

"I hope for your sake, Grimm," boomed Mr. Lewker, "that neither your theory nor Edward's is the right one. Both of them imply that this case is just beginning and that a great deal of hard work for Inspector Grimmett is in prospect."

Grimmett laughed shortly. "I'll say you're right there, sir. Now—if you've taken a shortcut—"

"Hardly that," interrupted Lewker severely. "I have merely grouped the facts into significant form. There is Mr. Truby's bield. We shall have to climb a little to reach it."

He continued to talk, a trifle breathlessly, as they struck up across the hillside towards the stone hut.

"The first group of facts includes Gay Johnson's last reported words, the clothing worn by Peel and Gay when they met their deaths, the fact that they were members of the same mountaineering club, and the electric lamp found in the bield. I must admit it was not until I observed one other thing on my climb with Hamish Macrae that I saw the only possible significance of these facts. Ah, here we are. I trust Mr. Truby is from home."

They walked round to the rickety door and Mr. Lewker pushed it open. The bield was deserted, as before.

"I do not think Ben has been here since last night," observed the actor-manager, leading the way into the gloomy little room. "He is probably sleeping off the effects of stretcher carrying." He bent down and pulled the flex and the attached lamp from beneath the pallet bed. "You see that the lamp is mounted on a square of leather. The sides of the leather have been roughly cut. Now, if I tell you that the thing I saw from Black Crag was a dark blotch down in the side of the Riggin gorge—"

He paused and raised his heavy brows inquiringly. The others stared at him.

"A blotch," he continued, "that reminded me of the mouth of Reynard's Cave in Dovedale—no? Then I must explain that this lamp—by the way, Edward, you saw nothing like this in Gay Johnson's possession?"

"No."

"Ah. But Peel might well have carried one. You see, do you not, that this has been cut from a broad band of leather? A band, I fancy, that had a buckle enabling the lamp to be worn on the forehead—"

"A pot holer's headlamp!" cried Ted.

"Midland *Cave* and Crag Club!" shouted the Inspector simultaneously. "By gum, sir—the full climbing kit on a hot day—they were going underground! But look here, there's no potholes hereabouts that I know of."

"That," beamed Mr. Lewker, rolling up the flex and handing the lamp to Grimmett, "was Gay Johnson's little secret. She had discovered a pothole or a cave. You recall her remark to Leonard? 'You can sign off, Orpheus! This is where Eurydice does her stuff!' In other words, Eurydice was going down into the Underworld and she didn't need her lover to bring her back."

"Wait a bit now, sir," begged the Inspector, frowning at the lamp and flex. "I take it you say this is part of some equipment belonging to either Peel or Johnson, and that therefore—"

"No, no, no, Grimm," Lewker interrupted firmly. "I say nothing of the kind. I merely say that the rather curious circumstance of the clothing, together with the fact that both the unfortunate wearers were members of a club that included pot holing among its activities, taken in conjunction with the cave or hole I observed in the wall of the gorge, added to—what a gorgeous sentence this is going to be!—added to the finding of this lamp, *suggests*, Grimm, that Peel and Miss Johnson may both have been exploring a cave or pot hole on the day of their death. I have a further reason for believing this lamp to have been the property of one of them. Why do you think it has been cut from its original headband?"

"To disguise what it was," said Ted.

"Perhaps. But there may have been another reason. The back and sides of the band have been removed, and probably destroyed. You remember what happened to the backs of the victims' heads."

There was a short silence. The Inspector started to nose round the little room, peering into corners and stirring the ashes in the fireplace.

"No coke, Grimm," said Mr. Lewker.

"No. But the place has been swept out recently."

"Yes."

Grimmett straightened himself. "If this bit about the lamp is right," he said slowly, "why did Ben Truby come to have it?"

"I think Ben had some idea of using it to light his mansion. He burned a battery in the fireplace, and it may have been the original battery."

"Gay—or Peel—would have the battery in a pocket," Ted put in. "I say, sir—d'you think Ben—he had opportunity, didn't he?"

"But where's his motive?" demanded Grimmett. "You can't tell me Ben Truby—"

"Shall we go out into the sunshine?" suggested the actor-manager abruptly. "This place likes me not."

They walked out on the grassy natural terrace before the bield. Mr. Lewker breathed deeply of the thyme-scented air and then took off the rucksack he carried and extracted from it an ordnance map on the six-inch scale.

"My second group of significant facts," he boomed as he knelt and spread it out on the ground, "relates itself to the first. Gay Johnson and Peel were pot hole enthusiasts—we have your report, Grimm, that Peel had done a lot of pot holing in Yorkshire—and your true pot holer must explore any hole he comes across. Gay, in Doctor Whitmore's opinion, died 'nearer midnight than seven o'clock.' Both were killed by being hit by a rock on the back of the head. Both were found in the pool under Riggin Spout with no other injury upon them but the smashed skull." He looked up at them. "Well?"

Grimmett opened his mouth, but Ted forestalled him.

"Gay being killed in the dark," he said eagerly, "could mean that she was killed underground. It wouldn't matter if it was night or day—she wanted to make Leonard anxious about her, which'd be just like her, and she could explore her pot hole with a lamp. And I can see what you're getting at, sir, about the cave mouth in the gorge. She was pitched out of that straight into the stream above the fall, and so was Peel. But could she have climbed down to this cave?"

The Inspector made a smacking sound with his lips. "The old lead mines," he said. "That's my guess. There's no other cave or hole round here."

Mr. Lewker nodded and stabbed a stubby forefinger at the map.

"The six-inch shows where the lode ran—this faint double line. A narrow seam, probably, running almost due north. To follow it they would have to drive a tunnel under this knoll here, and beyond. The map shows it as far as a point just short of the Riggin Beck." He folded the map and stood up. "I may say," he added, "that if Gay Johnson and Robert Peel did indeed explore the old lead mines, the link with my third and last group of significant facts is finally established."

"What about Bodfan Jones?" demanded Grimmett.

"He is a third grouper. If you will bear with me a little longer I will expound. Let us, with all our chivalry, to the lead mines."

"There's precious little proof in this," muttered the Inspector.

"You have that lamp, Grimm? Then come along."

He led the way on to the slope of the hillside. The Inspector, after blowing strongly through his mustache, followed with Ted.

The far hills beyond Bleaberry Dodd were already powder blue with the brume of waning afternoon. Down in its nest of trees Langthwaite farm shone white in the sun. Above and in front of them the rugged outline of Black Crag rose, the buttresses and columns of its face gleaming a dull gold against the pearly haze of the sky. Riggin Spout was hidden from them by an intervening shoulder of hill, but its deep voice, now loud, now hushed as the faint breeze bore it away, came to their ears like the never ending song of some guardian spirit of the hills. That song, reflected Mr. Lewker, had sounded when the immigrant Norsemen sacrificed virgins in the great waterfall; when a wrecked Armada galleon brought the progenitors of the famous Herdwick sheep to the shores of Cumberland; when Mr. Burton traveled north "in the time of the Late Wars" gathering material for his *True Record of Wizardrie*. The thought made him suddenly and sharply aware of the inevitable flight of time. He experienced a wave of revulsion against his present occupation of hunting murderers and a desire to have done with it so that he could enjoy the incomparable peace of these ageless hills.

"Seems sort of funny—detectives, up here," said Ted abruptly from behind him.

"You feel that, laddie? Yes. Mountains and murders are discongruent. Holidays and homicide likewise."

"I've got three days of holiday left," Ted meditated aloud. "Well, it'll be a memorable holiday, I suppose."

"My dear Edward! Let us hope you will remember it by something more pleasant than the violent death of a friend. You do not intend to stay on at Cauldmoor, I suppose?"

"No. I think the Macraes are going to stay in Wasdale Head and we'll do the same. We'll go to Gay's funeral tomorrow and then walk—oh, lord!" Ted interrupted himself. "I forgot about the police!"

"Don't mind us," said Grimmett from the rear. "Nobody does, round here. Three murders, one after the other, and I reckon we've still a long way to go."

"Is this my cheery Grimm that speaks?" boomed Lewker. "And do I sense a lack of faith in my surmises? Never mind, Edward. In two days' time—and Saint Christopher send I lie not—you and I will sit on the top of Napes Needle with Wasdale Head two thousand feet below. And there will be no room for dark memories in our minds."

"All very well, sir," grumbled the Inspector. "I want my murderer. What about Bertram Jarrett? What have the lead mines got to do with him?"

"Patience, Grimm. Ah, there is the track below. A well made road, in effect. And here are the mine buildings. I presume they crushed and sorted the ore here."

They had been traversing the indented hillside a little lower down than their first route, in the reverse direction, had taken them, and now they scrambled down a steep and boggy bank on to a flat shelf in the side of the hill. The metalled track came up from the left. Close against the slope of the fell stood the ruins of two buildings, roofless and derelict. Behind them a wooden double door closed what was evidently the entrance to the mine tunnel. They walked round the ruins and up to the door. The woodwork was old but stout and a bolt and staple, with a huge padlock attached, barred it effectively.

"They stored pictures or something here during the war," said the Inspector.

"Yes, Grimm. Look at this, though." Mr. Lewker pointed to the bolt. "Greased within the last month or so." He stepped back a few paces and scrutinized the boulder-strewn hillside above the tunnel. "Suppose you are an enthusiastic cave explorer. Here is an obvious underground tunnel, asking to be explored. The entrance is barred. But the roofs of old tunnels have a habit of falling in."

As he spoke he sprang with surprising energy at the rough slope beside the tunnel door and began to clamber up it, peering keenly among the mossy rocks that lay jumbled on the uneven mountainside. After a moment's pause Ted and the Inspector followed him. Mr. Lewker gesticulated at them, inviting them to spread out and search. It was only a minute later when Ted gave a shout.

"This is it, I think!"

The others joined him where he stood above a slight depression among the boulders. Rocks had been thrown into what had been a ragged hole.

"This wasn't done long ago," said Grimmett, stooping and sniffing like a terrier at a stopped earth.

"Since Gay Johnson's visit, Grimm, if I am not mistaken. Draw me this cork, my lads! With a will, now!"

Lewker's eagerness was contagious. Working swiftly, they threw out the rocks, none of which were larger than one man could handle. The last few, which were jammed across the narrow aperture, fell through on to rock five or six feet below and left a gaping black hole.

"The very spit and image of what pot holers call a swallet," boomed Mr. Lewker. "It is not hard to see Peel or Gay Johnson coming upon this and being impelled to investigate farther." He took off his rucksack and produced from it his flashlight. "I rely on you two to extract me if my rotundity becomes jammed. I have a fifty-foot line, but we can dispense with that."

"Here, hold on, sir!" exclaimed Grimmett. But Mr. Lewker was already lowering himself feet first into the hole. It was just wide enough to receive him, and he wriggled swiftly down until only the top of his bald head, glimmering faintly like some strange fungus, was visible below. His voice boomed in muffled sonority.

"There is a further descent, and it looks easy. Pray avoid sending down rocks upon me as you come in."

He disappeared entirely. Ted began to lower himself at once and disappeared more quickly than his bulkier leader. The Inspector scratched his head vigorously, made what appeared to be a determined effort to blow his mustache clean off his upper lip, and then inserted himself gingerly into the hole. It twisted to one side from the ledge on which he landed, and a gleam of reflected light shone from a further chasm below. This was vertical, but the projecting rocks of its narrow walls made a safe and easy ladder of descent for fifteen feet or more. Grimmett landed as the others had done on a pile of small fragments and stepped down into the mine tunnel.

Mr. Lewker's flashlight showed a straight and level shaft some twelve feet wide and seven feet high. At intervals timbers, in good repair, shored up the black rock of the roof. The walls glistened evilly, and water dripped with tinkling echoes in the farther reaches, but on the whole the tunnel was dry and easy to traverse. Lewker shone his light on the ground. Fallen fragments had formed a sort of soft earth, and a well-trodden track ran along it.

"One or two prints at the side there, Grimm," he said, his deep voice echoing strangely from the walls. "You may need them, so keep clear. On we go."

They had moved forward a few paces in single file when Ted, who was treading close behind Mr. Lewker, exclaimed loudly. The party halted. Ted was pointing to the ground at the side of the beaten track. The light of the flashlight showed a clear impression of a nailed boot.

"That's Gay's, all right," said Ted, trying to sound cool and collected. "It's her special pattern—ring clinkers, tricounis at the toe, small tricounis in a star on the heel. We had an argument about it one day."

"You'd swear that's her print?" demanded the Inspector.

"Yes, I would."

Grimmett scraped the debris into a little heap close to the footprint and they went on. The tunnel, after running straight and level for nearly a hundred yards, began to climb gently. Sometimes there were pools close under the walls, but always the path in the center was hard and dry and they walked dry-shod, following the bright beam of the flashlight. Grimmett began to speak his thoughts aloud, and the acoustics of the place made the quietly spoken words sound dramatic and significant.

"Gay Johnson came exploring here. Someone who was either here already or followed her in killed her, seemingly. Why? Because she'd seen something that someone didn't want her to see—something nobody must see and be let live. We can assume Peel had done the same a couple of months earlier. The murderer didn't spot where they'd got in until after Gay Johnson's death, and then he blocked the hole up. Funny if he blocks it up again while we're down here. Anyway, we're doing what those two youngsters did so we're like to see whatever they saw. But what about Bodfan Jones, or Jarrett? Did he—"

"Listen!" said Ted suddenly.

The party halted and listened.

"Sorry," Ted said with a nervous laugh. "Thought I heard footsteps, but it was the echo."

They went on again, still on a slight uphill gradient. Grimmett took up his monologue where he had been interrupted.

"What about Jarrett? Did he come down here too, and get killed for the same reason? If so, why was his body taken to the Bent Stones?"

Mr. Lewker's booming voice answered him.

"Jones, or Jarrett, knew the secret without coming down here to discover it."

"Oh. And do you know this precious secret too, sir?"

"I would venture a ducat or two that I could tell you what it is, Grimm." Mr. Lewker halted and flashed his light into a fissure in the right-hand wall; ten feet inside the fissure a stream tumbled down from above to disappear immediately below ground. "What is that contraption rigged across the stream? A water wheel?"

Grimmett peered into the wide crack.

"Water wheel it is, I reckon," he said. "Looks like a small dynamo, too. Miles told me they ran some lights and a small heater off an underground stream when that stuff from the art gallery was stored here—there go the wires, look, along the bottom of the wall."

"They appear in excellent repair," commented Lewker, walking on.

"They do, sir. Is this something to do with the murders? What *did* Jarrett know?"

"Let me give you my third and last group of interrelated facts, Grimm. They told me the secret that Jarrett knew, and why Jarrett's body was lying where we found it. There is the odd reluctance of Mr. George Roughten to talk about Jones, or Jarrett; the fact that Meirion and Ben Truby had quarreled; the story of Roughten's truck being tipped over the edge by the Old Ones; and the evidence found on Jarrett's body. Now if we add—"

He stopped speaking and came once again to a halt. The others, halting also, heard and felt what he had sensed. The ground beneath their feet seemed to vibrate slightly and a dull noise like the muffled sound of machinery trembled in their ears.

"It's the fall!" Ted exclaimed.

"The fall it is, laddie. We near the end of this dark entry."

They went forward, more quickly now. The floor of the tunnel leveled and bent to the right. With every step the reverberation of falling water increased. Mr. Lewker switched off his light for a second and a dim radiance, gray and cold, told of daylight somewhere ahead. The beam of the light, shooting forward again, lit the end of the tunnel. It narrowed to a few feet in width and was closed by an ordinary house door in a timber frame; but on the left of the door a ragged opening showed in the hewn rock of the tunnel wall, and through this came the white light of day. Grimmett made eagerly for the door, but Mr. Lewker caught his arm and pointed. Leaning against the side of the rift was a thin splinter of rock some four feet long. There was sufficient light to show a few streaks and patches of a dark substance, like tar, on the rough surface of its thicker end.

"The weapon!" gloated the Inspector. "Don't touch it, young feller—it's a bad surface for prints, but you never know. By gosh, he had the nerve to leave it here in full view!"

"No doubt he was keeping it for the next unwelcome visitor," remarked Mr. Lewker. "Here, I think, is the cave mouth I saw from Black Crag."

He stepped into the fissure, the others squeezing in after him. Four steps brought them into the blinding glare of daylight, with the cool air surging up from the stream that plunged over its fall far below.

They stood in a tall natural archway opening on the gorge of the Riggin Beck. Opposite them the vertical wall of the gorge rose to end at the scree slope at its top, and above, so high above that they could only see it by stooping and craning their necks, soared the sun-gilded precipice of Black Crag. At their feet the rock sloped steeply away, wet and slippery, for four or five feet, to end abruptly on the verge of the chasm. Up from the depths came the voice of Riggin Spout, filling that place with menacing sound.

"Look here," said Ted, stooping over a patch of soft earth in the mouth of the cave. "Another climbing boot—all clinkers. Its a bit fuzzy, but you can see it's not Gay's."

"You'd be safe to say it's Peel's," approved Grimmett, bending to examine it. "I reckon, Mr. Lewker, your theory's proved—as far as it goes. They both came here. They were both killed with that rock splinter and shoved over the edge."

The actor-manager nodded gravely. "Yes. Down this slab the bodies of Gay Johnson and Robert Peel were sent, to—"

"*Look out!*" screamed Ted, and flung himself away from the edge, flying like a bullet between Lewker and the Inspector.

Mr. Lewker swung round in time to see a murderer in the act of his crime. Ben Truby, his gaunt frame towering above them, stood there with the rock splinter swung aloft above his venerable head. His gray elf-locks and his craggy distorted face were those of some ogre of Norse legend. His pale eyes were wide and glittering. So much Lewker had time to note before Ted's skull took the shepherd in the pit of the stomach. Ben Truby's club fell harmlessly and went slithering over the edge into the gorge. He doubled up and crashed over backwards with Ted on top of him. Ted scrambled to his feet, but the old man lay still.

"I—I've killed him, haven't I?" Ted faltered.

"Hit his head on the rock wall," said Grimmett; he knelt swiftly beside the shepherd. "No—stunned, that's all. Reckon you saved my life, young feller," he added, looking up. "It was me he was aiming for."

Ted said nothing. He began to shiver violently.

"Edward," boomed Mr. Lewker sharply, "pull yourself together and help me with this."

He had taken the fifty-foot line from his rucksack and was already uncoiling it. Ted, mastering his trembling fingers, assisted him to secure the shepherd's arms and legs with neat and adequate lashings, while Grimmett examined the oozing wound on the back of the old man's skull.

"Look at the froth on his lips," said the Inspector disgustedly. "Who'd have thought it? Was he mad, then? What's he got hiding here? A hoard of Spanish gold or something?"

Mr. Lewker rose to his feet.

"I think he will do now," he said. "Edward, I congratulate you on your very prompt and courageous action. It is a solemn thought that if your young lady had succeeded in depriving us of your company, Inspector Grimmett's career might have ceased upon this spot." He turned to the Inspector. "In a sense, Grimm, Truby is mad—but he is not a lunatic. He had a reason for these murders, and now, I fancy, we can examine it undisturbed."

He went back through the fissure, switching on his flashlight. Ted and Grimmett followed. Lewker went straight to the door at the end of the tunnel and tried the handle. It opened easily. He flung it wide and sent the beam of the light flooding into the chamber beyond.

"And there," boomed Mr. Lewker with immense satisfaction, "is the reason."

CHAPTER XVI
THE BURTHEN OF IT ALL

NEARLY TWENTY-FOUR HOURS AFTER BEN TRUBY'S ATTEMPT to murder Inspector Grimmett, the Inspector himself, with Mr. Lewker, approached the door of Riding Mount. The Inspector knocked, and they stood waiting in silence.

Both of them looked tired. Grimmett had missed another night's sleep, and his companion, though he had done little beyond making a long telephone call to Liverpool and holding a conference with Dr. Whitmore, had passed a restless night. On the pouchy countenance of Mr. Lewker and the Inspector's brick-red features a distaste for their present business, the reporting to the Deputy Chief Constable of the successful termination of their man hunt, showed itself plainly.

A maid opened the door to them, but Sir Walter himself, lean and elegant in old but well-cut tweeds, came quickly along the hall before they had stated their business.

"Ah—you are here at last," he said, a certain impatience underlying his geniality. "Come to the study. I had expected you before this, Inspector." He ushered them into the little room and closed the door. "There is a rumor that Ben Truby has been taken into custody. I can hardly believe it."

Grimmett sat down heavily. "It's right enough, sir," he said. "Truby's a murderer, not a doubt of it."

"Do sit down, Lewker," said Sir Walter. Mr. Lewker, who had been frowning abstractedly out of the window at the dark fells that stood against the overcast sky of afternoon, obediently lowered himself into a chair. "This has been a considerable shock to me," added the Deputy Chief Constable, sitting down behind his desk. "I have known Ben for nearly forty years. He was a sergeant in my regiment in the first world war."

"You saved his life, I understand," put in Mr. Lewker.

"Well—yes. I tell you, Lewker, the poor old chap's quite harmless. A little queer in some ways, but not a homicidal maniac. There must be some mistake."

"I'd better tell you at once, sir," said Grimmett, "that Truby has made a statement."

"Confessing to the murder?"

"It amounts to a confession, sir—yes."

Sir Walter frowned in silence at the penholder he was twisting between his long fingers.

"Well?" he said suddenly. "Go on, Inspector. Let me have chapter and verse."

Grimmett shifted uneasily. "It was Mr. Lewker here who tumbled to it, sir," he said. "I'd suggest he gives you the matter in due order."

Sir Walter glanced at the actor-manager with a ghost of his impish grin.

"So the talented amateur scored, did he? Very well, Lewker—as Hamlet says to the Ghost, 'Speak; I am bound to hear.' "

"In the Ghost's words, then, 'Lend thy serious hearing to what I shall unfold,' " returned Mr. Lewker; but he did not return the other's smile. "I will be brief. The evidence led me to suspect that both Johnson and Peel had found their way into the old lead mines and had there been murdered, their bodies being flung down from the mouth of the cave which connects with the mine tunnel. With Grimm, I visited the mines and found evidence that bore out this theory. While there—"

"The lead mines!" ejaculated Sir Walter. "But why? Have you found anything to show why this should be so?"

"Bear with me, I beg, while I tell my tale in mine own manner. While we were there Truby, who I believe to have watched us enter the mine and followed us in, made a murderous attack on Inspector Grimmett, using the rock splinter which bore signs of having been used for the murders of Gay Johnson and Peel. In Truby's bield we found part of an electric head lamp which we hope to identify as having belonged to Peel."

"But—"

"A moment, Sir Walter, please."

Sir Walter bowed his head and continued to turn the penholder restlessly in his hands. Mr. Lewker turned his gaze to the window and the dark landscape beyond. For once his sonorous tones lost their expressiveness and became flat and monotonous.

"As Grimm has said, Truby's confession confirms his responsibility for the deaths of those two youngsters. I pass to the murder of Bodfan Jones. Here Truby made a bad slip. He disobeyed his instructions."

"His *instructions!* I beg your pardon, Lewker. Go on."

"The original idea, I think, was to deal with Jones' body as the others had been dealt with. The wound in the back of the head had been made in the same manner. But Truby—who, if not mad, is at least not wholly sane—had quarreled with Paul Meirion over the price charged for certain materials used in the latter's necromantic 'experiments.' In his vindictiveness, he thought to implicate the Warden. Instead of taking the body to the cave he placed it by the Bent Stones, where he knew Meirion was to perform his incantations that same night."

"Good heavens!" muttered Sir Walter, as if to the penholder. "The whole thing's fantastic! But go on—go on!"

"Thank you." There was perhaps a trace of irony in Mr. Lewker's voice. "With regard to Bodfan Jones, Inspector Grimmett here made some interesting discoveries. The man's real name was Bertram Jarrett and he had been in prison for blackmailing activities. It appears he was incorrigible, for his business in Birkerdale was blackmail. He used his Youth Hostel walking tour as cover for this, I think. Paul Meirion was afraid of him because he had made a veiled threat to inform Meirion's employers of the Warden's previous confinement in a mental home, and of his obsession with sorcery. But Jarrett's main blackmailing line was concerned with art."

The Deputy Chief Constable glanced up sharply, but Mr. Lewker's gaze was still fixed on the distant fells.

"On Jarrett's body," Lewker continued, "was found an art dealer's catalogue. Against one of the items—a picture by Thomas Girtin—was penciled the word 'fake.' This strengthened a theory I had already formed, and the Inspector has ascertained from the Liverpool police that Jarrett's conviction was in connection with the blackmailing of a man who faked valuable pictures. Another circumstance I found significant was the attempt of Mr. George Roughten of the Herdwick Arms to deny that Jarrett had visited the inn at Whitsuntide, and his subsequent avoidance of further discussion. I believe, Sir Walter, that Roughten is indebted to you for considerable financial help?"

"Why—yes, that is true. But—"

"You will remember that Roughten was the driver of the truck which was to convey the art treasures from storage in the lead mines to the Reynolds Gallery in Liverpool." Mr. Lewker was speaking more quickly now. "The truck overturned and burst into flames, and its contents were totally destroyed. The only other man present on that occasion was the art expert sent from the Gallery to supervise the packing. I have telephoned to the Reynolds Gallery this morning and find that this art expert lost his job a few weeks later. His name was Bertram Jarrett."

The penholder snapped in Sir Walter's fingers. He stared at the broken pieces in puzzled fashion for a second and then looked up.

"I see what this means," he said quietly. "The pictures—they were pictures, I believe—were not destroyed. Roughten and Jarrett connived at the fake accident and the pictures were actually preserved and concealed. Presumably Roughten was selling them one by one—Jarrett would know the likely markets, of course. Then I suppose Jarrett thought blackmail would be a quicker way of making money and he began to blackmail Roughten. It was Roughten who made Ben Truby the guardian of the hoard and instructed him, finally, to kill Jarrett." He stared penetratingly at Lewker, who was still gazing out of the window. "You found the pictures in the lead mine, I take it?"

Mr. Lewker turned slowly to meet his stare.

"So far as I have been able to ascertain," he boomed gravely, "they are all there. Not one is missing and they have been most carefully looked after."

Sir Walter breathed a sigh of relief. "Excellent," he said. "The nation has not, after all, suffered a great loss."

"I understand," said Mr. Lewker, "that the collection of watercolors is the finest in the country. I congratulate you," he added, "on so quickly formulating your theory of Roughten's guilt. It is not, however, the true one."

There was a knock at the door. Sir Walter's "Come in" sounded strained and unnatural. The maid entered, looking a trifle flustered.

"It's this policeman, sir," she began. "And there's three others messing about in—"

Sergeant Miles pushed past her and closed the study door firmly in her face. He stood stiffly inside the room, looking at the Inspector. A meaningful glance passed between them.

"Just a moment, sergeant," said Grimmett. "Mr. Lewker has not quite finished."

"I must protest, Inspector," said Sir Walter sharply. "This is very irregular. I—"

"If you will allow me," Mr. Lewker broke in with emphasis, "I will be very brief. To return to the finding of Jarrett's body. It was quite clear to me, from the various signs, that Jarrett had not been killed at the Bent Stones. The finding of a piece of coke in the shoe suggested that it had lain in a place where coke was present, since the man could not have walked with any comfort with the coke chafing his foot. He had been carried there, then. From where?"

"Hasn't Truby told you that in his confession?" demanded Sir Walter quickly.

"Truby's madness, Sir Walter, takes the form of an unreasoning loyalty. He has confessed to murdering Gay Johnson and Robert Peel. He has refused to say anything about the killing of Jarrett, and I believe that he did not kill Jarrett. I am reasonably certain, however, that he carried the body to where it was found. One word more and I have finished. Doctor Whitmore made a first examination of Jarrett's body at five o'clock yesterday morning. He said then that the body temperature indicated that the man had been killed between four and nine in the evening of the previous day, but he was puzzled by the very advanced state of the rigor mortis. Perhaps"—he raised his eyebrows at Sir Walter—"perhaps you knew that the human body loses heat at the rate of three and a half degrees Fahrenheit per hour for the first three hours after death, and three degrees for the second three hours?"

"No," said the Deputy Chief Constable shortly.

"I am informed that it does. Also that violent exertion just before death may hasten the advance of rigor. Whitmore suggested that this might have been the case, but he would not, at first credit my statement that when I myself touched the body, at midnight or thereabouts—five hours before Whitmore—rigor had already affected the whole body."

"My dear Lewker!" Sir Walter sounded contemptuous. "You can hardly claim to be a qualified medical witness."

Mr. Lewker nodded. "Quite. Yet the fact was as I say. And Whitmore's later examination established two other facts which supported my own explanation of this apparent discrepancy. There was coke dust in the hair and clothing of the corpse, and Jarrett had received, prior to the blow that killed him, a stunning blow on the side of the head."

He paused. Sir Walter's gaze seemed riveted to the actor-manager's face. His lips twisted in a forced smile.

"And what is your explanation of these—ah—facts, may I ask?" he demanded contemptuously.

Mr. Lewker seemed to recollect something.

"Pray forgive me," he boomed, "but I neglected to ask after your malaria. It is better, I trust—I notice your central heating is not on today. And was your journey to the vet in Gosforth satisfactorily concluded? I understand your car was seen taking the road over the moors after nine o'clock on Tuesday night—the road that passes within a mile of the Bent Stones, you know."

The other spoke without appearing to move a muscle of face or body. "What are you insinuating?"

"It is odd," continued Lewker evenly, "that no one but Ben Truby saw Jarrett after he left here on Tuesday morning. Your servants were out, of course, and in any case Truby's evidence is hardly admissible. All things considered, Sir Walter, I feel justified in—shall I say—painting a series of imaginary scenes." He leaned forward, his little eyes unwinking on the rigid face opposite him. "I see Bertram Jarrett standing in this room demanding blackmail, just as he had done at Whitsuntide. I see him knocked down by a blow from something like a poker—I notice yours is no longer in your fireplace—and carried into a boiler room, there to be finished off with a heavier blow on the back of the head. I see the body left there, lying on a heap of coke in the very warm atmosphere, until nearly nine o'clock at night. His murderer no doubt hopes to confuse the evidence as to time of death by maintaining the body temperature—but he fails to realize that the warmth will hasten the advance of rigor mortis, not retard it. I see the body lifted into the back of a car and covered with rug or tarpaulin, and the car driven up the hill road towards Gosforth. I see it stop on the crest of the pass and Ben Truby set off northwards into the mist carrying the body—to place it where his own angry whim dictates. Well, Sir Walter—you are a judge of pictures. Are these of mine true to life, or—should I say—true to death?"

Sir Walter did not answer. He had sunk farther and farther into his chair until he was crouched behind his desk like some trapped bird of prey. His face looked old and haggard. A trickle of moisture oozed from the side of his mouth; he smeared it aside with a trembling hand. His eyes were fixed on Lewker's face as though he were hypnotized.

The actor-manager turned his own gaze away quickly.

"That is all, Grimm," he said quietly.

Grimmett looked at the sergeant. "Let us have your report."

Miles cleared his throat loudly; the sound emphasized the tension that had grown in the little room.

"Acting on instructions," he began in an expressionless voice, "we have entered and examined the boiler room at the rear of this house, which is where the central heating is run from. On the heap of coke therein, having apparently percolated through the lumps, so to speak, we found congealed blood, of which samples have been taken. Several large pieces of timber, presoomably for firelighting purposes, were also found. None of these bore any sign of being used as a weapon, but a large piece partly consoomed by fire was found in the fireplace."

He paused and glanced at the Deputy Chief Constable, who had made a choking noise.

"Go on," Grimmett.

"Yes, sir. We have also examined the car, Rover ten-horse, in the garage. The upholstery of the rear seat has been scrubbed recently. Under the mat on the floor of the rear seat we found a large stain that may be a bloodstain. A portion of the mat has been taken for analysis. A tarpaulin was also——"

"Damn you!" Sir Walter was on his feet and waving his arms hysterically. "You have no right to pry about my house! You have no warrant!"

"I've a search warrant, sir," said Grimmett heavily. "And a—another warrant, too."

He took some papers from his pocket. Sir Walter fell back in his chair and covered his face with his hands.

"As God's my witness," he muttered, "I never intended it should—come to—this."

The Inspector stood up. Sergeant Miles moved forward.

"Walter Talbot Haythornthwaite," said Grimmett, "I arrest you for the murder of Bertram Jarrett, and I warn you that anything you say …"

"Well, he spoke the truth there, I'm certain," said Mrs. Lewker. "He didn't intend that his theft of the pictures should lead to three murders."

She was sitting on a bilberry-cushioned ledge at the foot of a soaring ridge of gray rock, and as usual she looked as though her surroundings had been made for her. Those surroundings were sufficiently remarkable, for the Napes Ridges of Great Gable provide some of the most impressive rock scenery in Great Britain. The bilberry ledge on which Georgie sat resembles in miniature the upper seating of a theater; it is, in fact, called the Dress Circle by the climbers and fell walkers of the Lake District, for it is perched directly opposite that most popular—and most photographed—of British rock climbs, the Napes Needle. Beyond the great pinnacle, on this still and hazy afternoon, the furrowed steeps of Lingmell, with Scafell itself above, loomed blue-green and gigantic across the wide valley. Far down to the westward, like a silver dish laid neatly between the precipices of the Screes and the lumpy fells of Copeland Forest, Wastwater gleamed dully. Beside Georgie sat Ted Somerset and Janet Macrae, both very silent and gazing solemnly across the steep scree gully below them at the sheer and menacing shape of the huge rock finger. Mr. Lewker lay flat on his back on the other side of his wife, enjoying a well-earned rest. He had maneuvered very cunningly to get the four of them away and up the hillside before Vera Crump and Hamish; by various shortcuts remembered from his younger days he had urged them onward and upward across the flanks of Great Gable, and now he had the satisfaction of having reached the Dress Circle a good half-hour before the others could arrive.

The two Macraes, with Ted and Vera, were spending the last two days of their eventful holiday at Wasdale Head, as they had planned. Leonard Bligh, sulky and self-centered as ever, had departed for Birmingham the day before. Mr. Lewker and his wife had walked over to stay for one night at the

Wasdale Head Hotel. Today, in theory, the party was to walk to the summit of Great Gable; but Mr. Lewker, having cast aside his part of Amateur Detective for that of Stage Manager, had other plans in mind.

"I suppose, in a way, he was mad," Georgie continued, following her train of thought. "That's the only way you can explain it."

Mr. Lewker stirred on his couch of bilberry.

"He was mad on one subject, as are most of us," he boomed. "He would have sold his soul to possess a private collection of precious watercolors, and when that chance presented itself he was tempted and fell. Roughten and old Truby were bound to him by ties of debt and devotion. He had to square Jarrett when he planned that fake accident, and Jarrett's propensities for blackmail proved his undoing. He was blackmailing Sir Walter, he tried to blackmail Roughten, I think, and he was feeling his way towards blackmailing the Warden, whose secret he had probably discovered from Roughten or Sir Walter himself."

"When did you first begin to suspect Sir Walter?" asked his wife curiously.

"When Mrs. Crake used that curious phrase about Sir Walter being wed to a lot of paintings and going after strange gods I began to wonder a little. Country folk in a small community are seldom ignorant of a neighbor's peculiarities, even when they are ignorant of the facts behind them. I remembered how the great watercolor authority had not a single decent watercolor on his walls, and how he shied away from the subject of watercolors when we dined there. That was odd. And when I found that it was Sir Walter who had presented the book on ancient sorceries to Sergeant Miles, I wondered again. It was clear that these superstitions about the Old Ones and the Bent Stones have only been revived in Birkerdale during the last five years—since the accident to Roughten's truck. In fact, Sir Walter made Ben Truby the guardian of his treasure, prompted him with stories which would keep the locals away from the neighborhood of Coffin's Pike as much as possible—especially at night, when he would go to gloat over his collection—and bolstered up the evil reputation of the Bent Stones by putting the *True Record of Wizardrie* into Miles' hands. He knew the legend would spread from there. Also, I believe, he egged Meirion on, through Truby, to persevere with his 'experiments,' hoping that the tale of weird rites and mysterious fires at the Bent Stones would still further frighten away the Birkerdalians. The opening of the Youth Hostel must have been a problem for him, endless parties of youngsters roaming over his forbidden territory."

"He didn't instruct Ben Truby to kill them, surely."

"No. I think Truby, the faithful watchdog, followed Peel into the mine and saw him discover the picture gallery. The place was rather amazing, you know—Turners, Girtins, Coxes, all beautifully hung and lit by electricity. A sort of Aladdin's Cave of art treasure. Truby, whose madness is nothing more than a singularly blind devotion, dealt with Peel in what he considered the only way. Sir Walter was doubtless shocked and dismayed when the old man told him, but he could do nothing. Revelation of his hoard would have meant imprisonment and ruin. The fact that Peel's death was smoothly passed over as accident soothed his conscience and encouraged Truby to treat the second intruder in the same way. There is," added Mr. Lewker, sitting up and throwing an arm across his wife's shoulder's, "a moral in all this, my dear, but blow me if I'll point it."

"I can see Hamish and Vera," said Janet suddenly.

Mr. Lewker stood up and peered downward. Two figures were toiling up the screes towards the Needle gully; Vera Crump was in front and making a fast pace while Hamish, smoking his pipe, followed at the reasonable plod of the mountaineer. Mr. Lewker took the coil of line from his rucksack.

"Edward, my young foiler of homicides," he boomed, "yonder pinnacle challenges us. You and I will take up the gage. Now are our brows bound with victorious wreaths, and we will crown our triumph with a noble climb. To the assault!"

He scrambled down into the gully without waiting for an answer.

"But—" began Ted, and stopped.

He looked at Janet, who carefully avoided his glance. He looked down at Vera, now only two or three hundred feet below and coming up fast. Without a word he climbed down after his leader. Mr. Lewker was already hoisting himself up on to the massive plinth from which the Needle rose. Ted, with some difficulty, joined him on the narrow shelf. Swiftly the actor-manager tied the bowlines round his own waist and Ted's and slipped a belaying loop over a spike.

"Pay the rope out over your shoulders, and let it run smoothly," he commanded; and stepped out at once on to the vertical rock face.

Ted, a prey to varying emotions, watched him creep out across the face like a huge bald-headed ape. He reached the sharp outer corner of the Needle and paused there a moment, silhouetted against space and with emptiness beneath him, to boom solemnly at Ted.

"Remember, laddie, these holds have been used by almost every great British mountaineer. You are to follow in the steps of Haskett Smith, of Winthrop Young, of Mallory of Everest. Fortune and victory sit on thy helm!"

He disappeared round the corner. The rope moved out swiftly and smoothly. Ted watched it slide up the sheer wall; he glanced down at the blue spaces beneath, and shivered. He would surely slip from those tiny holds—was it too late, even now, to cry off? He would say he had cramp, or felt sick. ... And there was Vera at the foot of the gully. He could see her red face upturned. She would be furious, and against her fury he could never find any defence but abasement. Her voice came faintly up to him. He could not hear the words, but undoubtedly she was very angry.

"Come along, laddie!"

That was Mr. Lewker's cheerful bellow from far overhead. Ted's stomach seemed to sink into the depths below him. He glanced across at the ledge where Georgie and Janet sat side by side. Janet waved an encouraging hand. Ted took a deep breath and removed his belaying loop. The slack of the rope went dangling up to the invisible Lewker and tightened gently on his body. He reached a shaking hand for the first handhold and began to climb.

That upward traverse was not so hard as he had expected; but once round the corner the world seemed to have fallen away from under him. He was clinging to the outside edge of the earth, with immense blue spaces on every side and nothing but tiny toe and finger holds between him and the void beneath. He glanced upward. Right overhead Mr. Lewker squatted on a kind of bracket under the impending apex of the Needle, at the top of a steep and horribly smooth-looking wall. He looked down, past the trembling edge of his left boot, and saw Vera, a little oddly foreshortened figure, straight below him. She was shouting something, but it didn't much matter what—because he was going to fall off.

He reached up desperately and his fingers closed on a good, friendly hold. His boot found another. His knees stopped shaking and he began to move upward. And quite suddenly he was not afraid. The soaring rock point overhead was no longer menacing—it was gloriously challenging him, not inimically but genially, offering him rough holds that needed only a confident user. He felt a surge of self-reliance, an assurance that new worlds of endeavor and triumph were his for the taking. This was life, this conquering of oneself in order to win a difficult summit!

"Ted!"

That was Vera. He had forgotten her.

"Ted! I thought I said you were not to climb!"

He paused, standing confidently on the steep slab, and looked down at her. Vera Crump seen in plan, a red angry face gaping and gasping, looked distinctly ridiculous.

"Ted Somerset," she was shouting, "if you go on up there I'll never speak to you again!"

From the ledge above her Janet was smiling up at him. That smile, he knew with sudden exhilaration, was a part of this new future of his. He nodded cheerfully at the furious countenance in the gully.

"That's okay by me, Miss Crump," said Ted Somerset.

THE END

If you enjoyed *The Youth Hostel Murders* be sure to ask your bookseller for *Murder on Milestone Buttress* (0-915230-29-1, $14.00). For more information on The Rue Morgue Press please turn the page.

About the Rue Morgue Press

"Rue Morgue Press is the old-mystery lover's best friend,
reprinting high quality books from the 1930s and '40s."
—*Ellery Queen's Mystery Magazine*

Since 1997, the Rue Morgue Press has reprinted scores of traditional mysteries, the kind of books that were the hallmark of the Golden Age of detective fiction. Authors reprinted or to be reprinted by the Rue Morgue include Catherine Aird, Dorothy Bowers, Pamela Branch, Joanna Cannan, Glyn Carr, Torrey Chanslor, Clyde B. Clason, Joan Coggin, Manning Coles, Lucy Cores, Frances Crane, Norbert Davis, Elizabeth Dean, Constance & Gwenyth Little, Marlys Millhiser, James Norman, Stuart Palmer, Craig Rice, Kelley Roos, Charlotte Murray Russell, Maureen Sarsfield, Margaret Scherf and Juanita Sheridan.

To suggest titles or to receive a catalog of Rue Morgue Press books write P.O. Box 4119, Boulder, CO 80306, telephone 800-699-6214, or check out our website, www.ruemorguepress.com, which lists complete descriptions of all of our titles, along with lengthy biographies of our writers.